Loathe Your Neighbor

by

D.A.Cairns

Square Pegs Publishing
Cover design: Mahedi Hasan

For my good friend, Delia McNamara

Acknowledgements

I would like to thank every editor who has either published my work, or rejected it constructively. I would also like to thank everyone who bought a copy of my first novel, *Devolution*. From that latter select group, I would really like to say a big thank you to those who offered words of encouragement and opinion. Especially my mum, Frances, my daughter, Alana, my sister, Justine, and my cousin, Ryan. My good friend, Delia, read the first draft of Loathe Your Neighbor, chapter by chapter, as it was being written, and offered invaluable feedback and encouragement. I can't thank her enough for believing in me.

Loathe Your Neighbor is the trim, well toned and muscular novel that you are about to read and hopefully enjoy because of the hard work of Jeanne Haskin and her team at Artema Press. Thank you for appreciating what I write and who I am. And thank you for publishing Loathe Your Neighbor.

CHAPTER ONE

There were no sirens, flashing lights, or screeching tires when the police arrived at number 1008 Princess Hwy. David Lavender felt offended.

The only sounds were of whirring steel blades and plastic cords as locals attacked the fast growing Buffalo grass on their lots in Chinaman's Hollow. Victa lawn mowers and Stihl line trimmers were the weapons of choice in the war against the humidity-fuelled growth in the yards of suburbia.

David had been refueling his lawnmower when he heard loud voices inside the house next door

Loud arguments were nothing unusual. They happened in his home as well, although outsiders would never have heard or even cared if they did. None of my business, David thought as he stood with straining ears to catch some of the words in the jumble of sound and anger.

'You did this and you did that. Fuck this and fuck you.' A stifled scream as though someone suffocated then a bang and another scream, which morphed into a growling yell. The noises became more animalistic, as if words were no longer effective. Perhaps anger robbed them of speech. A crash and another bang. He could feel the rage pulsing from the house. For a moment it paralyzed him. Should he keep his nose out of their business and keep mowing the lawn, or intervene? Knock on the door and ask for milk? Sugar? He had not been afraid to interrupt during previous arguments, even though he'd looked like a fool. Intervention, yes. Police? No, not yet.

David ran to knock at their door.

He wondered if they argued new material or just rehashed the same issues. He listened.

"Why don't you leave me the fuck alone? I'm tired. I don't want your shit."

"I don't want *your* shit and I wish you'd leave *me* alone."

"Well stop talking then. Fuck off!"

"*You* fuck off!"

"Why should I?"

"Because I want you to. I'm sick of your shit."

"I'm sick of *your* shit."

"Well fuck off then!"

"Why should I?"

David knocked again and realized he was still listening. He was fascinated; transfixed by their intellectual debate, its deep philosophical nature and their incredible range of vocabulary. A whole five minutes worth. Of what? I'm sick of your shit. David tried to imagine his wife, Lilijana, using that line with him. Not in a million years. Sure, she'd probably thought it but was far too self-controlled to ever speak that way.

A thud, like something or someone hitting the floor brought David back to attention He knocked again, this time to ominous silence. No one answered his knock. No face at the door, looking angry or sheepish. No one came to apologize or threaten him. David raced home to call the police.

So here they were. Two officers. The short, female cop tried steering her towering, male companion toward talking to David first. In response, the male officer gestured to the neighbor's house. David nodded then gave them the thumbs up. They'd found the right place.

Once the police passed the garage, which obscured his view of their front door, David crossed onto his neighbor's property to watch.

"Hello," said the male officer in a commanding voice. "Is any one there? It's the police."

David anticipated drawn guns, smashed doors and the cops charging in, yelling for weapons to be dropped. Instead, the male officer knocked a second time then tried the knob of the door. He called out as both officers entered and the screen door banged behind them.

What would the cops find once they navigated the garbage-strewn living room? Was the rest of the house in a similar state? A teenager dropped garbage wherever he pleased, but for adults to trash their own home?

"What are you doing, David?"

It was Lilijana.

"Nothing." David struggled to hide his irritation at having his watch interrupted.

"Are you going to finish mowing the lawn?"

"Yep."

He waited for the cops to emerge with a struggling Phil. Naydine would yell threats to protect her man, now forgiven after their war of words.

"Are you going to finish today? We're going out tonight, remember?"

Damn. He had tried to forget. Lilijana always wanted to go out or have people over. She loved to spread her sunshine, and the recipients of her graciousness and kindness lapped it up. Why not? There was no danger of sunburn. Zero possibility of melanoma. Five seconds in Lilijana's company and the hardest glacial heart was guaranteed to melt. Cares and worries washed away by her positivity. It gave him the shits sometimes. Worse, it was genuine and not just with others but with David and their children. She was like a bloody angel. There were times when David resented her for it.

"David?"

Resigned to speaking to make her go away and realizing he might have to move to authenticate his words, he answered in his most pleasant voice. "Yes dear, I'll get right on it. I'm nearly finished and then I'll have shower."

He glanced at her. If she believed he was going to do as he said, she didn't show it. David reluctantly wrenched his eyes, then his head and finally his whole body away from where he was to where he should be. He walked back to the mower, crouched beside it, and unscrewed the cap of the jerry can. David thought about what was going on inside 1008. Phil and Naydine would assure the police there was no problem. They would apologize for causing any trouble, and the police would accept the words of the former combatants, now enthusiastic allies.

David poured petrol in until it overflowed then cursed at his carelessness as though it was the first time he'd done it. After replacing both caps, he made sure Lilijana had gone inside before he returned to his former station. No sound. He waited a moment, sighed, and went to finish the lawn.

The Victa Lawnmaster 350 exploded back to life with a pull on the starter cord. David resumed his task.

Phil and Naydine moved into 1008 on a rainy Saturday two months ago, when David was at home due to the cancellation of his son's cricket match. He went out to welcome the newcomers to Chinaman's Hollow.

"G'day, I'm David."

Phil and Naydine were standing at the back of the removal truck. She looked at David who was holding out his hand. "I'm Naydine and this is John."

"Nardine and John," David repeated. It was a trick he had seen Lilijana use on numerous occasions. It helped her remember people's names. Despite his best efforts, nothing seemed to help David. Was he getting old or was he simply defective?

"*Nay*-dine," she corrected him with an exaggerated emphasis on the first syllable of her name.

"That's different," said David. She seemed to have lost interest. The man, John, gave him a perfunctory glance with a sharp lift of the chin as some sort of greeting. David disliked him immediately. He didn't look like a John. David knew lots of John's. Lilijana's church was full of them, and full of Davids as well. He often joked with the other Davids that they should change the name of the church to the House of David. David expected to find nice people in church even if they were all fakers and hypocrites. He didn't care if they were two-faced as long as they treated him with respect. And they did. His interactions with holy people were limited to an hour each week anyway, and that didn't amount to any sort of relationships in David's book. Live and let live.

The blade of the mower hit a rock and the awful noise arrested David's attention. He bent over, raised the blade one notch then went over the same patch of grass.

There was no way David could allow this new neighbor into the fraternity of good Johns. So he decided to call him Phil. One he remembered from his school days, called Phil Lewis, was a funny bloke. He pretended he was about to take a bite of an open jam sandwich and ploughed it into his cheek when someone called his name. That was his best party trick. Phil was a shifty sort of bloke, a bit too crafty and a real attention seeker. Next door John didn't exactly fit the Phil mold but it was a reasonable match because of the suspicion he aroused in David. There was much more to Phil Lewis at school than met the eye and David was sure that there was also much more to Phil next door.

They had run into each other at the train station about a week after he and Naydine moved in. David noticed him first and waited for Phil to look up so he could say G'day. David reckoned it was important to catch a person's eye before saying hello because they might not recognize him, or worse not even remember him. There was nothing worse than being looked through by people you knew. He was surprised when seen and commented that he must have forgotten to don the cloak of invisibility. On this occasion, he must have been wearing that extraordinary piece of attire because Phil raised his head, made a nanosecond of eye contact, then looked away as though he had seen something he shouldn't have. If it wasn't the cloak then Phil was either under the influence of some mighty powerful substance or just plain rude.

David had swallowed his greeting and walked on. Phil was certainly not a man to like or trust. So what the hell was going on at 1008? He found his attention wandering again to the possibilities next door.

He stared at the front door, having pushed the mower to a shorn patch of grass, which provided a clear view of the front door. David made same backwards and forwards movements that wouldn't have fooled anybody. The door opened and the two officers appeared: first the woman then the man.

The female officer looked at David so he spun the mower around and headed in the opposite direction. At the end of his stroll across the grass, he had return to the other side. Following that path took him straight to the police. Good. Maybe they would want to talk to him. Perhaps they would fill him in on what happened. He was the anxious neighbor so he had a right to know.

On his return voyage across the lawn, he noticed the two officers watching him. The male officer gestured for David to shut down the mower. David was happy to oblige.

"Thanks for calling us, Mr. Lavender. You did the right thing."

"Everything all right then?"

"We've spoken to both parties," began the female officer, "and they have given us a satisfactory explanation as to what transpired."

David became aware that she was kind of cute and the police talk sounded more than a little sexy coming from her lips. He struggled to concentrate while he imagined her as an aerobic instructor in a brightly colored leotard.

"Transpired?" he said, as though he didn't understand the word. "Yes, what did transpire?"

The male officer took over and he wasn't nearly as attractive. "There was a bit of an argument. They have calmed down now and given us an undertaking to do their utmost to maintain some tranquility."

As the smile broke across his face, David hoped it would not be misinterpreted. The situation was not amusing, but the language these cops used was hilarious. The preposterous understatement that Phil and Naydine had a bit of an argument was funny in itself but undertakings and utmost tranquilities? Was that part of their training?

"That's all very well for them to say," said David, "but if that shit fight was a bit of an argument, I'm going to need police protection if they ever have a real barney. And let's face it, that's pretty likely. I mean this isn't the first time they've had a blue, but it's for sure the worst. That's why I called."

The police looked at each other, apparently having a mental game of paper, scissors, rock to decide who should address David's concern. David had raised a fair point, and wasn't going to be fobbed off with police doublespeak.

He pressed on. "What assurances can you give that I won't get caught up in their domestic troubles? They're off their faces half the time, anyway. Aren't they stoned now? Did you check them out? You might think they can be trusted, but I don't and I want to know what you're going to do."

"Mr. Lavender," said the cute cop, whom David couldn't stop picturing in that leotard. "We have done all we can for now. If you have another situation, please call and we will return." Seeing the look of bemusement on David's face, she took a breath and continued. "Your neighbors have not broken the law. They had an argument. We can't arrest them without cause. I'm sure you understand, Mr. Lavender."

That was the end of the conversation. They turned to leave after a final nod.

Further words of protest evaporated on David's tongue. Phil and Naydine. Trouble, nothing but trouble. With the lawn finished off and the police gone, David had no reason to linger in the front yard. The path and the driveway needed to be swept and the edges were begging for attention, but David had had enough. Besides, he didn't have time, and if Lilijana challenged him, he would say so.

David pushed the Victa down the driveway. He recalled the time when he had been watching television and was interrupted by the squawking roar of a chainsaw. He assumed it was the property maintenance guy working at 1008. As he had never heard a chainsaw used there before, he was curious.

He headed down the stairs and out the back door. From there he could see into the backyard of 1008.

Phil was operating the chainsaw. He may as well have been wearing a hockey mask for the effect he had on David. He was feverishly cutting away at a shrub which lay at the foot of his back stairs. By the time David arrived to see the carnage, Phil had already reduced the once mighty plant to a husk, less than a quarter of its original size. His clothes hung as though they were two or three sizes too big and he never looked up. Phil just kept gunning the chainsaw and slashing it through the helpless shrub.

What made the incident more disturbing was that David had never seen Phil outside the house. Up until that moment, he had only heard him inside the house and seen him at the train station once. Not that David could assume Phil never left the house, but it was pretty suspicious. What does a person do inside a house all day? Perhaps he spent all his time planning acts of terror against trees.

David had beaten a hasty retreat, hoping that Phil the Chinaman's Hollow Chainsaw Maniac hadn't seen him. David was unsettled, dizzy with the fear that someone like Phil was living next door. Now, guiding the lawnmower down the ramp to the backyard shed, he glanced into their backyard. What would happen when Phil ran out of trees and shrubs to destroy? Was it just plant life he felt compelled to annihilate or was that only the beginning? People who committed acts of insane cruelty to animals often graduated to sickening violence toward people.

Time passed as he stood locked in a fuzzy disconnected state. When Lilijana's voice crashed through his torpor, he was startled and let a choice word slip from his mouth. With good grace as usual, she ignored his language and reminded him to hurry up.

"Lilijana, I'm worried about Phil next door."

"Why? Has he been attacking more plants?"

"I'm telling you something's not right about those two. They hardly ever leave the house. They have violent and raucous arguments. He wields a chainsaw like he's buttering bread and they look wrong."

"They look wrong? What does that mean?"

As David tried to explain, Lilijana began walking away. She cut off his words with, "David, would you please get a move on? We're going to be late."

"The police were just here, you know, and not for no reason," said David to Lilijana's back.

He parked the mower and closed the shed without being able to shake the feeling of dread. His family was in trouble.

CHAPTER TWO

The party had been a real hoot. Much more fun and interesting than David could have imagined, even if he wasn't the type who imagined good things. Every upcoming event, future party, or pending celebration was bound to be painful and mind numbingly dull: filled with ridiculous social charades and effusive sentiment. False smiles, fake laughs and frivolous conversations. What a joke. That's what he supposed. The truth was he always had a good time. Whether it was the company, the food or the alcohol he drank, he enjoyed himself. Lilijana had some extraordinary female friends and David delighted in their company. Although it attracted the ire of the men at these parties, it was harmless fun in David's eyes. The ladies did not seem to mind.

"That was fun," said David to Lilijana as he removed his shoes.

"I'm glad you enjoyed it. I had a good time, too."

David watched Lilijana slip out of her party dress and admired her figure. She had given birth to three children and you could tell. It was not the body of the Lilijana he had married ten years ago, but it was a beautiful body nonetheless. A bit of fat hung around her buttocks, thighs and tummy like an unwanted guest, and she was self-conscious about it. She preferred a one piece swimsuit and a pair of board shorts whenever they hit the beach. He hadn't seen her in a bikini since before Alen was born. Her matronly bra and knickers didn't match, but were close enough to a bikini to allow him a vision.

"Stop staring at me," she protested.

"You're beautiful."

"You're drunk and I'm tired."

There it was: the phrase of death for his exasperated libido. He wanted to complain or try to talk her around, but it seemed futile. David wanted to make love to his wife. Was that a crime? Sure, he wanted to make love every night, and during the day as well. What was wrong with that? It perplexed him that Lilijana found his constant interest strange and mostly inappropriate. Inappropriate was a hurtful word. At least she didn't think it was always inappropriate.

"Yeah," he said, feigning a resigned but cheerful tone, "I'm not sure I have enough energy to even remove my socks."

She smiled warmly. "Let me help you then. You know I can't share a bed with stinky socks."

Lilijana knelt before him, and he became aroused by the mundane action of her pulling off his socks. The sock thing was weird. She'd let him sleep with dirty underpants and even fully dressed in clothes he'd impregnated with body odor, yet she wouldn't allow soiled socks.

"There you go," she said. "I'm off to brush my teeth. Are you going to pick Danijela up from Amy's place tomorrow?"

"Uh-huh."

David watched Lilijana walk away and fought the urge to run after her. He really didn't have the strength for that. He summoned the power to raise himself off the chair, stagger over, fall on the bed and bury his head in the pillow. By the time Lilijana returned from the bathroom, her husband was fast asleep.

***

He blinked furiously, trying to pry open his eyes. They stung and his head hurt. Noise had rudely broken into his dreams. David couldn't work out what the racket was, or where it was coming from. When his eyes popped open he stared at the clock on the tall boy. It was 4:15 a.m. He sat up and listened. Quiet, but he'd heard something before. There it was again.

"Stop it. Stop it!"

The words were as clear as though spoken by Lilijana, who lay blissfully unaware beside him. It was a woman's voice. His tired and liquor-soaked brain warmed to the investigative task. He realized it was Naydine. It came again like a siren wailing.

"Stop it. Leave me alone."

Each word enunciated as though speaking to a classroom of new refugees from a non-English speaking country. Where was Phil? He always participated in these verbal stoushes, but he was not responding. He must be there, or who was Naydine yelling at?

David rubbed his temples and his face. The pain and fuzziness remained. He should get up and do something. What? Call the police again. They had said he should if there were any more disturbances. When was that? Yesterday? David threw the covers off, swung his legs onto the floor and stood. The police had visited less than twenty-four hours earlier.

"I'm useless," he said aloud. "Have to think clearly. Wake up!"

If Lilijana heard, she ignored him. She was also a sound sleeper. What a blessing for her.

David went to the bathroom and spun on the cold water. He scooped his hands underneath and splashed water onto his face. It felt terrific. A scream ripped through the gush and he froze. Another followed and swirled in a whoosh before dying. Dying? David raced to the phone, ignoring the rain of water from his face. He fumbled for the light switch. Phone in hand, he accessed the phonebook and found the number for the Chinaman's Hollow police station. He started to dial then realized no one would be there. The small station was only manned during business hours. Like all regional and outback cop shops, they were undermanned due to government cutbacks. The call would be diverted to Warrawong. While he wondered whether to dial to triple zero, a voice greeted him on the line.

"Warrawong Police. Constable Morrison."

"I've got a barney going on next door. Previous history of domestic disturbance."

In the silence that greeted his initial statement, David realized he was using copspeak and nearly laughed. Was Constable Morrison taken aback by the use of his profession's special language?

Morrison: "What's your name, sir?"

"David Lavender. They're fighting. Yelling and screaming, like they were yesterday arvo."

"Your address please?"

"1010 Princess Highway, Chinaman's Hollow, New—"

"Address where the disturbance is occurring?"

"1008 Princess Highway. Next door."

There was a smashing and bubbling clink of glass breaking, followed by another scream.

"Did you hear that?" asked David. "They broke something. That Phil he's a dangerous bastard. A psycho."

Morrison: "Your phone number, and an alternative contact number please."

David dutifully recited his numbers.

"We'll send a patrol car around as soon as possible. Do not leave your home."

Morrison disconnected. What exactly did as soon as possible mean? David recalled a time when he and a few of his mates were left as chaperones at his younger sister's birthday party. Mum and dad had gone out to dinner, entrusting David as the older, more responsible sibling to look after the place and keep order. As a seventeen-year-old, binge-drinking high school dropout, David was pleased they trusted him. It made him feel important and was a step towards regaining their respect after the stolen car incident eighteen months before.

There was a house full of teenagers drinking alcohol unsupervised and having a good time. It had been peaceful. David had spent most of it listening to his ex-girlfriend, Christine, tell him how Jesus changed her life, and could change David's. He didn't want to change his life, but he had the hots for Christine and hoped to win her back. Just to be with her, hear her voice and look into her big brown eyes was worth putting up with the Jesus talk. David kept an eye on things. The music was loud, as was the talking and laughing. However, it was a party so this was ordinary. Tables and chairs in the backyard were occupied by groups of happy partygoers. It seemed as though the night would proceed without incident and David would pass this test. He'd please his parents, who still distrusted him.

Then a group of young blokes arrived whom nobody seemed to know. David was called to check them out. They said they went to school with his sister, so he asked if she knew them. She did, but they weren't friends. It was at this point that his accumulated wisdom demonstrated nonexistence. He let them in, and things went downhill fast.

Two of them entered the aviary and tried to catch the budgies, so he went to get them out. With all the diplomacy of a pimply kid, David told them they were fuck sticks and should get the fuck out of the aviary. One was surprisingly offended, and returned some choice words of his own. A brawl ensued, and lasted for thirty minutes, during which David retreated into the house and advised everyone to stay inside. Doors were locked and the police were called. David saw fists and feet flying. A chair impacted the head of one of his friends. He saw the blood flow and did nothing.

When the police arrived, the crashers had gone. David warmly told the police they were fuck sticks for being too late. Experienced and unoffended, they allowed David to let off steam and then had a calm conversation about what transpired. What would his parents think? The police couldn't do anything.

David hung up the phone and sighed. He hadn't forgiven himself for being a coward at his sister's party. He wouldn't do nothing tonight. He'd stand up and be a man.

"What are you doing?"

Lilijana interrupted his progress to the front door.

"It's all right, love, go back to bed."

"I asked what you were doing."

His wife's persistence was a wonderful quality. At this moment it was a pain in the neck. "I had to call the police again. About next door."

Lilijana stared at him, waiting for explanation.

He paused, realizing how daft he'd probably sound. "I'm going to show them where the trouble is."

A heavy sigh preceded her reply. "Leave it to the police. Can't you mind your own business?"

"Can't you mind yours?"

Out through the opened door, David crossed the lawn. As he reached the invisible fence between his place and 1008, the police arrived. No lights and no siren. David was not disappointed. It was, after all, 4:00 a.m. He was glad he didn't have to knock on the neighbor's door again. It would have been necessary to prove that critical moments would be met with resolute bravery, not the cowardice he displayed at his sister's party and numerous times since.

The police left their vehicle and strolled over. David thought they should have been marching, not strolling. The scene was a virtual replay of the previous visit. Sadly, the cute female officer was absent.

When it was over, David went to bed where Lilijana was waiting.

"Well?"

"Everything's all right. They promised to behave themselves and the police said to call if it happens again."

"It will, won't it?"

"I reckon so."

David's biggest worry was not that Phil and Naydine would have another violent argument. Phil might actually hurt her, and then come looking for more action. Both neighbors would realize it was David who brought the police every time they had a blue. They would peg him as a nosy neighbor with too much time on his hands. David was prepared to live with the label, but not if he and his loved ones became targets; reasons why Phil should go after the troublesome stickybeak next door.

He could feel Lilijana's gaze pressing into his head. David didn't want to talk, so he rolled away and reached for the sanctity of sleep.

CHAPTER THREE

Creative was not a word people used to describe David Lavender, but there were times when he experienced the secret pleasure of conspiracy. Although he appeared to be clueless, David was, in fact, a genius at work. There were times when intense urges compelled him into enthusiastic endeavor.

This business with the psycho and his offsider living next door was one of those things that burst into his dull existence and threatened the peace he enjoyed. It was a catalyst for abnormal creativity. David decided he must do something about his neighbors. He couldn't discuss the issue with Lilijana because she thought he was meddling. She couldn't see the danger they were in. She hadn't looked into the eyes of the madman, Phil. Hadn't seen him wielding the chainsaw with sick pleasure. Though Lilijana didn't know what she was talking about, she seemed strangely impregnable to logical argument. Perhaps she believed rational debate was her domain. Not something he was adept at and therefore an unworthy opponent. He laughed out loud.

"What's so funny?" asked Lilijana.

David opened his eyes and blinked. It was light. He was awake. Lilijana had spoken to him. She had probably been talking to him for a while: trying to penetrate his oblivion. These morning chats in bed were sweet times for David and Lilijana. Yesterday was history. Each new morning was a fresh start in life. In another way it was a clash of civilizations. Lilijana's kingdom of sunshine versus David's empire of gloom.

"I was thinking about how much I love our morning chats."

"Really?"

David noted her tone of surprise. "Yes." He rolled over and snuggled close. "It feels like we're the only people in the world. It feels safe."

Lilijana shifted a little to press her body into his. Her breath smelled but he had gotten over that a long time ago. The promise of good morning sex was what he loved about morning chats because that was invariably where they ended up. If she stayed in bed and talked to him, she had something else in mind.

"It feels a bit dangerous," she said, with a kiss. "But I like talking to you as well." The reference to danger acknowledged his arousal.

David smiled. "The thing is, I can't think of anything to say."

"That's okay. Neither can I."

Later, at the breakfast table, with Cornflakes crunching inside his mouth, David was tallying up the frequency of good morning sex. Sadly, it was easy to count.

"Why don't we talk more often?" he asked, as she joined him at the table.

She sipped her coffee. "Don't be greedy, David."

There it was. A man wanting regular sex with his wife was considered greedy for his heinous desire. Maybe he should settle for twice a month. Damn it was difficult to accept. It wasn't wrong to desire Lilijana. What was abnormal was permission to express that desire only twice a month. It was a mystery to him how Lilijana could switch her libido on and off. Mostly off. If his sex drive came with an on off switch, it was definitely broken.

He ate another mouthful of Cornflakes then wiped off skim milk, which dribbled down his chin. A meaningful afterglow glance. She drank her coffee, alternating each sip with a spoonful of yogurt. He crunched. She sipped. They both swallowed. In silence. It was such a poignant moment that David was afraid to say anything lest the spell be smashed. He was seeing his life, their life together with clarity. Safe. Comfortable. Easy. Nice. Why wasn't this enough?

Now there were two catalysts for creativity in his life. The residents of 1008, and his wife. The first offended his sense of calm and order. The second denied his need for satisfaction and excitement. The neighbors from hell scared him but energized him. They made him feel like his purpose was to act, with whatever means necessary, to protect himself and his family. His wife from Heaven bored him. He winced. The thought was repugnant yet true. Lilijana bored him often, and annoyed him even more. He could imagine life without her. It wasn't all good, yet it wasn't all bad. He needed a woman to talk to whenever he wanted, about whatever he wanted. A woman to do things for him and never nag. A woman who lusted after him. Lilijana made him feel like he needed another woman.

The spoon clinked rudely against the bowl as he finished the last of his cornflakes. He could take his bowl to the counter, open the cereal box and shake in more cornflakes. He could have more if he wanted. David glanced at Lilijana and wondered what she would think of his cornflakes analogy. It wasn't perfect; no metaphor ever was.

"Breakfast philosophy," he said.

Half-standing, having finished her yogurt, she looked at David with confusion. "What?"

"I was just thinking that I could have more if I wanted."

"Aren't you going to be late for work?"

That was it. The bliss of the morning was over. Time to face the world. Time to apply some creative thinking to these festering problems. Time to get off his proverbial arse and do something. All the commitment was present, as was the eagerness. Unfortunately, the solutions to his problems weren't. He had no idea what to do about his neighbors or the unsettlingly strong feelings of marital discontent.

He shaved and dressed for work. Brushed his teeth and called goodbye. Lilijana may or may not have responded. He opened the garage door then settled into the car. Heavy hearted, he turned the key in the ignition, selected drive, released the handbrake, glanced through the windscreen and drove out. He remembered the training program at work which was due to start today. His spirits lifted.

Two weeks ago, the Human Resources manager at Dean & Branxton, had asked him to participate as part of a workplace literacy project. He protested that he knew how to read and write. Was the company looking for a way to get rid of him? Assured this was not the case, he agreed to a time and a date for a pre-training assessment. David felt anxious and was unable to shake the feeling that the assessment would prove him incompetent. Right-thinking David knew he was not incompetent in the execution of his work. Wrong-thinking David feared the exposure of hidden inadequacies.

He arrived at the staff training room and found a woman waiting, presumably for him. She had long thick hair restrained by a ponytail. The clasp of her bra hid beneath a slip. A thin gold chain encircled the back of her neck above the stiff white collar of her shirt.

He knocked softly on the open door. 'G'day. I'm David Lavender.'

She introduced herself then explained the assessment process in a reassuring voice. He absorbed it like a child listening to a bedtime story. His anxiety melted away and every time she smiled his heart started beating again. Several times she asked if he was okay. He lied and said he was fine. In fact, he was mesmerized. Her eyes were blue grey and bright. If not for their sparkle he might have thought they were made of steel. By the time he reached the end of the assessment and had ticked the required boxes, he had managed to overcome the intoxication of her perfume and her presence. She finished with encouraging words that went in one ear and out the other, then said she would see him again when the training started. He smiled. She smiled. He stood still, unaware it was time to leave, or just plain unwilling. She smiled some more. Then he left.

'What is her name?' he said aloud as he drove.

Moments passed before he remembered: Julia. His grip tightened on the steering wheel and his foot pressed harder on the accelerator.

***

The training session was due to start at 7:00 am. Early as usual, David found Julia writing on the whiteboard. She had changed the layout of the room. The table at the front was obviously hers, as it was covered with piles of paper, a folder and a drink bottle. The others were lined up against the wall opposite the whiteboard. He didn't know how many of his coworkers were going to attend. David hoped there were none. One and a half hours alone with Julia was a wonderful prospect, even if she delivered some mind-numbingly boring training program about communication skills.

"You're early," said Julia, continuing to write on the board.

David wondered about her tone. Was she glad he was early? Personally pleased or just professionally?

He watched as she finished writing: 'What the hell I am doing here?'

That was cute. It reminded him of Lilijana's recount of her first lecture in comparative religion at Sydney University where the words on the blackboard read: 'There is nothing interesting in all the world.'

A few minutes later, the lecturer made a dramatic entrance. With long hair and a ragged beard, many thought he looked like Jesus, or at least the Hollywood version. He strode to the board and completed what the students had not realized was only half a sentence.

'...except religion.'

It was a good attention grabber: a clever way to engage the audience, to arrest their apathy and lock it up. David pondered Julia's question as he sat.

"I'm always early to work. Years of habit. Like a machine."

He tried to suck the last back into his mouth like a runaway piece of spaghetti. Julia smiled enigmatically. David decided to press on.

"Gives me the choice of seats in here, anyway."

"Are your workmates similarly punctual?" she asked.

Similarly punctual? He liked that teacher talk. She could have simply asked if the others would be on time. He would have replied probably not, as they were a bunch of slack arsed bludgers who needed a boot in the backside to get them going. He allowed the words, 'similarly punctual,' to float inside his head. David was used to such speech. Lilijana had studied at university and willfully adopted sophisticated speech. It sounded weird sometimes. Out of place, like a ballet dancer at a heavy metal concert, but it was kind of cute. When he suggested she was stuck up, Lilijana would say, "If there are many ways to say something, why not try them all?" David suddenly realized that Julia waited for an answer. He opted for diplomatic with a dash of bullshit.

"They should probably be on time. They're a good bunch of blokes. Who are you expecting?"

She shuffled some papers on her desk then found her list. "Jake Frame."

"Good young fella," said David, though he hardly knew him.

"Jose Rivas."

"Yep."

"Sam Burnside. James Freeman. Nik Asimovski and Billy Trajezski."

David was about to answer that he knew and liked them all when a group of his workmates arrived. His time alone with Julia was over.

"Smelly," Nik said loudly as he sat down heavily next to David. "How's it going?"

They all thought it was hilarious to call him 'Smelly' because of his surname. The stupid bastards didn't even know what lavender was until he explained it. He had used gestures to indicate it smelled good. Unfortunately, they had interpreted his actions as applying to a bad smell and that cracked them up. The moniker 'Smelly' had been offered and its acceptance was inevitable. David had laughed along, even though he was offended. He could control himself well at times. This time, with Julia watching, David wanted to tell Nik he should shove his head in the toilet for a whiff of something stinky. His second thought was to remind Nik and buddies that people usually showered daily. His third thought was to let it slide, and impressively he did. Although he didn't want Julia to know his hated nickname, he reasoned she knew where it came from and would admire self control rather than childish abuse and threats.

"I like the smell of lavender," she said.

David flushed with embarrassment, relieved to discover that Nik had missed her comment. Dumb wog wouldn't have understood it anyway.

"Good morning, gentlemen," she began. "Welcome to Apply Basic Communication Skills."

Julia spoke with authority and commanded respectful silence. David could barely contain his interest in her voice, hair, eyes, breasts and legs. The others seemed unaffected by her obvious sexual power. From the way they talked about women, being married didn't stop them from lusting after snarling ladies in their hidden porno mags. Julia was beautiful: a goddess. Either his coworkers were mysteriously immune to her sexuality or they were good at covering up.

The hour and a half passed quickly while David played the role of diligent student. He left the room in a daze, uncertain of how he would make it through the rest of the day. A wildfire of ideas burned in his mind. He could not stop thinking about Julia. No matter how he tried, she exploded back into his consciousness. He began to count the hours until the next session. It couldn't come fast enough.

On the drive home, a dilemma emerged. If Lilijana remembered the training, she would ask how it went. David would have to decide how much he could safely tell her. Hopefully, she would not go into detective inspector mode. Her eyes would drill into his and a lie would be exposed as easily as peeling an overripe banana. Under the force of examination, he doubted he could deflect her suspicion. What if she connected his desire for more cornflakes with his new infatuation with the communications trainer?

David hit the steering wheel with his hand and shook his head. Unless he could extinguish these searing flames of lust, Lilijana would see right through him. Worse still, was the prophetic vision of him hunting Julia to satisfy his passions.

"Bloody hell," he said aloud, "and what about the neighbors?"

To maintain his sanity and keep his family safe, he had to get rid of Phil and Naydine. David's head throbbed. What to do? Nausea swirled as the pain in his head intensified. He pulled over to the side of the road and turned the ignition off. Trying to take deep breaths, he gulped and gasped like a fish out of water. Nothing helped. Panic rose like a flood. He reached for his phone and speed-dialed for an ambulance. After giving his location, he started to lose his peripheral sight. The operator spoke but her words sounded garbled and he didn't know how to respond. The pain. The pressure. Darkness closed in and swallowed him. He dropped the phone on the floor of the car.

CHAPTER FOUR

"Welcome back, David. How are you feeling?"

The voice sounded familiar but fuzzy, as though the speaker had their hand over their mouth. When David opened his eyes the white sterility of the room told him he was in hospital. His gaze honed in on a gray spot in the middle of the ceiling beside the stark fluorescent light. It looked like a water stain with a pattern he found intriguing.

"David? Can you hear me?"

More insistent, the nurse demanded his attention.

Without removing his gaze from the pattern, David imagined a face to go with her voice. Unfortunately, it wasn't pretty. His first thoughts were of a broad, wide face. Grey hair pulled back in a bun severe enough to cause nosebleeds. Rimmed spectacles with thick lenses in front of beady eyes. He shivered.

"David? Please say something."

A body came into view. Huge breasts; enough to compensate half a dozen flat-chested ladies. A name tag: Helga. He twitched violently.

"He's having a fit, Mum. Call the doctor. Press the button."

Now David was confused. Did the horrible Helga bring her son to work? It was extremely difficult to work out what to say. 'I'm all right.' Yes. When he tried to speak, he found his voice missing in action. It was being strangled or smothered by something. He reached for his mouth and found an oxygen mask. The burning dryness of his throat almost rendered him mute.

He pulled the mask off but it would not travel far due to the elastic around his head. Frantically, he pushed it onto his forehead.

"It's all right, David. The doctor is coming. Please try to stay calm."

He turned his head toward Lilijana. "Lili, baby." He coughed. "Hi. I'm all right."

Her arms opened and her head plunged onto his chest as Lilijana attempted a hug. Although the movement was frightening in speed and intensity, David could feel the strength of her love. Relief. Compassion. The warmth of her body infused him with life. When she broke the embrace, she took his face in her hands. He saw past the wet redness of her eyes to the passionate heart of the woman he loved. She kissed him softly on the mouth, then hard, as if she didn't do it properly the first time.

"Are you sure you're okay?" she asked.

"I feel okay but I'm not a doctor. I am in hospital, you know."

Lilijana smiled at the feeble joke.

"You had us worried there, Dave."

Looking past Lilijana, he saw his large-framed stepson, Tomo. David was surprised that he came at all and had spoken with concern. To avoid the sparks that usually flew between them, David returned his gaze to the ceiling.

"Thanks for your concern and for being with your mother. Appreciate it."

David heard Tomo's reply but it faded into the shadowy place from which Lilijana's voice had emerged. He felt the pattern calling for his undiluted attention. As he stared at the unusual swirling, he remembered the scene in Poltergeist when trinkets fell through the ceiling in the midst of eerie smoke. Later, a rope traveled through that hole from the bedroom to the living room, allowing the mother to rescue her daughter, Carol-Anne. Both of them covered in pink slime. David wondered if this place was a portal to another world.

A hand on his shoulder, firm but not rough.

"Doctor's here."

David muttered about not being able to breathe. The doctor replaced the oxygen mask over his mouth and nose. Relieved of the need to speak, he returned his gaze to the ceiling. Was there some connection between mischievous ghosts and his stepson? There were similarities. Both were less often seen than unseen and created their fair share of trouble. Maybe Tomo was a poltergeist. David made a conscious effort to think kindly towards his stepson by delving into the distant past.

When David met him eleven years ago, he had liked and empathized with Tomo, the seven-year-old son of the woman he loved. Lilijana had nervously introduced them. Tomo was old enough to have had a powerful bond with his father, and resisted any man who threatened to fill his shoes. Tomo's paternal attitude toward those who entered Lilijana's world stemmed from the need to protect her now that his father was gone. His dad had died as a soldier, something that Tomo was proud of. It had strengthened his mind and body, making Tomo fiercely loyal and alarmingly confident. He carried Lilijana through the trauma of loss due to a war she didn't believe in or even understand. Then they had to relocate to the other side of the world. Tomo's childhood ended, abruptly and violently, on the terrible day that letter announced his father's death on the battlefield.

"He just needs to rest," said Lilijana to Tomo.

"He needs to stop being an arsehole."

David focused on suppressing a smile. There he was. The Tomo he knew and loved. Or not. Tomo, his mother's defender, thinking the worst of David, as though his collapse was a deliberate act designed to upset Lilijana. Nineteen years old now and still a complete prick. David felt a tsunami of self justification surging in his mind. Tomo, the ungrateful smart-mouthed brat who does what he wants, exactly when he wants. The narrow-minded, hatred-driven tool who can't see past his bitterness to appreciate kindness in others. Especially in the man who cared for him, gave him a home, bought stuff for him, drove him to his sporting activities, and loved his mother unselfishly. It hurt to be unappreciated. David wanted to give his stepson a mouthful of angry resentment.

"That's not fair, Tomo. Maybe you should go. Thanks for bringing me in. I'll talk to you later."

Lilijana kissed away Tomo's protests and enveloped him in a hug. Tomo towered over her, so the sight of them embracing was awkward and amusing. Tomo left without a word.

David pushed the oxygen mask back onto to his forehead. "I'm sorry, baby."

"I understand. Forget about it. I'm just glad you're okay."

"I am," replied David. Lilijana was forgiving of the heavy soup that simmered on the stove of his and Tomo's relationship. Occasionally it boiled over and the pot needed to be removed but it was always returned to the stove. It lasted until the day Tomo left home and broke out on his own. Then David had turned off the stove and let the hotplate cool.

"The doctor said it was most likely an anxiety attack."

"When did he say that?"

"While you were lying there praying for a demon to burst from the ceiling and swallow Tomo."

"Damn," said David, "You know me too well."

"What was that movie you liked, Pootergoose?"

David laughed. "Poltergeist."

She sat carefully on the edge of his bed and began to stroke his arm. "I don't know why you like those scary movies. They're horrible."

"I like being scared," replied David, while thinking how much he liked this attention from Lilijana. What he felt was not sexual. He just felt nice. He felt loved and close to her. "Most of them are funny. Not scary at all."

She frowned. "I don't like being scared, David. I feel very afraid right now. Why did this happen to you? What are you worried about?"

The dilemma knocked on his door again. He couldn't tell her about Julia. Nor could he talk about the neighbors. Every time he did, Lilijana dismissed it as nonsense. She wasn't going to take his side just because he was in hospital. In fact, the scenario was absurd. He'd worked himself up over nothing. The potential threat of Phil evaporated like a raindrop on a scorching concrete road. So how could he explain? Should he fabricate something to satisfy her? Should he plead ignorance? Yes, ignorance.

"I don't know," he said, looking into her eyes to hide the lie. "I was driving and listening to the radio when I started to feel unwell and it suddenly got worse. I panicked because I didn't know what was wrong with me."

In silence, Lilijana continued to caress his arm. Then she stopped and took his hand. She squeezed it tightly and said, "You can be a real idiot, David."

He turned his attention to going home. The greedy man who lived inside experienced the first rumblings of renewed appetite and he knew that hospital food was unlikely to satisfy him.

"Do you want me to buy you a pizza for dinner?"

"Sure, we can grab one on the way home."

Lilijana smiled and shook her head, "Sorry, mate, they want you to spend the night."

"Damn," David said. Though an overnight stay was appalling, with pizza and his wife, he could cope. If only he could keep his mind off Julia. Even with Lilijana touching him and speaking to him, he could still see Julia. This was bad, evil in fact, but he allowed the other woman to share his personal head space in an unobtrusive way. What harm could there be in that?

CHAPTER FIVE

The holiday in hospital had afforded him a sanctuary that proved painfully brief. In the midst of a tempest of negativity, David was summoned by a knock to the front door two days after his release.

He and Lilijana had argued before she left to go shopping, which was not uncommon due to David's impulsivity. She would only buy what was on her list, and David wanted non-listed items. The tin of dynamite hot Stag chilli, which he insisted he buy and consume, was not on his radar at home. When he saw it on the shelf, though, it generated appetite. That was exactly the kind of purchase that riled Lilijana. She didn't think of things like light globes or plug-in room fresheners, and if he wanted a chocolate-covered vanilla ice cream then he just had to be there, so they'd agreed to shop together. This morning, however, she insisted that he rest. When he contended that he was fine and would appreciate being allowed to leave, Lilijana accused him of exaggerating his alleged incarceration and being frivolous with his health.

David smiled at Lilijana using a word like 'frivolous.' Upon arrival in Australia, she'd been a shy young woman who could barely string two sentences together in English. As David opened the door, the smile fell from his face like a rotten lemon.

"Morning, Mr. Lavender," said the mountainous police officer through the screen door.

It was the same cop who had addressed David's first emergency call. He was again accompanied by the cute female officer.

She spoke next. "Are you all right, sir? You look very pale."

Good, thought David. If I appear unwell they won't think my pallor is caused by guilt. Nothing to be guilty about, anyway. "I've been in hospital."

"Nothing serious I hope," she said. They both adopted concerned demeanors simultaneously.

"No," replied David, unsure how much information he should provide.

The male officer said, "Perhaps we could come in and talk. Then you could sit down if that will be more comfortable for you."

It was a good suggestion but David demurred. "No, I'm fine. What can I do for you?"

"Mr. Valentine next door has lodged a complaint against you," said the female officer.

David thought he was already white. Apparently there were different shades. As he stood in stunned silence, the cute police officer stepped closer and took his arm.

"Please sit down, Mr. Lavender. Before you fall down."

He allowed her to gently push him inside and guide him to the nearest chair. The giant followed them in, ducking through the doorway.

"Would you like some water?" the female officer asked.

When David nodded, she headed for the kitchen. The male cop stood uncomfortably, waiting for his partner. She returned and handed David the glass. He took it gratefully and drank it. When he lowered the glass, she spoke.

"Mr. Valentine alleges that you have been," she paused, searching for the right words, "stalking him."

"What?" exploded David. "Stalking that psycho? Why would I do that?"

Unperturbed by his outburst, she pulled a notepad from her breast pocket, flipped a few pages then began to read. "'Following me around the streets. Watching me over the back fence. Knocking on my door at inappropriate times of the day.' Those are his words. What do you say?"

"I say he's a fucking lunatic. I'm not following him anywhere. I saw him at the train station once but he didn't even recognize me. He doesn't leave the house except to chainsaw massacre the shrubs in his backyard. That's why I was looking over the fence. A bloke like that shouldn't be allowed to own a chainsaw."

The two officers stared at him, as though he were a dangerous - approach with severe caution - suspect.

"I only knocked on the door when I heard all that banging and shouting. I wanted to make sure everything was all right. Neighborly concern. Hasn't that prick ever heard of that?"

This irrational outburst wasn't doing him any favors. No doubt he appeared unstable, and they thought Phil was justified in lodging a complaint. David's ranting would have convinced anyone he was capable of stalking, or worse. It was too late to take back the words.

The police were trained to form opinions quickly, to assess people's weaknesses and culpability. The concerned expressions they wore earlier had morphed into frowns. He couldn't discern whether their eyes held pity, or fear, or something else.

"Mr. Lavender," said the male officer as he stepped closer. "I'm going to have to insist that you calm down and control your language. You are not helping yourself."

Strong words were brewing, but David resisted the urge to speak.

"We also have to insist that you leave Mr. Valentine and his partner alone. Stay off their property and mind your own business. They want to be left alone. They want you to respect their privacy."

David took a deep breath, and exhaled slowly. "I am minding my own business, but you've been called a couple of times to handle their domestic disputes. If what they do impacts my family, I'm not going to do nothing. I'm not going to bend over and get fucked. If I'm in danger, I'll do what I must. Understand?"

The mountainous man leaned down to make intimidating eye contact. David gulped and backed into his seat.

"You will be fucked if you don't pull your head in, Mr. Lavender. Understand?"

The words were cold and controlled. The cute female placed a hand on her partner's shoulder. No doubt she agreed with him.

New tides of resentment swelled. The police were supposed to defend law and order, support and protect the good guys. Wasn't he one of the good guys? Ten minutes ago he wouldn't have had any doubts. Now, as he watched the police leave, he suspected he might be crossing the line between good citizen and criminal.

The male officer ducked out through the door but his partner stopped and turned. "I apologize for his behavior, Mr. Lavender. However, next time we speak, and I seriously hope we don't, I want you to be more circumspect. Do we understand each other?"

David nodded. He received the message loud and clear. He was on his own in his war with Mr. Valentine.

The female officer left, closing the door behind her.

David remained seated, shocked and seething. How did he become the bad guy? His blood pressure medication didn't stop him from wanting a drink. David forced himself to rise. There was Chianti in the fridge. That would do the job.

The wine was sweet. His mood was sour. Mr. Valentine. Calling him that made him sound civilized and normal. The neighbors' domestic disputes were as far removed from civilized as crapping in a cardboard box, and no one wielding a chainsaw with such frenetic passion could possibly seem normal. Phil was an animal. Unless David could get rid of him, someone would be hurt.

As he drained his glass of Chianti, a cockroach scampered across the kitchen. He stomped on it. "Goodbye Phil."

"We're home," called Lilijana as she pushed open the front door.

David rinsed his glass in the sink before grabbing a cookie from the jar on the kitchen counter. He took a bite and mumbled, "That was quick."

"What did you say?"

"I said you didn't take long."

"I never take long."

Laden with plastic shopping bags, Lilijana shuffled inside, followed by Alen and Danijela who were also doing their part.

"Don't worry about helping us," said Lilijana. "We've got it covered."

Ordinarily, this would have been said with sarcasm. Now her remark seemed reasonable. David hoped she'd keep her distance until the smell of Chianti dissipated. He didn't have the energy for an argument, and would soon be hungry enough to feel faint. He slipped into the role of the appreciative recuperating husband, which in all honesty he was.

Lilijana arrived in the kitchen and laid her bags near the sink. "You didn't sneak a glass of Chianti, did you, David?"

There was no point denying it when Lilijana had seen the evidence. "Just one. The police were here."

"The police?"

David had not thought of using the police visit to divert attention but it worked. The problem was how much information to release. He may have jumped out of the frying pan but if he told her everything he would land in the fire and get burned.

"Apparently, our neighbor thinks I'm stalking him."

"Who, John?"

Lilijana knew his name and this worried him. David had only referred to the guy as Phil or with a number of unflattering epithets like weirdo or tool. Did Lilijana know him? No. Was she acquainted with him? He tried to eject the implications of her knowing Phil's real name.

"John. Yes, John Valentine."

"What have you done?"

There it was. The slap in the face. The punch in the stomach. He wanted her to protest in outrage on his behalf. Declare that the accusation was ridiculous, and couldn't possibly be true. Instead, she joined the baying crowd that circled with stones in their hands.

"Nothing!"

"Why are you shouting at me?"

"I'm not. Why do you assume I've done something? I told you Phil is mental. He doesn't look right or act right."

"What are you saying?"

"I'm saying that I'm your husband and Phil is a dickhead." David decided to stay on the offensive and not let her answer. "Why are you accusing me?"

"You do seem to have an unhealthy interest in their affairs."

"An unhealthy interest in their affairs? Is that what you think? I've tried to talk to you but you always brush me off."

"What our neighbors do is none of our business."

"It becomes our business when it becomes our business."

"What does that mean?"

David was running out of puff. Nausea gripped him and his head pounded. He hoped he looked as ill as he felt. Knowing he was going to lose this verbal joust, he decided it was time to retreat.

"I don't feel well, sorry. Can we talk about it later?"

Without waiting for her permission, he headed for the bathroom. He'd surrendered and hoped the issue would never come up again. Bile burned the back of his throat. He burped twice before he made it to the bathroom and knelt to take the wheel of the porcelain bus.

CHAPTER SIX

Sparks become flames and rage to wild blazes. Orange fingers of fire hunt you down as you run. Smoke suffocates you while it scratches your nose and throat. You feel faint and panic leads to helplessness. The fear that forced you to flee is replaced by an eerie calm: acceptance of your fate. The futility of action paralyses your legs. You fall. A different smell invades the air when you burn. The angry heat devours you.

David would never share this mindset with anyone. Not even Lilijana. These dark thoughts frightened and shook him violently when he tumbled down the well of despair. Unlike others, whose black dogs were ever present companions, his was an infrequent visitor. The idea of personifying depression struck David as reassuring. If it was a thing it seemed more threatening. At least with personality it had some semblance of humanity. He hoped so, anyway.

His room was dark. Lilijana had drawn the curtains, which were added when he worked the night shift years ago. David had never adjusted to sleeping during the day. Instead, it had ruined his health. He had lost ten kilograms and arguably ten points off his IQ. Despite the reduced income which followed his move back to day shifts, his health was more important. Lilijana found a casual job to help out. Now she worked full time.

There was a smothering stuffiness in the room. David's throat burned from vomiting. Such a violent action. The human body goes to extremes to expel unwanted substances. Even sneezing closes your eyes and stops your heart for a nano second.

David rolled out of bed, pulled on a bathrobe and slipped on his scuffs. He went to the kitchen to make himself tea and toast. He took his breakfast to the lounge room, where he switched on the television and settled down with the remote control. Half an hour later, someone knocked on the door twice before resorting to urgent bang. David hurried to the door, figuring it was the police. Not this time, though.

His stepson stood on the verandah with his fist cocked, ready to knock again. Tomo was an arsehole. No matter which way you looked at him, he was bag of unpleasantries. He had some pals but David couldn't imagine why they'd want such a bad mannered, bad tempered friend. His mates were probably arseholes, too. Or maybe David was the odd man out. In this crazy world where right could be turned into wrong and vice versa, maybe people appreciated and admired boorish louts.

Tomo's presence was not expected or welcomed. David wished Tomo would never visit. The day he moved out, swearing and threatening violence, brought happiness to David. Everything shitty in his life left the building. Lilijana had tried to engender closeness between them in an attempt to rebuild her family. Tomo had never been sold on the idea. As long as David remained outside himself and Lilijana, he could accept David's presence. All pretense of playing nice had departed in a huff of resentment when David and Lilijana informed the boy they were to be married.

David remembered nine-year-old Tomo's eloquent disapproval.

"Fuck that!"

"Tomo!" replied Lilijana in shock.

"I had a dad. I don't want another one!"

It was hard to know what to say. Arguing with an irate child, full of prepubescent rage, was neither wise nor productive.

The conversation between Lilijana and David afterwards was awkward. David wasn't sure how to proceed. Should he offer comfort and encouragement? Should he remain silent and wait for her to speak? Should he touch her? Embrace her? In the end he did nothing. Without looking at him she said, "He'll come around." Her low voice held conviction.

"So you still want to marry me?"

She raised her eyes to meet his, tears shimmering in her lower lids. The nod was imperceptible but sufficient.

"Dave!" said Tomo just below a shout. "Hello? You with me, man?" Tomo's deep masculine voice was tinged with an Eastern European accent, the vowels a little off center.

"Yep. Your mum's not here."

"Shit."

Tomo began to prowl as though Lilijana had deliberately aggravated him. David entertained the idea of getting in Tomo's face. However, Tomo was so tall that David would need a footstool to see eye to eye. Tomo believed his greater height equaled superior character. There was no way to educate a fool.

"You should call before you come. Save your time." David wondered about the tone of voice he'd used. Did he unconsciously growl every time he spoke to Tomo so it sounded like an insult or threat, or the condescension Tomo accused him of?

"When will she be back?"

"I don't know. I've only just crawled out of bed."

"You're no fucking help."

He wanted Tomo to leave. "Actually, I remember something about a party that Alen had been invited to. I don't know when she'll be back."

"I gotta go," grumbled Tomo. "Tell her I was here, all right?"

"Sure," said David, not intending to follow the order. "See ya."

Tomo left without another word.

Once his Subaru roared to life and exploded down the street, David relaxed. He had tried to befriend Tomo while providing what a stepfather should: a stable home, food on the table, clothes to wear. He'd fixed broken toys, repaired punctured tires, and provided taxi service for Tomo and his fan club during the six years Tomo played football. The last had been difficult because David was a rugby league man through and through. Having played rugby league as youth, then coached and refereed, it was disappointing that Tomo showed no interest. It seemed certain ethnic backgrounds virtually guaranteed a football career.

No matter how he tried, David never broke through. Tomo put up with his presence and was pleased to cooperate and be nice when it suited: if there was, in his eyes, sufficient return on investment. To purchase something for him, he would happily go to the mall. He refused to go grocery or clothes shopping, but, when he did, he showed the enthusiasm of a dog asleep in the shade on a hot day.

Though David was no psychologist, he knew at least this much. Tomo blamed the world and everyone in it for taking away his father. The chip on his shoulder was more like a sack of potatoes.

Lilijana had met Tomo's father, Petar, in 1988 at a social dance for the young Croat men of the Brezovica district in Zagreb. He had just come of age and was required to do two years of military service. Lilijana had not wanted to love a soldier but Petar was tall and handsome, charming and confident. He was a serious, passionate man who made her feel special, and he wanted a farm and a family. Their wedding was the kind of romantic event most young girls dreamed of. With the blessing of both families, they married with the wide-eyed, love-soaked dreaminess of idealistic youth. Lilijana's fears about losing Petar to the war convinced her to love him with all she had. She maximized their brief times together and forsook birth control. Born in 1992, Tomo was a surprise to Petar but not to Lilijana.

Petar's father offered them a parcel of land and money to build a house. It seemed another step toward the fulfillment of their dreams. Lilijana did not consider what might be lurking round the corner. Disaster became an abstract concept: something that happened to other people, in other places, at other times. She felt blessed.

After completing his tour of duty, Petar was recalled immediately to fight in the JNA against the Croat insurgency. Those were troubled times in the Yugoslav Republic of Croatia. The war raged for four years, and claimed up to twenty thousand causalities, Petar among them. Lilijana and Tomo joined the hundreds of thousands who were forced to leave their homeland as the bitter fighting continued.

Thoughts of Lilijana having to flee with her son in her arms made David both angry and sad. He wasn't one to take sides in other people's battles but he shared Lilijana's bitterness toward the Serbs for what they had done.

As the front door swung open, David started and sprang to his feet "Hi. How's it going?"

Lilijana looked at him and frowned. "What's wrong?"

David walked to her and kissed her before going to the car to help unload the shopping bags.

"What are you doing?"

David realized his mistake when he ran into Daniela. The shopping was over and done with. He'd forgotten what he told Tomo not more than half an hour ago. Why couldn't he focus and remember? Could it be an aftershock related to his panic attack? The doctor had not warned him. He'd expected only tiredness. Were these demented moments simply the result of exhaustion?

Lilijana stood in doorway watching him. "Are you all right?"

He didn't want to tell her what he'd been thinking. Lilijana would only worry, and she preferred not to speak of the past. She had wept when she told her story, making David feel useless and angry. Against the raw pain of her memories, talking did not help. Her scars remained and always would.

David tried to shift gears and ask Alen about the party. He was sucking on a musk stick and mumbled that it had been great. Lilijana stood waiting for an answer. She was going to make him talk and that presented a dilemma. His 'something is wrong with me' appearance had two causes. Which should he tell her about? Both were unstable fault lines, and the last thing he wanted was another earthquake.

"Tomo came to see you."

"Why doesn't he call first? It makes me think he's trying to avoid me."

"Don't be diriculous," said David adopting Lilijana's mispronunciation of the word ridiculous. She had never managed to break the habit and now it was a private joke.

"You think I'm being diriculous, do you?"

The word's fire-extinguishing qualities were overpowered by her anger. Lilijana stormed off when he smiled. If there was one thing she hated (and there wasn't only one thing) it was not to be taken seriously. He called her back to no avail.

Alen stood by the car bouncing a ball on the driveway. With respect to Alen and Danijela, Tomo referred to himself as their half-brother, the connotation one of distaste. Alen should have been able to look up to Tomo. Instead, Tomo had shut him out with disinterested sarcasm and hostility. Their ten-year age gap may as well have been a hundred and ten.

"Come play with me, Dad."

"Sorry, mate. I need to rest."

Agreeably, Alen returned to his solo game. He could be absentminded and detached, which Lilijana saw as laziness and insolence. Alen reminded David of himself. In juxtaposition to Tomo, David couldn't criticize Alen.

"Where's Danijela?"

Alen continued to bounce his ball. "I don't know. Inside?"

"Of course." As David turned, a car pulled into the next-door driveway. Phil and Naydine didn't own a car, and they never had visitors apart from the police. The white Commodore station wagon stopped abruptly before the garage. Covertly stickybeaking, David wandered over to Alen and called for the ball. He kept one eye on the noisily idling Commodore.

"Here, Dad," said Alen thrusting the ball in his direction. "What're you looking at?"

"Ever seen a car next door before? Besides a police car?"

Alen paused. "I don't know. Why?"

The passenger door popped open and Phil emerged from the station wagon. Looking his usual disheveled self, he leaned back inside then straightened and slammed the door. With a gravelly roar, the tires of the Commodore spun on the asphalt until the vehicle flew backwards onto the road. Phil disappeared into 1008.

"Dad?"

"I've never seen that car here."

"You're weird," was all Alen replied before he went inside.

His bizarre fascination with Phil and Naydine mystified David. There really was no reason for his intense curiosity, nor any justification for such an unhealthy interest in other people's business. He enjoyed it. Why? Was it the same vicarious thrill women derived from reading *New Idea* or watching Desperate Housewives? Was it that his own life, had settled into the rut of domestic routine, and he needed something else? Some spark. Some passion. Julia.

"Shit!" said David. His brain was a mixed grill, jumping from one dangerous obsession to another. Throw a sausage on the barbecue. Then a steak. What about a kebab? Can I eat that much? Who cares. Have an egg. A lamb chop. Sizzle, crack, pop! Insanity seemed to be lurking. David felt he was losing control. He laughed. Another sign of madness? No. He wasn't crazy, not even close. Phil and Naydine are trouble, he reasserted. They cannot be trusted. Julia is hot and I want her, but I won't have her. I love my wife and my life. I don't have to endure Tomo's presence often. I like my job. I feel better. I can return to work next week. He pulled himself from the inferno; safe, alive, and unharmed by the furnace of depression.

He went inside to find Lilijana and see if she was all right. He hoped so because he felt like a million dollars. No, a billion dollars.

CHAPTER SEVEN

With the new day came the stowaway of anxiety, and David was pissed off about it. He wished his happiness could last for twenty-four hours. Why did sleep have to agitate his mind? He felt victim to a conspiracy of insanity by slow fade.

Today was Sunday, The Lord's Day, as Lilijana called it. She would come and ask in the sweetest voice, primed just below begging, if David would join her at church. Usually, he mumbled a lame apology about having stayed up too late or needing to work around the house. Lilijana was always on his case about working around the house, so she could hardly complain. His wife would say it could wait until the afternoon.

"Morning, honey," said Lilijana softly and cheerfully, "Are you coming to church today?"

David hadn't had time to work out his excuse. He was caught in her sights. "Uh-huh."

"Better get ready then." She leaned down to kiss his forehead. His skin tingled at the touch of her lips. He reached out, hoping to grab her around the waist and pull her down. Instead, his hand cannoned into her breast. It was clumsy but he was determined.

"No time for that now. Up you get," she said as she gently slapped his hand.

Her tone betrayed a transient resistance. Hopefully, a promise of future fulfillment. Did she realize how he ached for her? How every woman he saw became Lilijana and, ipso facto, the object of his desire? David loved women. He savored their appearances, their aromas, the liquid beauty of their voices, though it was Lilijana he wanted to be with. Every exchange of pleasantries was tainted. Stained by the impurity of his fantasies.

"Come on, we don't want to be late."

Lilijana hated being late, and David tested her limits often. He always needed more time in bed and spent forever in their bathroom. He was an infuriating nuisance.

Reluctantly, he threw the bedcovers off and swung his legs to the floor. He marveled at the fairies dancing on the sunlight poking through the blinds. Finally, he trudged to the bathroom where he relieved himself without bothering to close the door.

Church was an odd place, like another planet. The building was an unremarkable yet functional edifice which catered to the faithful and faithless with a variety of activities and get-togethers. It was not dissimilar to the plethora of other clubs which provided services to make money. That was a sore point. Don't mention that Lilijana, who'd say, 'It's not a business or club. It's not an institution. The church is group of people who love God and recognize their need for Him and each other. They want to serve Him and show their love by helping others.' His wife's definition of church was more appealing than his own. Unfortunately, his personal experience did not dovetail with her perception.

"I think you've finished there, Dad," said Alen as he strolled past the open bathroom door.

David looked at his son, then down at his penis which was still outside his boxers in his hand. He had finished.

Lilijana was the next to offer commentary as David put it away and flushed the toilet. "You should shut the door, honey. Nobody wants to see you use the toilet."

"I think they do," replied David. "Some people would pay to see it."

Her laugh exploded backward as she moved down hall. David stood in front of the mirror, turning his face this way and that, before lifting his shirt to examine his forty-year paunch. He looked all right for his age. He felt okay. At his last visit, the doctor had said he was fine.

Lilijana passed on her way to the kitchen. "Hurry up dear. I'd like to leave soon. Fifteen minutes, all right?"

It wasn't a question. David washed his face and applied deodorant to his underarms. He checked his nose for the long white hairs that had started arriving when he turned forty. Very white. Fast growing and straight as arrows. They caused a need to wipe and pick when they tickled his nostrils. David owned a nose hair trimmer but a snip from a sharp pair of scissors was the most effective eliminator.

"Let's go," called Lilijana.

Hunger was calling to David. He would have to grab something at church. The café which operated between the morning services served awesome coffee and thick slices of raisin toast. Their muffins were also good. Good service and food made for a good business. David smiled as he semi-hurried back to change his clothes.

Five minutes later, his family sat in the car. Danijela was also there under protest. She had grown too old for games and story time in kid's church.

"Could drive a little faster, David? We're running late."

"We have plenty of time," replied David. "Besides I'm traveling the speed limit. You wouldn't want me to break the law, would you?"

"Just a little bit over won't matter."

"It won't change our arrival time either." They'd had this conversation often. Lilijana would eventually get angry and tell him politely to shut up. He strove for that moment because it represented victory. He felt competitive this morning. Maybe he just liked trouble. "Isn't breaking the law a sin?"

"It's not a sin to go five kilometers over the speed limit. Don't be diriculous."

"Is it a sin to go ten k's over?"

"Stop it, David."

He could feel her pre-rage glare burning into his cheeks. "If breaking the law is a sin then you can't pick and chose which laws are okay to break. That's why people get accused of hypocrisy."

"David."

Feeling exhilarated, David trampled her objections with more verbal bricks in the high wall of the case he was building. "I know a Christian man who boasts of regularly speeding. Not by five or ten k's, mind you. I'm talking serious hooning around and he laughs at not getting caught. Can you believe that? He thinks flouting the law is fun and says, 'that's what cars are for.'"

David faced forward as he realized he was looking at Lilijana instead of watching the road. A white Commodore station wagon had stopped at the red light. David hit the brakes too late.

Lilijana screamed, as did the tires on the asphalt. The impact jolted them forward. Pulling on the handbrake, David threw the transmission into park and killed the ignition. He breathed slowly before turning to check on his family.

"Everyone all right?"

It was a low speed crash. David's reflexes hadn't been sharp enough to avoid hitting the Commodore: a white station wagon. He hoped it was a coincidence. David tried to think, to break each action down into components. To get out of the car. Step one: unfasten seatbelt. Step two: ensure handbrake is engaged and engine switched off. Step three.

"What's wrong with you? Are you blind?"

The voice was muffled by the rush of blood inside David's head and the window of the car.

"Hey! Wake up, sleepy!"

David reached for the door handle. The other man stepped back. David's thoughts were still muddled. Lilijana and the children were okay. He was not hurt either. The driver of the Commodore appeared to be fine as well. They had only the vehicles to concern them.

"I think 'sorry' is the word you're searching for," the other man demanded.

Walking to the front of his Accord, David ignored the man. He was angry and David was at fault, but there seemed to be no point in speaking while he was livid. Though silence might aggravate him further, David became calmer by the second. Someone had pulled the plug of his mental sink. The dirty water of confusion and shock ran down the drain. Step three, he resumed thinking: assess other driver's mood and determine how to respond.

"Didn't you see the red light? Or my brake lights? Or my car stopped?"

David studied the front bumper of his Accord then the rear bumper of the Commodore. Both had done their jobs but would need to be replaced. The Commodore's hung down on the right side.

"Do you want me to help you take this off?" asked David, gesturing to the bumper.

The man's mouth hung open. Feeling more in control, David turned back to his Accord. Lilijana left the car. She opened the rear door for Alen and Danijela, beckoning them out. David was relieved to see them standing unassisted. Turning back to the Commodore, he noticed someone in the front passenger seat. Although he could only see the back of his head, David knew it was Phil.

"What's happened here?" said a familiar voice from behind him.

He heard Lilijana's gracious response. "Hi Keith, just a little accident."

"Everyone all right?"

Lilijana and both children nodded in unison. The Samaritan was Keith Green from church. He'd stopped his Statesman behind them and switched on his hazard lights. David approached Keith, ignoring the driver of the Commodore. The heat of his mounting rage was like a hot wind blowing at David's back.

"G'day, Keith."

"G'day, Dave." The two men shook hands. "Had a little accident, I see."

"Uh-huh."

"Would you like me to take Lilijana and the kids to church while you sort it out?"

"That would be great," Lilijana said. "Are you sure you don't mind?"

Why would he mind? He would not have offered if he did and they were going to the same place. It made sense for David to be left to sort things out. Still, he felt annoyed. Lilijana interrupted his self pity with a kiss.

"We'll see you later then."

"See you, Dad."

David waved farewell, noting Danijela's reluctance. Keith waved back before they piled into the Statesman and drove past him on the inside lane.

The driver of the Commodore had followed David over and now stood in his face. David caught a whiff of smoky-sweet breath.

"Back off a bit please. That weed's a bit strong."

"Are you going to stop being a smart arse or do I have to hurt you?"

David laughed at the blatant bluff. If this guy was going to do anything he would have already done it.

"I tell you what," said David confidently. "I'll help you pull off the bumper and chuck it in the back of your wagon, and I won't involve the police. Then you and I can be on our merry way. Okay?"

"You rear-ended me."

"You're stoned."

The man's position was hopeless. Even with witnesses to say that David had failed to stop, the marijuana would land him in trouble. He didn't cause the accident but he was under the influence of an illicit drug while operating a motor vehicle. David smiled at his use of police jargon.

"You're a prick," said the man with a menacing jab of his finger.

"You're a druggo."

The man growled and turned away. David nearly wet himself as he looked at the back of Phil's head. If he'd recognized David then he would tell his mate. What would happen the next time he pulled into1008? Would he recognize David? Remember what had happened? Would they conspire to pay him back? He had felt threatened by Phil without cause according to everyone else. Now his neighbor had ammunition. Possibly? Potentially. He did not know whether Phil had seen him or not.

"Hang on, mate," said David as he hurried after the man. "I'm sorry. I won't call the police."

His words vaporized on the way to the man's ears. He jumped behind the wheel and the Commodore burst down the road. Aware of curious onlookers, David stared until the Commodore was out of sight. Then he looked back at his Accord. Only a few months old, it was the first new car they'd owned. Lilijana had agreed they needed to replace their old Falcon. Having determined they could afford a new vehicle, they had to decide which one. Lilijana was keen on a Toyota Camry. David, on a new Falcon. The Camry was overpriced and he didn't like the look of it. The Falcon was not fuel efficient. The Honda Accord was a compromise. It looked good, drove well and was economical. Those looks had been tarnished by David's carelessness. David refocused.

Step five: if car is drivable, and the driver of the other vehicle takes off stoned, resume journey.

As he got in and re-fired the engine, David fought the nagging feeling that Phil and his pothead mate would be coming after him. The dread was overwhelming, smothering. Instead of going to church, he'd be better off protecting his home. Scary thoughts based on the tenuous suspicion that Phil might have seen him. There was nothing worse than fear from the vacuum of ignorance. He was going to church, so maybe he should have a chat with God. Sadly, David realized he didn't know God: if He got involved in stuff like this. Surely, God was too busy for petty disagreements and minor car accidents. He would be tied up with war and fatal multi-car pile-ups, with famine and disasters. If ignorance was cash, David was wealthy.

Resume journey, he thought. Maybe someone at church could help him. Maybe not. Maybe Phil would hunt him. Maybe not. Maybe I'm a bloody idiot, thought David. Yes, that's it. I am.

CHAPTER EIGHT

One week later, nothing happened. Life rolled on in its usual fashion. The Commodore appeared next door a few times but the driver did not alight and Phil never noticed David. The Accord had been repaired. The Commodore had not. All the incident cost had David was five hundred bucks for a new bumper and a week's peace of mind.

At church that previous Sunday, David had looked for one of the older men to talk to. One of the guys who hung around in the foyer after the service started, complaining about the music and the sermon being too long. David felt solidarity with these men who seemed compelled to be present at church yet strangely immune to its Spirit. Most of them were called John or Bruce. There was even a fellow called John Bruce, and he was the one David found when he arrived that morning wearing a cloak of guilt and anxiety.

"What's the matter with you, young David?" he asked once David had seen him.

"Minor car accident on the way here."

"Never had one of those," said John. "What's it like?"

David stood beside John who was staring through the glass entry doors to the auditorium. "Aren't you going in?"

"Music's too loud," he said, tapping one of his large ears. "Tell me about your accident."

Not inclined to enter the auditorium, David welcomed the chance to talk. He wondered, however, if John really never had an accident. The man was eighty-five years old and still held a driver's license.

"You were a sales rep, weren't you? You must have clocked up thousands of kilometers. How did you manage to avoid an accident?"

John smiled. "I didn't say I had no accidents. I was talking about minor accidents."

David laughed. He told John about his latest bingle, including the problem with Phil, then asked for his advice.

"Why don't we sit down?" suggested John.

Old people's advice came in two varieties: very short 'Snap out of it' advice or counsel attached to long, irrelevant stories. John Bruce's advice was likely the latter type, so David took a seat in the lounge.

"These neighborhood disputes can get pretty serious," said John. "Boy, have I heard some stories. I read about this guy in Virginia. Did you know I spent time there as a youngster?"

David groaned inwardly.

"Anyway, this guy had a speed bump installed in front of his house, and some bloke didn't like it so he beat the guy up."

This sounded like something which occur between him and Phil, but John wasn't finished.

"They were supposed to go to court, but the guy broke into Mr. Speed Bump's home and tied up him and his girlfriend at gunpoint. The papers reported a struggle which resulted in the man's death."

"Which man?"

"The guy who had the speed bump installed."

"The other guy killed him because of a speed bump?"

John nodded and David gulped. He wished he hadn't brought up this subject. If he thought his fears were groundless and fantastic then John Bruce had just transformed them into an imminent and terrifying probability.

"That's a worst case scenario," said David. "Mostly these disagreements get sorted out less violently, don't they?"

"Sure," said John. "But don't get to thinking they're isolated incidents. Google neighborhood disputes and see how many hits you get, especially those which lead to murder. And don't think it only happens in America."

"No?" said David as he struggled with the idea of old John Bruce surfing the World Wide Web.

"Young fella named Gunns ended up in court for being a public nuisance after egging his neighbor's front door then pissing off his balcony toward her home. Funny, eh? Funnier still was the name of the suburb."

He paused as if David was meant to supply the punchline to his joke.

"Enoggera," he said before laughter flooded his words. "It sounds like Eggnog –era. Get it?"

David joined the laugh out of courtesy, desperately wanting to know what happened to the perpetrator.

"This was the result of a dispute between neighbors?"

"Yeah, the woman had been vomiting in his toilet when he wanted to use it."

"What?"

"Gunns admitted to the eggs but not the urine. You know what the magistrate said after he fined Gunns two hundred bucks?"

Another pause, which left David feeling like he'd been enlisted to play the straight man: Lou Costello to John's Bud Abbott.

"He said, 'It was a dreadful waste of eggs.'"

John gave him a satisfied look, as though the key to David's solutions was in that story somewhere. David ruminated over the details, desperately searching for meaning so he could give John a look which shouted revelation. Was John presenting him with a choice between murder and egging? David nodded.

"You're a wise man, John."

"Wisdom is God's gift to the aged," he replied modestly.

The service still had half an hour to run so David decided to sound John out on another matter.

"Can I ask you something personal, John?"

"Uh-huh."

"When did you stop caring about, or thinking about, sex?"

John's laughter was so disheartening that it sliced through the empathy David felt they had built between them. After a coughing fit, John said, "You're making a pretty big assumption there, Dave."

David's face reddened and he felt hot in the silence. Should have quit while I was ahead.

"You're not getting any, are you?" John said.

"I'm getting some, just not enough."

John laughed so David braced for another coughing fit, hoping it would not herald John's demise.

"It's never enough for us."

John's pause was clothed in a sagacity which David found intense. His original question no longer seemed of any consequence.

"You want to know what to do about it," said John who waited for David to nod. "You've got three options. One is virtually impossible while another is bloody dangerous. The third option is your best choice. It's also the one you have the least control over."

Was this a third category of advice giving? A middle path of something approaching sensitive rationalism? Deep fried empathy with a side order of realism please.

"You'd better give me the best one then," said David.

"Does your wife, what's her name?"

"Lilijana."

"Lilijana? Where's she from? Serbia? Croatia?"

David fought to hide his impatience. "Croatia. You were about to ask me something?"

He frowned and David feared the moment had passed as he watched the train leave the station and run off the track.

"Does your wife...?" David prompted.

"I fought side by side with some Slavs in 1941. 6th division was in Crete to take on the Nazis after they rolled over Yugoslavia in eleven days. These Slavs were on the run after some fascist bastard called Pavelic bent over for Hitler and was allowed to declare an independent Croatia. They said he was a puppet of the Germans but he was a vicious son of a bitch. I don't understand all that racial bullshit. We're all the same, aren't we?"

"Pretty much," replied David with more conviction than he felt. He was amused by John's lapse into Aussie digger speak.

It was eleven o'clock and the sermon had finished. David was running out of time to scrape John's brain for valuable information. Should he try again, or take what he had and run? He decided to start again.

"Can I ask you something personal?"

John was taken aback at the interruption but nevertheless acceded. The conversation proceeded as it had before. Verbatim. In search of a devastating truth, David asked John for the best option first.

"Does your wife...?"

David held his breath. He gambled. "Does my wife know how I feel?"

"Hmm."

"She says so, but it hasn't resulted in action."

"Do everything in your power to make her want you and create the right environment for her to feel like she can have you."

David needed a suggestion. "Can you give me an example?"

"Ever heard the ladies rabbit on about a six-pack and how good someone looks with his shirt off?"

"Yep."

"They say they aren't motivated or attracted by appearances. That's crap. Don't let anyone tell you different. So you," he poked David in the gut, "lose that and get some definition in those arms."

Had David discovered the world's most savvy sex counselor right in his own backyard?

"Okay," said David thoughtfully. "Option two?"

"Do everything you can to not think about it. Distract yourself."

"I can't do that," blurted David. "I mean even if I wanted to, I couldn't. You don't know how often I think about sex."

John smiled. "Sure, I do." He laid his hand on David's shoulder. "You think about it *all* the time."

"Not *all* the time," David conceded. "I couldn't really function if that was the only thing I thought about."

"Is there some sort of pattern to your most intrusive thoughts?"

The wording of the question stunned David.

John pressed on, "Well, is there? Have you ever thought about it?"

"Are you a psychologist, John?"

That knowing smiled flickered again. "Are there certain times of the day or certain situations in which you think more about sex? More than normal?"

David glanced at his watch. "I'll have to get back to you on that one. Can you give me number three? Quickly?"

John raised an eyebrow, as if wanting to know why David avoided his question.

David ignored the inquiry. "Service is nearly over. We'll be overrun in a minute."

Turning toward the auditorium, John was reminded of where they were. "Of course," he said hastily.

The next pause was agonizing. David could not help hoping that the last option was the best one. The first wasn't too bad. Even if he didn't think it would work, it was possible, at least. He would benefit from increased fitness. He'd always wanted to be stronger and lose some weight, so option one was good, except Lilijana wouldn't go for it She wasn't that superficial. David had never heard her remark about nice abs or chests. Option two? David didn't understand it. How was it possible to control his most basic thoughts?

"Option three?" pleaded David as he watched the congregation break into conversation cliques.

"Option three," said John with a disturbing tone of reluctance, "is the worst option."

"Uh-huh," said David with half an eye on the people pushing through the doors into the foyer. If anyone recognized him they would come straight over and he would have to wait to hear about option three. He hoped John could hear the urgency in his voice. "What is it?"

"Get it somewhere else. Have an affair or go and pay for it."

David instantly thought of Julia. He stood stupefied that a man of God would suggest such a course of action, in church of all places.

John struggled to his feet. "Be careful. A double life is dangerous, bloody hard work. Let me tell you. Be careful."

"Be careful about what?" Lilijana arrived in time to hear the last.

How much more did she hear? Think quick. Bizarrely, David thought this could be practice for the deceitful double life he suddenly ached for. "I was just telling John about the accident."

"Yes," said Lilijana smiling at John, "he should be more careful."

The foyer teemed with buzzing parishioners. Conversation overlaid with laughter swirled around them. David recognized the spirit, the good cheer, and he appreciated it. He did not understand God or spiritual things but happiness and peace were treasures which even pagans like him could enjoy.

A young woman slipped her left arm inside John's right. "There you are, Grandad," she said. "Mum asked me to find you. We've got to go."

John placed his hand over hers and introduced his granddaughter. She was attractive, though the wrinkles around her eyes placed her near her forties.

David looked at her too long.

Lilijana nudged him as she took the woman's hand and said it was nice to meet her.

David wondered if John's suggestion was going to ruin his life. Would he look at every woman he fancied as a prospective partner? That was madness. He wished he'd never heard option three.

Lilijana and John's granddaughter were conversing. He had no idea what they discussed so Lilijana's question left him exposed.

"Huh? Sorry?"

"I asked what you thought of changing from two morning services to one?"

"I didn't know they were going to do that."

The use of the word 'they' sounded wrong and David regretted it. He had inadvertently put distance between the believers and himself. In football you always used the pronoun *we* when talking about your team and *they,* when speaking of the opposition. He knew Lilijana would notice.

"Yes," said Lilijana, "*We* are going to change. It was announced this morning in service. Where have you been?"

John's granddaughter must have sensed a shift in the atmosphere. "Come on, Granddad," she said cheerfully. "We really must get going."

She smiled politely at Lilijana then warmly at David.

"Be careful, Dave," said John, before disappearing into the throng.

The old man's departure left David vulnerable.

"You didn't answer my question," Lilijana said.

There was no need for her to be angry, or for David to defend himself. He had done nothing wrong. The post worship service glow was falling off Lilijana's shoulders like a hurriedly discarded coat. She had willfully suppressed whatever negative emotion had resulted from the crash. She could do that. She was strong minded. In this area and many others, David depended on her. He wondered if she relied on him at all. Or believed that he compensated for any weaknesses in her character. Did she even have any weaknesses?

"David?"

"I was just talking to John and we lost track of time. I'm not even sure when I arrived. Let's go. We can talk in the car. I can see you're upset."

She appeared temporarily mollified by David's empathy. They moved towards the exit.

"Where's Alen?"

"He's going to spend the afternoon with Lachlan."

"And Danijela?"

"Abbey's."

"So we're child-free this afternoon," said David, insinuating this could be a good thing.

"Don't get any ideas," said Lilijana coldly.

"Of course not."

The walk from the foyer, out the door, down the steps and to the carpark seemed to take forever. It felt like his shoes were sticking to the asphalt, or he was walking knee deep in mud. Silence accompanied them. David wondered what Lilijana was thinking and what he could say to make her feel better. Then his attention wandered. John's tone of warning when he spoke of a double life as dangerous, bloody hard work was daunting but not off-putting. The idea of an affair with Julia was not a new one. David had only managed to shelve it, courtesy of his panic attack and the need to recuperate under Lilijana's loving care. David was certain of two things. He would speak with John in more detail about this double life and, no matter what John said, David would pursue option three.

CHAPTER NINE

Some people call them watershed moments. Some call them turning points. Others call them epiphanies. David was having such a moment. It was good. He was breaking through. John Bruce's words had worn away his resistance like water on sandstone, shaping him and transforming him. He was aware of the alteration and its importance. David made a monumental, life-changing decision. He was going to have an affair.

Curiously, Julia's participation was taken for granted. It was as though she had made an offer that merited consideration, despite being impossible to resist. Impulsivity unwelcomed, blocked by thoughtful deliberation. Julia had done no such thing. According to David's interpretation, Julia was hot for him. However, he had no evidence to support his belief. It was pure unadulterated fancy. David heard the word unadulterated in his head and chuckled. Delicious irony.

It was Monday morning and David was driving to work. He looked forward to it. His health had returned and his depression had lifted. If he wasn't afraid of its connotations he would have used the term 'born again' to describe how he felt. If they knew what he planned, the born-again Christians he spent time with would bar him from their presence and label him a recalcitrant sinner. He liked the sound of that.

Lilijana had referred to the accident over breakfast with a vague recommendation to take extra care. He could not remember what he'd answered and it didn't seem to matter. David was moving Lilijana to the periphery of his concerns. He would interact with her as much as she allowed and totally on her terms. He would be dutiful, attentive and affectionate. There was a danger of overdoing the good husband act, which, if too good, might expose him to Lilijana's suspicions. She was confident of knowing him inside out.

That could work to his advantage.

When he parked the car at Dean & Branxton, he felt relaxed and at home. He was in his element at work. There was nothing here to challenge or attack him. No chainsaw-wielding, drug-addled neighbors. It was a safe place. He was free to carry out his business with as much brainpower as he required, and use the rest to ponder and to plan. The thrill of his intentions tingled along his spine.

Thursday rolled around and David's euphoria held strong. In fact, it was more intoxicating because this was training day. He would see Julia again. As he thought of hearing her voice and drowning in the warmth of her smile, he realized how much he'd missed her. How much he wanted her. He didn't recognize this as lust. He had fallen in love with Julia and wanted to be with her. To soak in the sunlight of her eyes and block out the world, floating in a happy little bubble, talking to her, smelling the fragrance of her hair, being bounced on her girlish laugh. It was hard to describe. There was no precedent for the nature of his emotions. Nothing like it had been aroused by Lilijana, or was he choosing to forget that he had once been in love with her, too? Lilijana was an intruder. He grabbed her roughly and pushed her out of his mind. Julia made him think of words like lovely and delightful. Strange, flowery words that seemed intrinsic to Julia and time spent thinking about her.

As usual, David was first into the training room.

"Hello David," said Julia, "Missed you last week. How are you?"

The sound of her voice wrapped him in a net, but unlike a fish which resists because it knows it's in trouble, David surrendered. Did she say his name differently than others? Did she really miss him or was that a throwaway line? A pleasantry? Did she care how he was? She watched him as if he really was a fish in a net.

"I missed you, too," he blurted. Although he had so much to say, there was little time to talk. "I'm all right now. Just had a bit of a scare with my heart."

She looked shocked.

"It's nothing really. More of an anxiety attack. Imagine that? I don't know what I've got to be anxious about." His babbling was interrupted by the arrival of some colleagues.

"Hey, Smelly. How are ya? Heard you had a heart attack?"

Julia turned her attention to the papers on the desk in front of her. She glanced at her watch.

"Not a heart attack," David said. "There's nothing wrong with my heart."

"That's good to know," said his disinterested coworker.

David wanted to tell him to fuck himself. He felt inexplicably angry so he looked at Julia again, hoping she could banish his wrath with one of her smiles.

"Nothing wrong with my heart," he said to her. "I'm fit and healthy."

Julia looked up and their eyes met. He smiled and hoped it came across as warm and friendly rather than embarrassed and awkward. The wait for her response was agonizingly long. She spoke softly, "Let's get started gentlemen."

"Sit down, Smelly, you're blocking my view."

David assumed his normal position and began to doodle. He could hear Julia's voice, which had recovered its authoritative volume and cadence, but the words seemed only for him. He was afraid to look up. What do you want from me, sweet princess, my angel? Ask anything and it shall be yours.

"That's what we covered last week, David. It was also a useful review for those of you who were here."

"No doubt," said one of the men sarcastically.

"This week we are looking at lines of communication." Julia's voice was easy to listen to, which made the subject matter more tolerable. When she turned to write on the board, David wanted to look away because he knew every man had their eyes in the same place. The movement of her buttocks beneath her skirt was mesmerizing. David didn't want to leer like the others. Yet he couldn't resist. An oft-quoted piece of scripture sprang to mind. 'The spirit is willing but the flesh is weak.' David flinched. Not now, Lilijana.

"When you cannot speak directly to someone, you may need to use a secretary or personal assistant as a line of communication. Things like bulletins, memos, letters and emails can be used to pass on information."

David began writing as soon as she mentioned letters.

He began with 'Dear Julia,' then crossed that out immediately. Deciding that no names would be better, he focused on the message. What had Julia said about being succinct? Use only the words you need to get your message across.

He started over. 'This is going to sound crazy but if I don't tell you how I feel I will go insane. I expect nothing from you and apologize in advance if this causes you embarrassment or offends you. Actually, I'm hoping you will take it as a compliment.'

He crossed out the last sentence. Not necessary. If she isn't offended then she will be flattered whether I suggest it or not. He continued: 'I like you.'

That's good, he praised himself. To the point. More of the same. 'I was wondering if you would like to meet me for coffee?'

"Events," said Julia, unaware of the proposal being scribed by David, "can also be lines of communication. A sales conference, for example."

David re-read the note. He wondered if he needed more compliments to win her over or could he assume that his interest in her was matched by her interest in him? How presumptuous. More flattery.

'I think you are very intelligent and beautiful. I would like to get to know you. As friends.'

He looked at the last two words. Will that tell her I want to have sex with her? Too obvious? Not necessary. He crossed it out.

'If you are interested you can write back. Just say yes and we'll work out a time and place. If you don't want to and I have misread the situation, then I'm sorry. Please ignore this letter and my advances.'

Advances? What will she make of that? He deliberated for a moment then decided to keep it. It was, after all, honest. If asking a woman out for a coffee was not an advance, what was it?

"Let's look at more examples of lines of communication."

David rewrote the note in his neatest writing. Read it again then a second time for good measure. His heart raced. Did he actually have the balls to hand the note to her? His mouth went dry and a little beast punched his stomach. Snap out of it, David. It's only a letter, an invitation, which Julia will accept or refuse. That's it.

He folded the paper in half and left it on the table then tried to concentrate on what Julia was saying instead of what she might say in response to his proposition. He had never felt such anticipation. It was unbearable. To dispel some of the tension, he twisted his head then lowered his chin before tilting his head back as far as it would go. Dizziness washed over him. He focused on Julia's voice to jumpstart his flagging strength.

"Are you all right, David?" asked Julia.

The question leapt out of a sentence about Minnie, who worked in a police station and had received a delivery of truncheons. David was wondering how Julia would solve her dilemma of how best to distribute the truncheons when he suddenly became aware he was the center of attention.

"Don't have another heart attack, Smelly. We're busy learning in here."

A burst of laughter followed. David ignored it and kept his eyes closed. Spinning in a maelstrom, he sensed Julia approaching. She asked him again if he felt okay and he realized he hadn't answered. Silence drew her to him. He imagined receiving her touch and opening his eyes to smile a thank you.

When Julia did place her hand on his shoulder, David half-jumped from his seat, as though she'd electrified him. His knees banged the table and tipped it over. Laughter filled the room, but all David could think about was the note which lay on the floor with his papers, phone and pen. He prayed for Julia not to be curious with the retrieval of his belongings. He should gather them before she did, but he was busy righting the table.

Julia picked up the items and placed them on David's desk, more concerned with his health than their nature. He needed to say something to diffuse the alarming tension.

"Sorry, Miss. I nodded off."

For once, his workmates laughed with him instead of at him. However, Julia's expression was mortifying. Its concoction of pity and disappointment reminded him of Lilijana. This was a devastating blow to his confidence

He searched Julia's eyes for some sign of forgiveness. She shook her head slowly and turned away.

"Let's get back to Minnie and her truncheons, shall we?"

David said, "I'm sorry, Julia. I felt dizzy for a bit but I'm okay. Thanks."

Julia did not acknowledge his apology. Perhaps she had not expected a reply to her question but was redirecting her own thoughts. Removing the spotlight from David and shining it back on the subject.

While she spoke, David fingered the invitation. It could also function as an apology if the timing was right and the planets aligned. Ignoring Minnie and her truncheons, David decided he would pursue Julia, seduce her, and do whatever it took to have her. With the skill of one accustomed to fooling himself, he dismissed her Lilijana-like expression as an aberration. He may have even imagined it, projecting Lilijana's reaction to his clumsiness and childish cheek onto Julia out of habit.

"What did you decide, David?"

He scanned the paper in front of him. "I reckon option 'C'. She should speak to the staff sergeant, and let him know the truncheons arrived so he can hand them out to the officers during their daily briefing."

Julia smiled and righted the whole world. Had he seen admiration in her eyes? Had he impressed her? As Julia addressed the others, he picked up the note and held it tightly.

"What's wrong with her standing in the foyer and banging the side of the box?" Julia asked.

When Julia finished her summary, David's workmates left in a rush.

David stood with this heart in his mouth, approached Julia, and cleared his throat. She looked at him and the words he'd prepared vaporized.

"Did you want to say something?"

"I-I," he stammered like a schoolboy. "I'm really sorry for what I said before."

"It's okay," she said sincerely. "You were embarrassed and needed to get the eyes of the world off you."

Grace was like a hot shower: cleansing, warming, invigorating and life-giving. Julia understood and forgave him.

David placed the note on her desk and said "This is for you. Please read it. See you next week." Then he rushed out of the room and nearly fell through the door. His face burned and his mouth was full of cotton. He had done it. Now to await Julia's reply.

CHAPTER TEN

Coming home had become symbolic for David: a recurring motif. There were layers of meaning in every part of the process and these had increased in poignancy over the years. The act of pulling into his driveway had mystical significance. Unfortunately, the connotations were not happy or peaceful. For most people, the turn of the steering wheel which pointed you onto your property was an act accompanied by relief. If the world was a battleground, then home was a refuge. It was where you felt safe and could recuperate, refresh your mind and rest your body in preparation for another day.

When David returned home, he left the happy friendly world which encouraged and entertained him while providing satisfaction and purpose. The knot which untangled each time he drove away, retied itself in his stomach and a sense of dread drenched him. He had never understood why coming home felt so painful. He hadn't noticed the insidious creep of malcontent and despair until one day revelation fell on him like bird crap.

Today was different because David was distracted by anticipation. The fence did not remind him of a prison nor did the front door conjure images of hellish red light within. The overgrown, unwelcome pine tree in the center of the yard did not speak about how his life was out of control. Today, his thoughts were on Julia, until he noticed the activity in the front yard next door.

Having only caught a glimpse, David was anxious to see more and forgot about discretion. The tires screeched as the car came to a stop a centimeter from the garage. David exited and headed for the front gate. Then he realized he was being too obvious so he veered toward the letterbox. Facing 1008, he lifted the lid and removed his mail. Phil stood with his back to David, talking the driver of the Commodore. Where was the car? He always parked it in the driveway or on the footpath. David needed an excuse to get closer. He noticed the local newspaper lying near the front gate. Lilijana didn't read it and neither did he usually.

"G'day Phil," said David as he marched over to pick up the newspaper.

Phil did not acknowledge him because his name wasn't Phil. The other man glanced at David with menace. Phil's posture changed, and David suddenly felt afraid. He snatched the newspaper then hurried to his porch. As he searched his pockets for the house keys, he noticed Phil turning to look. The other man followed his gaze. David continued his frantic search. Where were his keys?

When the mail dropped from his hands, David remembered that his keys were still in the car. Moving to his car, he saw the driver of the Commodore walk away toward town. Phil spun around and half-ran, half-walked from his driveway to David's.

The distance between them shrank. Phil clenched his nicotine-stained fingers in a fist and cocked his arm ready to punch. David braced himself. The fist burst towards his face. Block? Duck? Counterpunch? Run? There was no time to run through options. It was too late. David tensed to receive the blow. He closed his eyes. Nothing.

"Mind your own fucking business," said Phil, spitting the words out as though they tasted bitter. "You've been told."

David opened his eyes to see a finger aimed at his face. Had he leaned forward it might have entered his eye. It was withdrawn then jabbed forward.

"This," said Phil, "is your last warning. Next time I see you spying on me. I'm going to poke your fucking eyes out." With one last thrust of his finger, Phil was done. "Got it?" he said. "Do you understand what I'm saying?"

David nodded. Phil turned and strode away without another word.

The solution to the problem of Julia had begun. Now he had to do something about Phil. Despite painting himself as a victim in the neighborhood dispute with David, Phil was the aggressor. The threat which David perceived but could not justify had become real. Phil's violent pointing had not been a figment of imagination. How far would the man go? Would he back up his threats with action? How much brutality was he capable of? Until now, David had not felt afraid of Phil. The feeling was better described as disquiet; an eerie sense that something was not right. Now there was flesh on those bones of menace. The danger he had perceived was imminent. David shuddered.

"David?"

He turned toward Lilijana's voice.

"What are you doing? I heard you pull in five minutes ago. Why haven't you come inside?"

There were times when David felt paralyzed by the burdens of decision making. Even little choices assumed monumental complexity. The consequences of his choices loomed large in his mind. The thought of failing scared the shit out of him.

Had five minutes really expired since he arrived? Was five minutes a long time?

"David?"

He transformed the blank stare of contemplation to alert interaction, and smiled to disarm her. "Hi, baby."

"What's wrong with you?" Her voice was harsh, her stare interrogative.

David collected the fallen mail and gathered his thoughts. There was no way he was going to share the latest incident with Phil. He would have to deal with that alone. This awareness was not overbearing. He accepted the challenge presented with assurance in his resourcefulness and strength. He would use any tactics and whatever tools he could find to protect his family. That was the bottom line. Despite the widening chasm between him and Lilijana, he still loved and wanted her. Wanted to be with her, and to be married to her. The voice which told him to cut and run was insipid and scarcely audible. It was a pathetic attempt at seduction. He wasn't going to allow anything to take what he had. He would fight.

"Nothing," he lied. "I'm good. It's good to be back at work. Back to normal, you know. Whatever normal is." He smiled at her again.

She grinned with substantial effort and said, "Not you, that's for sure."

With that arrow dispelled into David's heart, she went back inside. He stood for a moment, gently massaging his chest. Then he looked across the driveway to the front yard of 1008. Phil and his wife were the fourth family to live next door to them in three years. Rental properties were like that; shabby and maintained at the minimum standard, occupied by low class tenants who came and went with predictable monotony.

The first tenants had seemed normal, though. Kevin, aged in his late twenties, looked like a typical waxhead with his lean muscular build, bronzed skin and blonde hair. Sure enough, he had a couple of surfboards stored in the garage. He worked long hours and wasn't around the house much. His other prized possession was a Harley Davidson. It had come up in their first conversation. Kevin said it was a 2003 Fatboy, and David had feigned admiration. He'd thought of how much noise the damn things made and hoped Kevin had little time for riding. Kevin worked to support his girlfriend, who was then between jobs. His girlfriend was intriguing and not just because she was beautiful. Although quiet to the point of shyness, Melanie appeared calm and confident. She and Kevin had dated for eighteen months. Melanie's parents did not approve of them living together. David supposed he would feel the same way when his little princess, Danijela, decided to leave. How could that not be hurtful? He didn't want her to grow up.

David and Melanie became friendly over time, courtesy of chats over the fence while tending laundry on their lines. As time passed, she opened up a little, but David did most of the talking. He babbled about nothing important and did a lot of complaining, which he tried to couch in humor. Mel listened and smiled, even laughed occasionally. David became addicted to the attention and found excuses to knock on their door when Kevin was out. It never occurred to him that he was flirting. He'd never thought he was that kind of guy.

One day, he was home from work early. Lilijana had taken the children and would be gone for more than an hour, so David picked some lemons from the tree in their backyard, put them in plastic bag, and took them to 1008.

Right now, David wondered if this nostalgia was appropriate to the moment. It was a bittersweet memory that would disable his faculties for as long as he indulged it. Mechanically, he went into the house, crossed to the kitchen, made himself a cup of tea and grabbed some Venetian biscuits. All the while he remembered.

Mel had answered the door in her dressing gown.

"Sorry, Mel, did I wake you?"

She smiled. "It's half past three in the afternoon."

He averted his gaze from the red liquid tinge of her eyes. "Sorry for just rocking up. I...brought you some lemons."

Mel laughed, which threw David off guard. "Better than onions," she said and gestured for him to enter. "Come in."

"You've been peeling onions?"

She pointed to a seat in the lounge and then sat opposite him. David felt hot. He had been in this position before but something was different this time.

"Peeling onions and crying."

"Because of the onions. You should soak them in water before you cut them."

An awkward silence fell. David tried not to look at her or notice the haphazard way she'd fastened her dressing gown. He didn't know if he should leave. He waited, feeling hotter by the second.

"You look hot, Dave. Would you like a drink?"

"Yes," said David too eagerly.

Mel stood and walked to the kitchen. David followed and saw her leaning on the bench as if in pain.

"Are you all right?"

When she turned, she was crying again. David wished he hadn't come. If it was Lilijana or one of the children, then a hug would have been appropriate. Trying to appear calm and compassionate, David placed his hand on her shoulder. Mel fell sobbing into his arms. She squeezed him tightly then released her grip only her to squeeze him again. The heat from her miserable body made him feel like he'd burst into flames. He had a vision of Mel throwing open her dressing gown to reveal her nakedness. This had to stop. He had to say something or do something.

"What's wrong?" he asked lamely. "Do you want to talk about it?"

After fiercely regaining control, Mel replied, "Kevin called to say he's working late again. He's always at work."

She stepped back and broke their embrace. David concentrated on her face, even though her dressing gown bared parts of her breasts and stomach. She looked angry. He was thoroughly aroused.

"He's always at fucking work," she said before falling back into his arms.

Twenty minutes later, David left 1008 with a barely subsiding erection and a gargantuan sense of guilt. It took every ounce of strength to keep from falling to the ground and being flattened by his shame.

Back in the present, he shook his head at the recollection. What a terrible mistake that had been. He remembered the horrible awkwardness of every subsequent meeting. That twenty minutes had shipwrecked their friendship, and each of them blamed themselves. They never talked about it. It was taboo.

Three months later, Mel was unmistakably pregnant. In a moment of rare unsullied friendship, she told him the child was Kevin's. She was fourteen weeks along. David congratulated her.

'We sorted things out when he came home,' she said. "I was so upset and ashamed I could barely put two words together."

David nodded.

"I told him why I was upset." Mel's eyes suddenly widened. "Not that."

Sensing she needed to say more, David gave her time.

"I told him I was lonely and needed him around more. That I felt lost and useless. He hugged me so tenderly it squeezed the pain right out of me. He didn't even say anything. There was such depth of feeling I nearly fainted with relief."

"Relief?"

"His touch made everything all right. It totally obliterated my shame and guilt. I felt forgiven, though I hadn't confessed to what we did. I nearly did tell him, but I held back."

"Why?" asked David, dry-mouthed and curious.

"Did you tell your wife?"

"No."

"Do you plan to?"

David shook his head. He understood.

After a long pause, Mel looked up. "We can still be friends, can't we? Over the fence, I mean."

David's smile was uncertain and apt to be misunderstood, but it was the best he could do. "Just over the fence then."

Lilijana stormed back into his world with all the subtlety of a twenty-one gun salute. "Don't you have something useful to do besides stare at the table?"

These days it felt like he and Lilijana barely communicated. The words they exchanged were like rock throwing between schoolyard gangs. Each word designed to attack and repel. Who was to blame? Would it end soon? Was it a phase or was this the new status quo?

"It's our tenth wedding anniversary next year," said David.

"I know."

"Good on us, eh?"

"Let's not count our chickens, honey."

If that was intended as a joke it could not have been any less funny. Ordinarily, Lilijana's use of English idioms amused him, but this one hurt. It wasn't a rock, it was a boulder. He sagged in his seat and stared into the mug where a remnant of brown liquid lay resigned to its fate. Much like David: doomed.

"What do you mean by that?"

"Nothing," came her voice from the kitchen where she had moved to avoid his presence. Was she trying to get away from him? And saying their marriage might not last?

"Just kidding," she said with finality.

How David hated those words. How many cruel barbs and sarcastic, vicious taunts had been thrust into people's hearts and minds only to be withdrawn as though the initial wound was of no consequence? David could feel the blood oozing from every previous wound he received in the name of 'just kidding.'

He rose and walked to the kitchen, where Lilijana bent over the sink rinsing dirty dishes. David didn't know if this was good time but he needed to talk.

"Are we okay?"

"What do you mean?" she asked without taking her eyes off the dishes.

"I don't feel like we talk to each other anymore. Not properly. We say stuff in passing and throw words and sentences like a food fight at a birthday party. There's no real connection."

"'No connection,' that's an interesting phrase."

Lilijana was a true champion of the put down, shutdown comment. Here he was trying to open up and all she could think to do was make another remark. As if he was a joke. As if his feelings were a joke. Belittled, he considered retreat, but in thinking of Mel and Julia, he felt a surge of confidence. Inexplicably he sensed a confession brewing and behind it a challenge to Lilijana: a word of defiance, even a threat. He wanted to test her. Would she forgive him? Was she the good Christian woman she purported to be? Previous forgiveness from Lilijana was like that given to a puppy you've brought home from the pet store which desecrates your sofa and devours your favorite shoes. You recognize that the animal can't help itself, that there's no malice in its actions, so you forgive, you demonstrate grace. What David was about to confess was in a different ball park.

Red lights flashed and alarm bells rang in his mind. He battled not to speak. This would not go well. Lilijana would explode. He would be crushed, incinerated by her response. He willed himself to back down. Retreat. But his ego goaded him. Weakness. Tiredness. Lack of will. He was losing this battle as Lilijana turned to look at him. She waited patiently as David found the right words.

"Baby, there's something I need to tell you."

CHAPTER ELEVEN

The white knight of common sense pulled David from the fire just as he was about to be burned. With Lilijana watching him hawkishly, he had begun to tell her about Mel. He had rationalized the confession in hopes that enough time had passed for the impact and the significance of the event to be of virtually no interest. It was irrelevant now. The counter argument was that no time was sufficient to allow the turgid waters of sex with another woman to flow under the proverbial bridge. It had happened with a neighbor no less. A younger woman whom Lilijana would have felt threatened by back then: superior in looks, and by virtue of her native English language, superior in intelligence as well. A whole book could not have contained the thoughts in David's mind as he opened his mouth to speak. Then came his savior.

The phone took them by surprise. An atmosphere of expectancy had grown in the kitchen. Now the ringing made him jump. As one, they unlocked their charged gazes to regard the telephone. Lilijana, who was a master at moving out of awkward and uncomfortable situations, did not move to answer it. Instead she looked at him. She was really allowing him to talk. A sign from Heaven that this was the right moment. Yet David's resolve shriveled. Drowned by the cold water of the persistent ringing, he lost his nerve and picked up the phone.

David listened then handed the phone to Lilijana. "It's for you."

"Who is it?"

David shrugged and walked to the lounge room where he planned to recover watching television.

As he left the room, her voice faded and he began to feel better. What had he hoped to achieve by confessing to a one-off sexual romp with their neighbor six years ago? The adage about letting sleeping dogs lie sprang to mind.

The lounge chair swallowed him in a familiar embrace as he sat and reached for the remote control. No sooner had he pressed the button than there came a knock on the door.

When ignoring it resulted in a more insistent knock, David grudgingly rose and answered the door. On opening it, he could think of no one he wanted to see less, not only now but ever. Tomo.

"Mum home?"

"G'day David, how are you?" mumbled David.

"Is she home or not, Dave?"

"You're a shit, Tomo," said David as he unlocked the screen door and opened it for his stepson. "Would it kill you to try and be nice? To at least say G'day?"

Tomo looked at David like he was an idiot. "G'day David, how are you?"

Deciding Tomo's tone did not deserve the respect of an answer, David trudged back to the TV and the comfort of the lounge.

"What's on?"

"Millionaire's coming on in a tick."

"Shit show. Whaddaya watch that for?"

"Fuck off, Tomo. Your mum's in the kitchen. She, unlike me, will be happy to see you."

Tomo chuckled as though pleased about something and left David to Millionaire.

He often wondered if he should register for the show. It couldn't hurt, and why shouldn't he have a bit of the action? You had to be lucky to get on the show and then you needed more luck to answer correctly and hope for mongrel questions that would stump your competitors. There was the possibility of running against another Barry Jones or Fran Bailey. That could mess you up. But the last man or woman only had to answer one more question correctly to win a hundred thousand dollars.

"One hundred thousand dollars." David liked the sound.

Lilijana reappeared with her golden boy. Why would she never listen to a bad word about Tomo? Not from him or anyone. He knew love could be blind but Lilijana appeared to have no eyes. She always took Tomo's side. Even when the evidence stacked up as high as Sydney Tower and was irrefutable, she still found some way to absolve him.

"I asked Tomo to stay for dinner, but I don't want him hanging around in the kitchen while I'm cooking."

Before David could protest about being a babysitter, Mrs. Lavender was gone. What a set up. This sucked. In David's mind, a vision formed of planting a knuckle sandwich right on Tomo's mouth and knocking loose some teeth. That would shut him up.

"Whadda they up to?"

"Eh?" said David.

"How much are they playing for now?"

"Watch this show, do you?"

"Nah. But I've seen it before."

David eyed Tomo suspiciously while his stepson stared at the television. "Fifty thousand."

"They're dumb shits aren't they? Some of these contestants?"

Although he agreed, David didn't say so. He was impressed by Tomo's use of a word with so many syllables.

After chit chat between newly arrived Amber and the host Eddie, the question was about the nationality of Roger Federer. Both men groaned. They groaned even more as Amber considered her options.

"The greatest tennis player of all time and she doesn't know who he is let alone where he comes from," said David. He liked talking to the television because it never talked back.

"You know Croats are shit hot at tennis, Dave?"

"Swiss," said David. "Swiss." He threw his hands in the air and cried, "Just take a stab and put us out of our misery, Amber."

He was aware of Tomo's observation but he ignored it. This was his lounge room and if he wanted to talk to the TV, he damn well would. Tomo had seen it all before anyway. When Tomo was younger he used to try to emulate David's TV banter, and it occasionally got them both in big trouble. David had figured out how far he could push Lilijana before she switched the television off. Tomo had no such control. He was a novice and crossed the line more frequently than not. This, too, was an area where Tomo was excused while David was blasted.

Eddie counted down from ten and when he hit two Amber locked in option C, which was Swiss. David was relieved for her, and everyone else watching. Who wouldn't know Roger Federer when everybody loved him?

"What did you say about Serbs, Tomo?"

"Croats, not fucking Serbs," snapped Tomo in response to David's deliberate provocation. "I said they're good at tennis."

"Shit hot you said, didn't you?"

Tomo paused, sensing that David was baiting him. "Shit hot."

David smiled, "But not the best. Not number one. Has there ever been a Croat ranked number one in world tennis?"

"Has there ever been an Australian ranked number one?"

"Don't sign up for this show, Tomo. You don't know half as much as you think you do."

"Fuck off, Dave."

David's suppressed groan could have shifted a mountain. This was going to be an evening of infantile boorishness, courtesy of the evil Peter Pan, also known as Tomo. He was locked in to a couple of hours of torture. Miraculously, the telephone saved him again.

'Yeah,' he said as he took the call. Lilijana spent hours every day trying to get him to identify himself when he answered the phone. She said it was polite and saved the caller from being unsure of to whom they were speaking. To David, if someone called his house and didn't know the male voice belonged to the master of the house then that call was not welcome.

"Feel like a beer?" said a familiar voice.

"Mate," replied David with turbocharged exasperation, "I really do, but I'm sort of locked in."

"Bullshit! Tell her it's an emergency."

"What sort of emergency?"

"I've just broken up with my girlfriend and I'm feeling suicidal."

"That's not gonna work. You go through women like—"

"Are you coming or not?"

"I'll see what I can do. I'll call you if I'm not coming."

"How long?"

"See you in ten if you don't hear from me in five."

"All right but don't piss around. I'm dying here."

David pressed end call and put the phone on the coffee table. Lilijana would never buy that line about Matt wanting to kill himself because she thought he was a heartless and gutless user. Funny how highly his wife regarded one of his best mates. Assuming Lilijana would object because she always did, David entered the kitchen and tried the direct approach. He was going to go anyway but he didn't want to leave with her rage ringing in his ears.

"Thought I'd duck down to the local for a quick drink or two."

"What's that?" Lilijana faced him with a faraway look, her train of thought interrupted.

"Would you mind if I went for a quick beer at the pub?"

"Dinner will be ready in an hour. Why don't you take Tomo with you?"

Like hell, thought David. I'd rather flush my head in the toilet. "Okay, I'll ask him. Thanks."

"One hour. Don't be late," she said. He left without saying a word to Tomo.

***

"How'd you escape, Dave?"

Matt was halfway through a schooner and sitting at the bar beside Chalkie. Chalkie was Dave's other best mate, so named because in school he had been a champion lines writer thanks to pissing off all the teachers. That was before whiteboards replaced chalkboards. The constant use of chalk to carry out his sentence left him with powder-coated hands and a nickname to last a lifetime. He made everyone red in the face with laughter with some of the things he got up to. Like the time he had the students move their desks toward the front of the room whenever the math teacher turned to write on the blackboard. David would never forget the look on Mr. Koona's face when he realized all the desks were pushed up against his table. As an Indian, he wasn't able to display beetroot shades. David and his classmates had never seen a whiter face.

"Chalkie," said David as punched his friend's shoulder before taking a seat next to Matt. "I didn't know it was a party. What's the occasion?"

"Serendipity," replied Chalkie.

Matt spat his beer on to the bar mat and nearly choked. David smiled at the comment and the reaction it received. No surprises with these boys. This was comfort. This was more home than his home. And to think Lilijana wanted him to contaminate it with Tomo germs.

"Good to be here, boys," said David, "I've only got an hour."

His mates booed simultaneously.

When Matt suggested they move, the three men rose in unison, secured their schooners and walked to the nearest table where they sat and resumed their conversation.

"What's new with you, Dave?" asked Chalkie.

"Mate, I nearly spilled the beans to Lilijana about me and the neighbor."

"You and the neighbor?"

"Does, 'I brought you some lemons' ring a bell for you, Chalkie?" said Matt.

"Oh yeah. That was years ago."

"When did you *nearly* tell her?" asked Matt, wanting to know not only when but exactly how close David had come to a full confession.

"Tonight." David took a mouthful of Victoria Bitter and placed his glass back on the table. "About an hour ago."

"Why, mate?" asked Chalkie. "What good would it do now?"

"What good would it have ever done?" added Matt.

David downed more of his drink. He had been thinking about Mel after his run in with Phil. Did the shock of Phil's threat push him toward confession? That didn't make sense.

"Ten seconds," said Matt. "Nine, eight..."

"I don't know. I'm having a problem with my neighbor."

"Your current neighbors?" asked Chalkie.

"Yeah."

"How long have they been there?"

"A couple of months,' replied David before draining his glass. 'Must be my shout then."

"Shit," exclaimed Matt. "How many of those are you planning to put away in this hour of freedom?"

David smiled as he rose and walked to the bar. If only he had more time this conversation could prove useful. These were the men he trusted and respected. More than his own father. Matt and Chalkie had been with him since high school. They'd experimented with drugs, alcohol and crime, and nearly ruined their lives by pushing the boundaries too far. They had somehow survived adolescence and become men together.

Back at the table, he set down three schooners and resumed his seat.

"Speak on, big man," said Matt.

David gave them the run down, beginning with the day one hello and the indifferent response he received. He told them about the chainsawing of the hedge, the strange comings and goings on, the white Commodore and the rear ender with the same vehicle, which made Matt and Chalkie laugh. David concluded with the latest incident on the driveway.

They drank their beers in thoughtful silence.

"And then there's Julia," David said.

The mention of a woman neither friend recognized caused them to freeze in comical fashion. Matt's hand remained plastered to the glass as he meant to place on the table. Chalkie's glass was halfway to his mouth when it became stuck. David had not intended to mention Julia but she was part of the reason he'd wanted to make a confession.

Slowly, Chalkie's glass finished its journey to his mouth. He drank and swallowed hard before fixing David with a curious stare.

"Julia?"

"Who the fuck is Julia?" said Matt, "and what does she have to do with your neighbors? Is she married to this Phil guy?"

"Pay attention, Matt," said Chalkie. "Phil's married to Naydine."

David glanced at his watch and was immediately set upon by Matt. "No you don't, buddy. You're not going to drop a bomb like that and run off. Who's Julia?"

"How many women have you loved, Matt?"

The question seemed to punch the air from his lungs. A look of confusion arrested his features.

"He's probably lost count," offered Chalkie.

"I don't mean had sex with. I mean been in love with."

There was no need to explain the difference. They'd frequently discussed the issue. David maintained that a man could love more than one woman whereas Matt had never really loved a woman and couldn't comment. Chalkie's position was the opposite of David's. One man, one woman.

"I've been in love with a few ladies. Maybe four that come to mind," said Matt. "Do teenage romances count?"

"Yes," said David. He recalled the overwhelming emotion associated with a girl named Jasmine when he was fifteen years old.

"Okay, make it five. The first one always leaves an eternal impression."

Chalkie looked troubled and tired of the philosophy. "Are you going to answer the question, Dave?"

"Julia is a trainer who's been coming to work to teach us how to be better communicators and have good working relationships."

"Give me her number," said Matt. "I'm about to kill the dickhead of manager I work for."

"I've fallen in love with her."

"Why?" The question was delivered in stereo.

"I don't know exactly. There's something about her."

"It's infatuation," suggested Chalkie. "She's hot looking and she's nice to you. She's probably intelligent and has a good sense of humor."

"Sounds good so far," said Matt. "I say again, give me her number."

Chalkie fired a warning glance at Matt. "You imagined being with her and how good it would be. You said to yourself, Julia and I could have fun. She wouldn't nag me and she would want to listen and hang out with me. She would want to make love to me. Then you started visualizing that sex."

"Steady on," said Matt with a note of alarm in his voice.

How different these two men were. Matt wanted to blow the froth off every beer of seriousness. He never wanted to dig too deep. Although supportive and encouraging, Matt would never challenge him on heavy moral issues. 'Each to his own' was Matt's philosophy. Acutely aware of his own flaws, he'd rarely point them out in others. Chalkie was a thinker with deeply held convictions, sensitive and empathetic. He would readily wield the knife of sobriety and slice through any bullshit. He had an uncanny knack for identifying the truth. On this occasion he nailed it.

"Things between you and Lilijana are still bad, aren't they?" he probed.

"Shit house."

Chalkie sipped his beer as though it were hot tea. "Dave, Lilijana's your wife. You have to give her all your love and right now you're not."

"How is thinking of another woman taking love away from your wife?" asked Matt.

"It depends on what you think love is."

"More philosophy," said Matt dismissively while David pondered the question. It was a good one.

David stole another look at his watch. "I can't help it," he said, "but I'm not going to do anything about it."

"Famous last words?"

"Seriously," said David, hoping he sounded convincing. "What am I going to do?" When there was no response, David answered his own question. "Nothing."

Matt looked as though he believed him. Chalkie's face was creased with concern.

"We should talk about this some more, don't you reckon?" said Chalkie.

"Sure," replied David, "I really have to go, though. I don't want any more trouble at home. Tomo's over for dinner so thanks for rescuing me temporarily." He stood and emptied the last of the Victoria Bitter.

"How are you and Tomo getting on these days?" asked Matt.

"He's a prick. I want to punch him every time he opens his mouth."

"So things are good then. Glad to hear it."

Matt made them laugh as always, and they parted in high spirits. David thanked his mates for listening and they agreed to meet up on Saturday at the Leagues Club for a drink.

As David walked back to his car, he wondered if much was likely to change before he talked with his friends again. No doubt he would come under intense scrutiny at their next meeting. He half-expected Chalkie to call him before Saturday to see how things were going. Two things troubled him. He did not say why he had wanted to confess his one-off infidelity with Mel to Lilijana, and he had lied about not having done anything about Julia. That lie sat in his stomach like a heap of greasy cheeseburgers. He felt sick. Both Matt and Chalkie would have said in the strongest terms that he was making a huge mistake. Chalkie was right when he said that David was stealing love from his wife. As far as his friends knew, the whole affair was imaginary, but Julia's acceptance of David's note had moved that fantasy to reality. This realization excited and frightened him. Its wrongness was part of its appeal. Even though Chalkie was right, it did not guarantee that the right thing would be done. Life was infinitely more complicated.

As David drove home, he could not shake the guilt he felt over the lie he told his friends. With every bump in the road, he expected to eject those greasy hamburgers. Pulling his mobile phone from his pocket, he dialed Chalkie's number.

"About Julia?"

"Yes?" Chalkie's tone was neutral.

"I actually have done something about acting on my feelings."

The silence on the other end made David uncertain of what to say or if he should speak at all.

Finally Chalkie said, "I'm listening, mate."

"The reason I wanted to confess to Lilijana is because I might do it again. With Mel I hadn't planned it and it was a one-off. I was naive and stupid, but it was wrong and I regret it. I thought if I told Lilijana she would blow her stack. Then I could use her anger as ammunition in against this desire to cheat on her with Julia."

"Makes sense," said Chalkie. "What have you done about Julia?"

No judgment. No anger. Chalkie didn't need to say anything. David was so appreciative he was speechless for a moment.

"Dave? You still there?"

"Yeah. I wrote her an invitation for coffee and she accepted."

Chalkie said, "You and I both know you didn't invite her for coffee. Nor did she accept an invitation for coffee. Ring her and tell her you changed your mind or you'll get burned. Do you hear me?"

"Yeah."

"Call it off," said Chalkie before disconnecting.

As David wheeled the car into his driveway he tested his resolve by telling himself out loud, "I should call it off." The words sounded lame and insincere.

CHAPTER TWELVE

The Sky Blue Café was located on the Esplanade at Thirroul in the northern suburbs between the steep Illawarra escarpment and the Pacific Ocean. Visitors enjoyed the scenery and holiday atmosphere. The beach side suburb offered trendy eateries and shops. David was anonymous as he pushed open the door of the Sky Blue and headed for a table towards the back right corner.

It was Saturday and David had arrived fifteen minutes early. He glanced at his watch as he sat with his back to the wall. Julia had suggested the Sky Blue because she had read about it in a newspaper article. Thirroul was halfway between where she lived in the Southern Suburbs of Sydney and Chinaman's Hollow, where David had lived in peace until recently. Was this a good time to have coffee with another woman? David changed the subject before he could answer. Walking out now on Julia and whatever sweet opportunities might arise from this meeting was no longer an option.

Fortunately the Sky Blue was not as packed as he'd feared. Cafes that received publicity tended to expand dramatically. There were those who made a sport of sampling food from the chefs whose praises were sung in important publications. This represented an explicit challenge to the food critics from the patrons: is this place as good as you say it is? David wondered if the Sky Blue had paid for the priceless advertising. Did any of the featured eateries pay to have a critic sample their food and tell readers about it? If they did, they must be supremely confident of their offering. Otherwise they'd be courting commercial homicide: death by bad review.

The patronage was just right. Too many people caused a noisy buzz of conversation and too few left a hollow unwelcoming ambience. It was also easier to blend with a café half-full of people, against the chance of being recognized. Alone, he might as well have worn a sandwich board to announce his meeting with a married woman. David squirmed and looked at his watch. Five minutes had passed.

The walls of the sky-blue interior were tastefully adorned with framed black and white photographs of beach and town scenes. He liked their simple beauty and might have performed a closer inspection in other circumstances. Three young ladies shared one of the small tables, giggling and gesturing as they sipped their lattes. Near the window, an elderly couple sat quietly side by side, staring out at the ocean. Other couples and a few single people had their faces buried in books or newspapers.

He felt he wore a flashing neon sign by sitting inactive so long. Should he buy a drink? Or would it be rude to order before Julia's arrival?

Nearly ten minutes had passed when he checked his watch the third time. Was the staff wondering why he hadn't ordered? Were the girls behind the counter speculating? Had they determined David's purpose? Could they read his mind? David shook his head. He had an overblown view of his own importance. Why should anyone care about him?

'It's not just coffee,' Chalkie had said.

David's thoughts bumbled in and out of his head. He recognized the signs of panic and rising anxiety. The tide could be halted, if only he had the power. He concentrated on a random spot in the Pacific. The temperature was cool on the surface, the motion gently undulating on this clear calm day. Calm and clear. Cool. He repeated the three words as though reciting a magic formula to throw a wet towel over fiery thoughts. He felt the change as he continued to speak the words: clear, calm and cool.

A bell tinkled as the door of the café opened. His gaze was pulled away from that transformative speck in the ocean. The elderly man held the door for his wife to exit. He followed her and was about to close the door when he made way for Julia. David's heart leapt.

He threw his hand up to catch her eye. She gave him a sly little wave and headed to meet him. He had never seen her in jeans before, and she wore a bone-colored sweater. She looked so wonderful his mouth fell open. David quickly closed it and called forth a smile. Julia smiled back. Spellbound, he realized her arrival had changed his world forever. Until he saw her it was possible to believe he'd been mistaken. That he imagined her accepting his invitation, or that she had changed her mind. He could have changed his mind as he sat and waited for her. That ever-present thought was insidious. Why insidious? Because he wanted her. There was no turning back.

David stood and half-extended his hand to greet her. She didn't notice so he withdrew it. He sat after she did, her gaze meeting his. Though no words had passed between them, their silence held joyful serenity. In that moment there were no outsiders. There was no outside world. No Pacific Ocean, no beach, no Sky Blue Café, no Thirroul, no other people. Nothing but David and Julia.

Reluctantly, David spoke. "Thanks for coming."

"Thanks for inviting me. Sorry I'm late."

She sat opposite him with her bag clutched to her chest, as though she needed protection or comfort. Her eyes twinkled, but her posture suggested uncertainty, if not fear. Her voice, though, was warm and fluid as ever. He would have waited for her all day, not that he would tell her.

"Coffee?"

"I guess so. That's why we came, isn't it?"

"Just coffee?"

"It's never just coffee," she said casually. "You have to have something with it."

"Something sweet." David gestured to the menu and Julia picked it up. He felt as though the conversation needed to be normalized. The salacious tone, which he may only have imagined, struck him as inappropriate. It was like ordering dessert before the main course.

"See anything you like?" asked David.

"Lots. It's hard to choose. I fancy the triple chocolate mudcake but they have a thing called mango butter cake." She looked at him. "How good does that sound?"

David watched her, amused by her intensity.

"I've got to try the mango butter cake," she said almost breathlessly. "What will you have?"

"I'll order the chocolate cake and then you'll have a backup if the mango is no good."

Julia smiled. They held each other's gaze again. "You're so sweet," she said.

David left to place their order then returned to ask Julia what sort of coffee she wanted. A soy cappuccino.

"Soy?"

"Soy," she said.

David didn't know anyone who drank soy milk. He didn't like the taste. After high school, he had worked in a soy milk factory. The smell had eventually melted into a sickly association with hard work and long nights. In a few months, he quit, pretending he was going to university. He had wanted a high-paying job away from factory floors, but his marks weren't high enough for university admittance.

Back at the table, David sat and said, "I used to make soy milk."

"Did you?"

"I had to leave early my very first shift because I cracked my head open."

Unaware of the exaggeration, Julia leaned forward to hear the full story.

"I was cleaning the floor underneath a hopper, so I was bent over and when I straightened my head hit the corner of the steel frame supporting it. It was careless." David pointed to his left eyebrow. "Right here it got me. At first I just felt dizzy. Then I felt pain and touched the impact spot. My hand came away bloody."

"Off to the doctor for stitches?"

"Four."

"Poor baby," said Julia.

Lilijana said 'poor baby' whenever he hurt himself at home. She felt no sympathy, though, and he knew it. To Lilijana, who'd been through war and childbirth, David had no idea what pain and suffering were. Any man with half a brain would never tell a woman his pain was worse than childbirth. Did Julia have children? She never referred to them in the training room. That did not mean they were nonexistent. Some people never discussed their private lives with strangers.

"Thanks for your sympathy," said David. He was unable to read her sentiment but he doubted it was dismissive, as it would have been for Lilijana. He knew of only one exception when Lilijana had shown him sympathy: after his suspected heart attack, when he hadn't really been hurt.

"I'm sure it was very painful," Julia said.

The coffee and cakes arrived, bringing an end to his thoughts.

"As a result of my time making soy milk, I don't like the stuff. Or coffee."

Julia tore open two packets of sugar and stirred them into her cup. She appeared unable to focus on anything besides her cappuccino. He watched and enjoyed her movements. For the first time he noticed her perfume: subtle and exotic. She spoke before he could ask about it.

"I love coffee and I'm allergic to lactose."

"No dairy products for you then. What about the butter in the cake?"

"Too bad."

"How severe is the allergy?"

"It's nothing," said Julia absently. While she lifted her fork, cut the cake and raised a piece to her mouth, he admired her graceful movements. The fork stopped as she met his gaze. Drowning in those sparkling pools, David felt giddiness creep over him. With a smile, she opened her mouth and placed the cake inside it. She closed her eyes and withdrew the fork. David felt a rush of blood in his crotch and quickly looked away. He shifted in his seat and grabbed the chocolate cake. After he took a bite, he realized Julia was watching him and discomfort stormed in again.

"What was that look all about?" he asked to escape the uneasiness.

"It's good cake. Very good."

Instantly, they were back in everyday land. This meeting was like a rollercoaster ride, and David loved it, despite the occasional awkwardness. Having come to this point it seemed illogical to be cautious. Why not relax and go with the flow? Let go. Enjoy the ride.

Out of the blue, Julia asked, "Do you think we'll do this again?"

"I hope so but it's going to be hard. We'll need to be discreet."

"Of course."

"We should probably discuss the rules of engagement."

Julia's fork froze in mid air. "Why? Are we going to war?"

David considered his answer as Julia finished her cake. It was imperative to be clear. They needed to understand their respective expectations. All relationships required rules, otherwise they failed. It was fine to talk about living in the moment and letting people be free but anarchy was bad. Order was good. Had Julia bristled because she didn't like rules? Or because she didn't think they were necessary? This was something he needed to clarify. David was beginning an adulterous affair. There was no point in calling it anything else. Honesty was critical and David needed to start with himself. He was not in love with Lilijana anymore. Any affection he felt was residual and platonic. He had the hots for Julia, was obsessed, in love. He wanted to be with her and eventually make love to her.

"David?"

Her words brought him back to the table.

He began, "Is it fair to say you perceived my note as more than an invitation for coffee?'

"Convoluted question," she replied, "but the answer is yes."

"Why?"

"Why what?"

David wasn't sure if she was being deliberately obtuse. "Why did you say yes to me?"

"I like coffee."

"Meaning you like me?"

When Julia's hand fell on his, it startled him. She rubbed his fingers gently and slowly. Then she smiled and looked into his eyes. He swallowed hard.

"I've never done this before," said Julia. She pulled her hand away. "Part of me thinks it's a bad idea. It fact, it's insane. Another part of me craves it. Yearns for you. I haven't stopped thinking about you since you handed me the note."

This time David reached for her hand and simply held it. "I feel the same way. I'm shocking myself but I don't want to stop. I want to be with you, Julia. I'm not in love with my wife and she doesn't give a shit about me, so I'm reaching out to a woman I find incredibly attractive and thoroughly desirable.'

"Who is she?"

They laughed together in relief. Something had broken and it was good. There was an extra radiance in their faces as they held hands and contemplated the future with exuberant, concupiscent hope.

"Now," said David, "Let's talk about those rules."

CHAPTER THIRTEEN

"I know it was wrong now," said David apologetically, "but at the time I thought he got what he deserved."

Chalkie was enthusiastic. "Tell us the full story."

"Haven't we heard this a thousand times before?" asked Matt.

David loaded a mouthful of Victoria Bitter and smiled at his friends. This was how their meetings often went: story after story. Some heard before and fondly remembered, enough to hear it repeated every time they got together. Some not heard, or long forgotten and eagerly anticipated. Their appetite for glorious tales of the past was voracious.

It was Wednesday night. They were parked on bar stools inside the Illawarra Workers Club. This venue had become a new tradition ever since Chalkie introduced it. The beer was cheap, the atmosphere cozy and Wednesday was hump day: the middle of the week. They all needed a debrief. David had met with Julia four days ago. He hadn't spoken to her since but he knew the anticipation he felt toward seeing her tomorrow would be matched by her own desire. Their affair had begun

"Hey," said Chalkie, hitting David's arm with his hand. "Are you going to tell the story or not?"

Matt rolled his eyes.

"Arthur Gardener was our neighbor when I was in high school. He lived alone, and was a crotchety old fart who detested children. He also seemed to have an immense distaste for fun. Never saw him smile or crack a joke. Hardly heard a peep out of him apart from telling us off for allowing our balls into his yard. Cricket or footy. Whatever. You know when you're playing in the yard that balls are going to sail over the fence. No big deal, right? Happens all over the country, every day of the week."

"All over the world every day of the week," agreed Chalkie.

"So we were always apologizing and having to kiss his boots to enter his yard and retrieve the balls. At first he allowed one of us in, it was usually me, but after a while, he ceased blessing us with admission into his hallowed turf. He would simply get the ball himself and throw it back over. Not hand it over, but chuck it randomly. He had a favorite saying which accompanied our requests: 'It's not the fucking Sydney Cricket Ground, you know.'"

"Nice way to speak to kids," said Matt, deciding to reengage.

"He swore at us other times, in other contexts and it was often under his breath. Bitter and twisted he was. Old Arthur Gardener. He even ripped the choko vine off his side of the fence and tossed it back over ours."

"Possession is ninth tenths of the law," said Chalkie. 'He could have kept those chokoes."

"He should have too, because chokoes are tasty," added Matt.

"Anyway, this went on for years and we just learned to cop it sweet. Mum and Dad reminded us to be careful and said Arthur was within his rights, even though they didn't regard him very highly. There were occasions after I was sworn at when Dad was ready to rock over to Arthur's place and fire a few choice words back. Mum forbade him though because she said it would make matters worse."

"Neighbors, eh?" said Chalkie wistfully, as though he was relating to this story in a personally potent way.

"Around that time a mate of mine introduced us to pipe bombs. Crackers were still legal and we all loved cracker night but bigger thrills could be had by making and detonating our own explosive devices. We didn't give a shit about the colors or the pretty patterns, we just wanted the noise and destruction. Letterboxes were perfect targets for our homemade incendiary devices."

"Don't be such a wanker, Dave," said Matt. "Just call them bombs."

"By the time I was fourteen, I'd had a gutful of Arthur Gardner and his arsehole attitude."

"You blew up his letterbox," said Chalkie.

David noted there was no congratulatory tone and Chalkie's expression was laced with concern.

"Completely annihilated it. One whole side was sent cartwheeling into his house and it pierced the wall just beside his front door. The bang was incredible. We nearly pissed ourselves laughing."

"Did that stop Arthur from swearing at you and complaining about the balls in his yard?" asked Chalkie.

"No," said David defensively, "But I didn't think it would. I just wanted to teach the old bugger a lesson."

"What did it teach him?"

"Shit you're a party pooper, Chalkie," said Matt. "Dave was just a stupid kid."

Chalkie was undaunted. "I don't reckon you taught him anything. You reinforced what he already believed: children are troublemakers. Selfish good for nothings."

"That's it," said David.

The silence which followed was not uncomfortable. They were grown men, used to each other's company. They could be hard on each other when necessary but grace was never far away. Lingering at the back of every word, every sentence and shared look was the knowledge they loved each other. Chalkie was the only one who had ever said the words but they all felt it. This was a priceless treasure.

Matt broke into their thoughts. "Now, as an adult, you still have troubles with the neighbors."

"This time it's not my fault, though. This is the way it is when you have a rental property next door. The tenants come and go, and sometimes they are nice, quiet people. Other times they aren't."

"What's the latest on the Phil situation?" asked Chalkie.

"There is no latest. I haven't since him since last week, when he threatened me on the driveway. Most of the time you wouldn't know anyone lives at 1008 but every now and then, there they are, disturbing my peace."

"You could always blow up their letter box," suggested Matt.

They laughed easily. Then Chalkie stood and offered to buy the next round of drinks.

Matt looked at David with serious intent. "Chalkie can be bloody self righteous sometimes, can't he?"

David nodded. "The problem is he's always right. If he ever fucks up in word or deed, I'll have a heart attack."

"Too perfect if you ask me."

"Shut up, Matt. You're just jealous. Chalkie is the most together bloke either of us know."

"He makes sure we know it, and the reason for it."

"Too harsh, my man. He's a good mate."

When Chalkie returned he looked as though he knew what they'd discussed. It was a dead giveaway when they ceased talking as soon as he came within earshot. Nothing says 'we discussed you behind your back' better than an abruptly choked conversation.

"Talking about me again, eh?"

"Yep," confessed Matt casually, and that was that.

"Did you have that coffee on Saturday, Dave?" asked Chalkie.

"I had tea actually and she had coffee."

"What were you thinking?" asked Matt.

Chalkie quietly drank his beer while watching David intently.

"What do you mean?" asked David.

"What were you thinking while you were with her?"

'It was pretty awkward at first,' replied David evasively. 'I arrived early and spent the whole time wondering if she would show up. And part of the time wondering if..."

"If you should leave before it was too late?" suggested Chalkie.

David shook his head. "If I should order a drink while I was waiting."

Without further interruption apart from an occasional question, David told his mates about the time he spent with Julia and did it without guilt. He contemplated his lack of shame, not just in meeting another woman and planning to see her again, but also in telling his mates. He could have been describing a night out with Lilijana. Recounting the sweet lightness of being with the woman he loved, except the woman he loved was no longer his wife. The weight of affection for the woman he'd spent eleven years with was feather light. It was as though he'd cast it off like an unwanted load. A chilling coldness remained. Strangely, he was calm and untroubled. If he was going to freeze to death in the ice of infidelity, then he was going willingly, joyfully.

"I don't want to hear anymore," said Chalkie. "You are doing the wrong thing and I won't encourage it."

David noted the sadness in his eyes. Maybe there was also a flicker of anger. He couldn't be sure. "Fair enough."

"So Julia is an off-limits topic?"

Reluctantly David agreed. He respected Chalkie, and knew his friend was dead right. Matt would still listen. He had form with regard to adultery, and he would be interested. Those conversations would have to occur without Chalkie.

Matt asked Chalkie about work, which led to a discussion on politics. David was able to participate without effort or real interest. He was thinking of Julia. He remembered every detail of their meeting and was imagining the next one. Would it be more of the same: a little bit awkward yet fun and exciting? Or would the luster of forbidden friendship wear off? He had no idea how this would play out. David was pioneering new territory. Even fearful, he was willing to travel this road as far as he could. Until it ended, however it ended, he would run free, yelling and whooping, without a thought to the ramifications.

Was this freedom or just another type of prison? Lilijana often said all people were locked in a jail. In one way or another, most created their own prisons. David had never felt like a captive until recently. His life had seemed to flow like a river through a lush forest. There were twists and turns, ups and downs, and times when the flow ebbed for reasons beyond his control, but it never stopped its march to the sea. His choices had ultimately resulted in progress, success and bounty. He had a hell of a lot to be thankful for, and it had always been enough in the past. Now, he was beginning to see that the banks of the river were prison bars and he wanted to break free so he could flow wherever he wanted. David wanted to be a flood, not a river.

"Still with us, Dave?" said Chalkie.

"Yeah," he replied flatly before glancing at his watch. "Bout time to go."

When David began to rise, Chalkie's hand grabbed his arm.

"Are we cool, Dave? You understand what I mean about the Julia thing?"

'The Julia thing' was a jarring expression which ignited a spark of anger. David suppressed it. He really wanted to tell Chalkie the thoughts that compelled him, but nothing more could, or should, be said. He had to accept that the door was closed.

"Of course, we're cool."

He gulped his remaining beer. "See you later, boys."

Handshakes all around, and then he left. As he passed the bar and headed toward the exit, he passed a painting he had never noticed before. Stopping, he stared at the artwork: a river overflowing its banks. A couple of cows stood belly-deep in water. In the distance, a house floated on the miscreant water.

The painting was titled: Flood. David imagined a better title: Freedom. For the water itself. Freedom.

CHAPTER FOURTEEN

Like the screaming of his alarm clock, familiar and equally unwelcome sounds penetrated David's peaceful sleep. He pried open one eye to look at the clock. 12:30 a.m. and all was quiet within the house. Outside was something else. The discordant notes of heated argument emanated from 1008.

A knot tied itself in his stomach. His recurrent dilemma presented itself again. To listen in the dark while trying to not listen. As the knot tightened into a fist and began pummeling his insides, David knew he would have to act. Going next door was out of the question. He had been warned off by the police, not to mention Phil. If his threats were only hot air, David would have happily banged on the door and told them to cork it or he'd call the cops again. He couldn't be certain, though, what Phil was capable of. Again. How often must this happen before the demon got his due?

At 12:35 a.m., David left the warmth of his bed. On the way to the kitchen, he conducted a mental coin toss. Heads, call the police. Tails, invade the neighbors' space. The first toss came up tails, which meant defying the police. He tossed again. Heads. If he called the police they would come but the argument would be over by then. Best of three, David thought. He was staring at the telephone when the third toss came up tails. He laughed quietly, nervous with indecision. The churning in his gut made him dizzy. Make a choice, he told himself. Make a choice.

"Expecting a call?"

Lilijana had followed him out, curious no doubt.

"They're fighting again."

Lilijana stepped closer and touched his arm. "Are you going to call the police again?"

"I can't just ignore it."

"Why?"

David had a million reasons but each one was vulnerable to counterattack. Was it any of his concern? Live and let live. He liked the title of the Bond film better: Live and Let Die. That would be a permanent solution. Lilijana's questioning stare bored into his back. Maybe she'd get sick of waiting, blow out exasperation and return to bed.

"Why do you care so much?" She gripped his arm harder. "Leave them alone."

"You have more empathy for them than me," David said. "That' a bit out of a whack, isn't it?"

She released his arm and moved her hands to her hips. "You're the one who's a bit out of whack, David. I'm going back to bed. Are you coming?"

Her words stung his face like a slap. Every perceived threat was attributed to his imagination. He had not imagined Phil swinging the chainsaw like a psychopath, nor the bony finger which had pierced his personal space in an undisguised threat. Phil was dangerous but David could not prove it. He had no allies in this war.

David looked at the kitchen clock. 12:45 a.m. He listened and heard silence: a temporary cure.

As he climbed back into bed, he felt Lilijana's gaze. David was no longer tired or irritated so he attempted to converse. "I'm not imagining things, baby. I'm not crazy. When did you learn the words 'out of whack?'"

Lilijana groaned, as though dealing with a child's tantrum.

"Since I'm *awake now*," she began, with emphasis on awake, "we might as well talk."

At last, thought David, drenched in relief.

"John and Naydine moved in four weeks ago. The day after, you went to say hello, which you do for all new neighbors. That's nice of you, by the way."

David resisted the powerful urge to maraud into her monologue and insert his proverbial two cents. She'd set a record for the most consecutive words said to him in a month.

"After you returned, you complained about their attitude, as though you were a school principle meeting two new students. Prejudge is the word that comes to mind. Not everybody fits into our molds or meets our standards. John and Naydine are perfectly decent people who simply live an alternative lifestyle."

David uttered the word "bullshit," muffled into a cough.

"After a two minute conversation, saying the man is a drug addict and a menace to society, is a bit rich, don't you think?"

David stiffened. Lilijana had gone overboard with her embellishment of the facts. Rhetoric. Don't answer, he warned himself.

"Well?"

"Nothing. Carry on."

The unpleasant pause which followed was a familiar one to David. Lilijana sent a probe into his mind and attempted to read his thoughts. He activated his force field and blocked her.

"Then came a series of reports on their devilish behavior. They have some pretty intense arguments but calling the police seems excessive when there is no physical proof of violence, which I suspect is what concerns you, as a knight in shining armor. Naydine doesn't need rescuing, and John is no threat to you or anyone else. He's harmless. When he warned you to leave him alone, he was just reacting in fear to your interference in his business. You can see that, right?"

Lilijana was inviting him to agree with her. He didn't. Anger invaded his heart as she defended strangers instead of him. This was the ultimate betrayal. She might have been a defense lawyer dismissing the alleged facts and cautioning the jury not to be bamboozled by fancy-sounding arguments to disguise wafer-thin evidence. David sighed.

"Uh-huh."

"I know you've been under a lot of stress. Changes at work. The panic attack and your ongoing feud with Tomo, but John and Naydine aren't to blame so stop scapegoating them. Concentrate on us, your family and your friends. I'm won't stop you from meeting Matt and Chalkie anymore. It's good to let off steam, and I'm sorry I haven't been interested in making love to you. I'm just tired. I expect my sex drive to return and we'll resume normal relations."

David could no longer remain silent. "I can't remember what normal relations are, and I'm cut that you're defending Phil and Naydine. I'm your husband, for fuck's sake!"

It slipped out before he could stop it, on a tidal wave of anger. Now that it had hit, devastation would follow.

"Sorry, baby." David laid a soothing hand on Lilijana. "I didn't mean to swear."

"You can't keep excusing your bad behavior. I never speak to you like that. It's so disrespectful."

David apologized again because there was nothing else he could do. Neither his words nor his tone mollified Lilijana. She shrugged off his hand and rolled away. The conversation was terminated.

In the darkness that surrounded and invaded, David's situation seemed unredeemable. He was done looking for hope. She understood he was under more stress but didn't acknowledge her role in the creation and maintenance of that stress. The possible return of her libido was of no solace either. David had lost interest. Sometimes he fantasized about her as he relieved his sexual tension. Usually, he imagined someone else. A lump swelled in his throat. His eyes burned with desperate tears.

***

Worn out with grieving frustration, David had slept deeply. He didn't want to wake up. He thought about feigning illness but wasn't up to the challenge. In fact, he felt good: energized and light. Perhaps the tears he'd shed had cleansed him. His thoughts were resolute and clear. He would give himself to Julia. She wanted him as he wanted her. There was no need to add complications. Lingering doubts, nourished by Chalkie's admonishment, were vanquished. He would also remove Phil from the violent scene of his life, and replace him with serenity. David did not know how, but the necessity to act was a snowball running downhill.

Refreshed in mind and body, David left his bed. He bounced into the bathroom, where he washed his face and smiled. As the mirror steamed over, he wrote on it with his finger.

Love your neighbor

Loathe your neighbor

David liked that. It was poignant and poetic. Julia, he would love. Phil, he would act against. An image of a bomb in a letterbox popped into his mind. Matt had thrown it out as a joke. It would be as ineffective as pissing on their wall, stealing from their clothesline, or ordering an unwanted pizza delivery. These were all childish pranks. They might make thirteen year old happy but David was a grown man. What did he want? How would he get it? David didn't know.

He used a hand towel to wipe off the mirror. Then he lathered his face with shaving cream. With the twin blade pressed against his face, he drew it halfway along his jaw. Lost in the security of routine, David was able to concentrate on finding a solution for Phil.

What outcome would be ideal? He wanted Phil and Naydine to leave. He didn't want to hurt them, but they wouldn't leave of their own accord. David had no means to force them out. He couldn't kill them.

"Kill," he said aloud.

Like a magic formula, it arrested his attention and busted his cocoon. Staring at his reflection like it could provide additional options proved fruitless. They would have to be evicted. For breach of their lease the landlord could kick them out. An exciting new line of thought opened up. What were the standard rental conditions? Only people specified on the lease could live on the premises. No dogs or cats. No unauthorized alterations. What else? Failure to pay rent on time. Use of premises for illegal purposes. Bingo. Drugs were a definite possibility. If Phil and Naydine were producing illicit drugs and dealing from 1008, it would definitely get them evicted. Proof was the fly in that ointment. Though nothing else came to mind, David knew he was on the right track. He resumed shaving.

"Did you forget how to do it?"

Lilijana's question was meant to be a joke. David offered a weak laugh.

"You know me. Somewhat incompetent."

"But loveable."

"Ow!" exclaimed David as Lilijana's compliment caused the blade to bite into his neck.

"Be careful, honey," she said then moved into the bathroom and past him to the toilet.

David finished shaving and washed the soap from his face. The slight nick on his neck had already stopped bleeding, courtesy of tissue paper. He removed it and examined the wound.

"Do you want me to call an ambulance?"

He'd assumed Lilijana was reading. Instead he was disconcerted to find she'd been watching. Her mood was bizarre and troubling. David wanted to escape her investigative glare and facetious barbs.

"I'll be fine," he said as he exited the bathroom.

Lilijana probably thought she was funny: keeping it light and bubbly after the conflict the night before. Maybe it was her way of saying they should move on. The issue has been dealt with. She was delusional if that's what she thought. The situation was intolerable and maddening. Lilijana's attempt to sweep their problems under the rug solidified his resolve. Love your neighbor. Loathe your neighbor. This was his new mantra. It would sustain him through adversity and discouragement. It would satisfy and strengthen him. It would keep him focused. It would bring him victory. He hooted as he strode into the kitchen.

Alen and Danijela shifted their gazes from the television, their faces adorned with surprise.

"Morning, guys," said David cheerily as he went about organizing breakfast.

They mumbled something in response then returned their attention to the television while shoveling Rice Bubbles into their mouths.

CHAPTER FIFTEEN

"Governments do not trust people to behave properly and maintain peaceful relationships. A healthy society is only achievable through rules and regulations. We can't be trusted. It's that simple."

David smiled at Julia but was too busy worshipping her to reply.

Big Al's Diner was a tribute to the classic American diner featured in Five Easy Pieces, Pulp Fiction, When Harry Met Sally, Happy Days and Seinfeld. David had never been in a diner. After their separate arrival, he and Julia greeted each other with clandestine affection. Although the weirdness of their meeting at Sky Blue was gone, they were light years away from public displays of affection. Julia had ordered a coffee, and David a Coke. After some sugary small talk, David had raised the subject of rules, which had set Julia off. She needed to be coerced into serious conversation, shepherded like cattle which preferred to roam free and frolic rather than be corralled.

"I need a law to punish me if I don't wear my seatbelt or ensure that my passengers wear seatbelts. I need a law to remind me to lock my car when I leave it unattended. If the law did not forbid murder, I would kill my enemies."

"You don't have any enemies, do you?"

It was Julia's turn to smile. Although she had built up a head of steam during her sermon, she was not so enraptured that she missed his amusement.

"I might have hundreds of enemies."

A raised eyebrow from David had Julia backpedaling. "Would you believe scores?"

David shook his head.

"Would you believe a few?"

"No Agent Eighty-Six. I don't believe anyone would want to hurt you or that you ever caused offense to a single living soul."

"That's right. All my enemies are dead."

This banter was enjoyable. David felt mesmerized in Julia's presence, enchanted by her sparkling eyes. He felt lost and didn't want to be found.

"Tell me more about the stupidity of our laws."

Julia straightened, inadvertently creating more distance between them. "I heard that a person could be fined three thousand dollars for not filling out a log book of their frog-keeping activities.'

David gagged and coughed a spray of Coke onto the table. When he resumed normal breathing, he laughed. Julia also laughed as she snatched up napkins and used them to clean the table. Tenderly, she reached out with a clean napkin and dabbed his mouth. David realized the importance of not looking at Julia until she fully recovered. Laughing fits were devils to subdue.

"What's so funny?" said Julia, through a hole in the wall of their hysteria.

"The look on your face when you said that. It was the biggest parody of earnest outrage I've ever seen."

Julia feigned a hurt look. "You don't take me seriously, do you?"

"No," replied David as laughter swelled again. He covered his mouth to stop more unauthorized escapees.

"That's good, except you don't know me well enough to judge when I'm having fun or being serious."

"If I get it wrong you can say 'I'm serious' or 'seriously.' Just don't make that face when you say it otherwise I'll laugh."

Julia grabbed his left hand and held it tightly in both of hers. She fixed him with a look of passion, something mysterious, wild and desperate, combined with fragments of fear. David held her gaze for a long time, barely conscious of her violent grip. He felt breathless and fearful. He wanted her to say something. She was suffocating him, like an anaconda using its powerful coils. He needed an exit, an escape route.

"If you sell a mouse to someone who feeds it alive to a snake, you can be fined eight thousand dollars." Julia released his hand and laughed a little too loud. "That's outrageous. The fine should be doubled. It's inhumane. Poor little mice."

David glanced around Big Al's. No one paid them any attention. There were no furtive glances or whispers, no elbowing or knowing nods. David and Julia might not have been there at all, despite the laughter that made them conspicuous. They weren't the center of the universe. Nobody knew them, and nobody cared. Julia could have murdered him and gotten away with it. She did say she'd killed all her enemies.

"Don't take me too seriously," said Julia, taking his hand more gently. "Life can be very full on, and I like to let off steam when I can."

The problem with steam is that it can burn people, thought David.

"I don't want," continued Julia, "to have a serious relationship with you. I've already got one of those."

At last they were back on track. Although many ridiculous laws were an insult to intelligence, without them there would be chaos. Only deranged anarchists thought that was good. The affair between David and Julia had yet to be sealed with sex. It was still a flirtatious friendship, albeit with intent. Before he dove into her ocean, he needed to know she wouldn't hold him, refusing to let him surface, denying him breath. Rules were necessary. He needed to know he could trust her. Chalkie's admonition reverberated in his head.

"I don't want that either," said David. "I'm not going to leave Lilijana. I won't hurt her or my children. I'm not motivated by revenge."

"Why are you here?"

"I crave your attention. When your eyes are on me, when you're listening to me, when you speak, I feel real. You're like water to my thirsty soul." The words sounded corny and too potent. He may as well have pointed a gun and told Julia to run for her life.

"Don't you mean Coke?"

Bang! The gun went off but it fired a blank. Julia had disarmed him with a joke.

He laughed. "I'm here because I like you and want to have some fun."

"Me too," replied Julia. "That's exactly what I want."

"Okay," said David, "I haven't thought about these rules in any particular order. I hope you've had similar ideas."

Julia sipped her coffee and nodded.

"There are two issues," said David. First is discretion and second is time."

"What do you mean by time?"

"This can't go on forever."

"Of course not."

"The thing is, how will we know when to stop and will we be able to stop? What's going to happen if I say in couple of weeks that I don't want to play?"

"That's cute," said Julia.

David struggled to put his thoughts in organized sentences. The need for clarity was paramount. These rules were critical, even if no else had ever started an affair with such deliberation. Weren't they always spontaneous and surprising? Didn't the participants get swept off the feet, carried along by a tide of passion to the total exclusion of logic? David's experience with romance was derived from the plots of romantic comedies. Julia might have been Sandra Bullock or Drew Barrymore or Jennifer Aniston. She waited for him to continue.

"This sounds crazy," said David. "Why don't we just do it? Don't we both know what we want?"

"We do."

"But I need some sort of safety net. I keep thinking of *Fatal Attraction*. You know, the movie with Michael Douglas and Glenn Close?"

Julia's sigh seemed to dim the lights. "If you tell me it's over, I might try to destroy your life. I could say that's not going to happen but I might lie. We barely know each other. There is undeniable risk. Isn't that part of the appeal? Isn't the danger exciting? You think I'm worth it otherwise you wouldn't be here. You've already made up your mind and so have I. We've passed the point of no return."

He wanted Julia. He had to have her. "Then when one of us wants out, it's over. If you or I decide to stop, the other accepts the decision. No follow up calls or text messages."

"No stalking," added Julia.

"Agreed."

Julia offered her hand to seal the arrangement.

"When it's over, it's over," David said. "Do you want to suggest a rule?"

She shook her head and drained her coffee.

"Next rule," David said, "don't call me, either at home or on the mobile. If you want to talk, send a text and let me know if I can call you or if you want a messaged reply. Like I said, discretion is crucial. When you text me, use a code."

"A coded message?" Julia's voice betrayed incredulity. "What are we? Spies?"

"If my phone goes off and it's lying around, Lilijana will answer it, or if it's a text message, she'll read it. I can't tell her to stop. How would I justify my sudden need for privacy?"

"Point taken," said Julia. "What sort of code did you have in mind?"

"Lilijana won't check the number nor will she read the message carefully. Most of the messages I get are trivial time-wasters anyway: advertising and special promotions from Vodafone or VideoEzy."

"What's the most common one?"

"I hear from Vodafone often, so if you text something like 'special offer from Vodafone: see website for details,' I would know it's you because they always use the words 'go to' followed by the URL."

Julia looked thoughtful. "If I want you to call me, what should I add?"

"Call now."

If eyebrows had powerful legs they would leap like Julia's did. Her mouth dropped open. "That's it? Call now?"

"Vodafone never says that. I'll also assume you mean 'now' when you say so."

"Fair assumption," replied Julia. "What if I can't talk, but want you to respond?'

"Add the words 'SMS now.'"

Julia lifted her empty coffee cup and stared into it. A smile crossed her face. She put the cup down and looked into David's eyes. "You've really given this some thought, haven't you?"

"I don't know if it's a weakness or a strength. I think really deeply about stuff, always have. Driving when I was a rep let me ponder and reflect, analyze and philosophize. It's annoying sometimes, and leaves me susceptible to aberrant thoughts and insanity."

A loud crack of laughter burst inside the diner. A dozen heads snapped toward the sound. Sitting opposite her overly amused companion, a thin young woman raised her hand apologetically. The interest of the other patrons disappeared like leaves on a gust of wind.

David and Julia looked at each other.

"Rule number three," said Julia. 'No outrageous headline-grabbing laughter in public places."

David did his best imitation of the man's explosive laugh. Mortified, Julia smacked his hand. She lowered her head as if that would make her invisible to anyone staring at David.

"I agree with that rule," said David, "but sometimes I can't help myself."

"Bullshit," said Julia softly.

"What about PDAs?"

"PDAs?"

"Public Displays of Affection. Should we ban those, too? We don't want to draw attention, do we?"

"What was that then? A second ago, that laugh. What was that?"

David returned to the issue. "Wherever we are, there might be someone who knows us. The risk fades the further we are from home, but we'd be hard pressed to explain if we were holding hands or smooching."

"Smooching?" said Julia as she leaned closer to David. He could smell coffee on her breath and perfume on her skin. He wanted to kiss her.

"I'm not smooching," she said. "Not even behind closed doors. No smooching."

"No Public Displays of Affection or Amusement then?"

"We can laugh, for God's sake, just not like a demonic clown or a sanitarium inmate."

"Agreed."

Julia said, "I'm too hungry to carry on with all this wicked plotting. Let's order."

Big Al's offered the widest and best selection of hamburgers in the country, and David had always been a massive fan of hamburgers. Ever since the monolithic burger with egg he'd attempted to eat with his dad, David had loved the texture and taste, the barely controlled chaos of the hamburger. The fast food chains with their cookie-cutter hamburgers and processed insipid ingredients didn't have a clue what the real thing was. That first one David ate had been a massive struggle because his mouth had been too small. Bill Lavender had laughed, pointing out that more of the burger hit the ground than his mouth. Sauce squirted onto his cheeks, dribbling down his chin. David had known he was out of his depth with a true Australian hamburger but his father's laughter wasn't derisive. It stated that he was happy to share the moment with his son. Those occasions were rare treasures. Looking back,

David wasn't sure whether it was hamburgers he loved or memories of time spent with his dad. They were inextricably entwined.

After briefly perusing the menu, Julia said, "I think I'll have a hamburger."

"Are you sure they sell them here?"

David decided on the Insane burger, which came with every imaginable filling. Julia opted for the slightly more sensible Hawaiian Super Burger. He placed their orders at the counter then returned with a couple of Cokes.

"Now," said David, "back to the rules of engagement."

"You've told me how to contact you and I accept that. It sounds safe. I need to think of some code for you to use. I'm not with Vodafone."

"Does your husband..." David paused for Julia to insert her husband's name.

Julia overlooked his inquisitive pause. "Should we be allowed to talk about our spouses?"

"I need food to deal with that one. Do you receive any regular texts? From clients? Businesses?"

"Not that I can think of."

"Does your husband read your messages or answer your phone?"

"Rarely. If I can't, or if I ask him to, but not usually."

Their hamburgers arrived to be ogled by greedy eyes.

"It's huge," said Julia. "How am I going to eat it?"

"I recommend a knife and fork to amateurs."

Julia shot him a look which half-heartedly warned him against cheekiness. He picked up his Insane Burger, hyper-extended his jaw and gouged a huge chunk out of its side. Fillers drenched with smoky barbecue sauce rained onto his plate.

"So that's how professionals eat hamburgers, is it?"

David nodded enthusiastically because his mouth was too full to speak. After thirty seconds of energetic mastication, he swallowed and chased the burger with a mouthful of Coke.

He said, "What about Best Flights special holiday deals? For the coded message. Same deal, see website for details then call now, or SMS now."

Julia held her cutlery at the ready. She seemed unsure of where to make the first cut. David was fascinated by how people ate, and he was generally fascinated by her. Stabbing the edge of the burger with her fork, she sawed through it with her knife. The mouth-sized bite was placed delicately in her mouth.

David said, "If you receive a text from Best Flights, it's me."

The Insane Burger stopped on its way to David's mouth. "We should have times on the messages or the delay could get us in trouble. The call has to be in five minutes or we revert to SMS."

Julia smiled. He wondered if he would ever tire of its warmth, not to mention the promise of contact with her lips. As a river of sauce flowed down his chin, he lashed it with his tongue then grabbed a napkin to wipe it off.

"I agree with the five minute rule but I may need to take some notes. Is there much more?"

David asked about mentioning spouses in conversation.

"Okay," said Julia, "but only when we're fully clothed."

David nearly choked on his burger. He felt a tingling in his pants, and tried to banish the blush he felt. Maybe it wasn't embarrassment. Perhaps it was shock or excitement. This was her first direct mention of their inevitable coupling. Whatever the case, he strove to master himself.

"Anymore rules?" he asked.

"Just one," said Julia, leaning in to take his hand. "No more rules."

CHAPTER SIXTEEN

When David walked out to the car which Lilijana had been unable to park in the garage, he felt aggravation swell. The discomfort manifested physically but it was internal unrest distorting his view of reality. There should be a law compelling people with garages to properly park their cars. Opening the door, he noticed bird crap on the roof, and knew no one would clean it off. It was stupid to park the car under a tree full of Noisy Miner birds. Proof that David was right and Lilijana was wrong.

His rightness and increasing need for self defense, against people in general and his wife in particular, was becoming a driving force. Even slight offenses, like people who stood in front of him while he watched his son's swimming lesson, were becoming less tolerable. The previous day, he'd arrived with Alen for his lesson and secured a seat at the end of the pool, where he could keep half an eye on Alen and half an eye on his latest read, *The Two of Me,* by Andrew Johns. A sign on the pool fence instructed parents not to block the view of others. Lessons were extended inexplicably to half-drowning babies and toddlers, and frightened children who screamed for their mummies. The more competent swimmers swam endless laps to improve their speed and endurance. Alen was in the middle category, which David referred to as 'getting the hang of it.'

Although his son would never challenge Ian Thorpe's world records, it was agreed he should learn to swim. Lilijana had taken lessons with Tomo after she arrived in Australia, and felt this skill was essential. David concurred.

David had settled into position and readied Alen with his swimming goggles. The lesson began with a typically reticent Alen easing into the water. He listened to the soothing encouragement of his rotund instructor, who wore a T-shirt with Flippers printed on it over a one piece swimsuit. She looked incredibly buoyant which inspired confidence in David, and importantly, Alen liked her.

The Two of Me was a fascinating look inside the private world of arguably the greatest Rugby League player ever. The book was a confession and an explanation. While demonstrating genius on the playing field, the man had battled depression since he was a teenager and was later diagnosed as Bipolar. His famous televised confession of using illegal drugs was controversy maxima. While many felt the revelations detracted from John's aura as a legend, David felt the weakness and illness made him more admirable. Not a saint, nor an angel but a man who achieved great things despite the kind of chronic mental illness that crushed so many people.

Halfway through the lesson, David looked up to see how Alen was doing. A woman had moved herself in front of him, not for a quick and better view, but with a chair that trumpeted permanence. This not only flouted the rules, it was sheer rudeness. David had felt invisible before but he'd endured it and excused it. It was hard work overcoming the etiquette breaches of others. Just once he wanted to tell these people off.

On this occasion, he had taken all he could. In hindsight, he could have handled it better. He remembered the exact words, though he wished he could forget them.

"I must be invisible."

No response.

David repeated his words, louder. "I must be invisible."

David neglected calm and the need to say 'please.' "Can you move? You're blocking my view."

The woman looked at him before standing, collecting her chair and obeying David's directive. He felt pleased until another woman's voice sounded behind him. She also forgot, or deliberately omitted, calm and the magic word.

"You don't have to be rude."

David was always outnumbered by women, here, in the supermarket and at the school at pick up time. He felt intimidated. Most women were efficient managers of businesses, households, and family. They possessed a fiery passion where it concerned their children. Menacing, in fact.

"Rude would be blocking someone's view," replied David.

"Like I said," stated the woman, as though she had been appointed as the anti- rudeness spokesperson.

"Why don't you mind you own business?"

"Why don't you stop being a dickhead?"

"Why don't you shut the fuck up and leave me in peace?"

'Fuck' sometimes works like a magic charm. It has the power to silence people. Sometimes it acts like petrol on a fire. The woman, who was very attractive, felt dickhead was okay but fuck was over the top. By the shocked look on her face, he might just as well have slapped her. Oddly, David felt pleased and returned to *The Two of Me.*

The heat was fading from his face, along with the burning on the back of his neck caused by the angry glares of every woman in the room. Although he looked at the words, David wasn't able to read them. He couldn't concentrate at all. He sensed someone approaching behind him and knew it to be the woman who called him a dickhead. She tapped him on the shoulder. As he was sitting and she was standing, he turned to face her belt buckle. The woman was out of uniform; young mothers wore three-quarter track or bike pants and T-shirts, which were loose if the woman carried excess baggage but tight if she was trim and toned.

"Can't look me in the face, huh?"

David raised his eyes too slowly over her stomach and across her mountainous breasts. Eventually he arrived at her face.

"You're a very rude man. You should apologize to me and everyone here."

There are times when appropriate responses go missing in action, when the right words are nowhere to be found even though they exist. Absurdly, David felt a flush of desire, and would have been whacked by her open palm if he spoke what he thought aloud. David was speechless, paralyzed. The woman scorched his retinas with her rage while David stared back like a possum caught in the headlights of an oncoming car.

"Stop staring at me!" she demanded.

"What's your name?" asked David softly, without knowing why.

The woman's crimson ire blanched. Then she turned and walked away. David didn't understand what happened but an overwhelming urge to apologize twisted a sincere tone into his voice. He held up both hands, palms out: first to the woman with the belt buckle, then to the woman who had blocked his view, and finally to everyone else. They had all been watching with interest.

"I'm sorry, everyone. I was out of line. I apologize."

This was the most theatrical apology David had ever performed. He wondered if anyone bought it as genuine. Before resuming his seat, he stole one last look at the woman with the belt buckle. His smile was intended to convey warmth but her response was inscrutable. David sat down and reopened *The Two of Me.* He tried to block out everything except the words on the page. The next thing he knew, Alen was standing in front of him, dripping water on his shoes.

Now, in the present, David ignored the bird crap, opened the car door and climbed in. This growing intolerance was going to get him in trouble. What was causing it? Lilijana and the neighbors, or was there something else?

As he fired the ignition, a song roared from the speakers. It was Nickelback. S.E.X. David hadn't understood why the word was spelled like an acronym until the lyrics of the song explained:

S is for the simple need, E is for the Ecstasy and X is just to mark the spot, cos that's the one you really want.

Very profound. The chorus of the song asserted that:

Sex is always the answer, it's never a question, cos the answer's yes. It's always yes.

Chad Kroeger had probably penned the song during a period of sexual frustration. It certainly got David thinking. Is sex always the answer? Could his lack of it be the reason for his increasing inability to roll with the proverbial punches? Apart from the aberration with Mel, David had only made love to Lilijana. Now sex was so infrequent he might not recall how to do it. His wife was an unobtainable stranger. That was wrong. He shouldn't have to go without. That's what a wife was for. It was not the only thing, but...

David was going to arrive at work at knock-off time if he didn't shake his sluggishness. As he drove to the end of the driveway, he saw the white Commodore parked on the footpath. The distance between his neighbor's front fence and the road was about three meters. The distance between the footpath and the road was zero. A car parked in that space forced pedestrians onto the road and impeded David's view of traffic. Had he not been running late, he might have gone to 1008, asked them to move the car and warned them not to park there again. All in an obnoxious manner which would have ignited tensions between he and Phil. David decided it was a good thing he was late for work.

Inching forward to gain a clearer view, David watched cars approach and pass in a never-ending stream. He was forced to back into the driveway. Agitation. Irritation. Half out of the driveway, then back in again. Everyone wanted to use the road when he was running late. Where the fuck did they come from? For the umpteenth time, David selected reverse and moved his car off the road. The ropes restraining his anger frayed then snapped. A blurry haze swallowed him; a personal fog of vehemence. He threw the shifter into park and jerked on the handbrake before killing the engine. Pushing open the door open hard, he left the car but not the fog. It followed him: swirling, pulling and propelling him. His fist extended through the cloud and banged on Phil's door. He banged until the door shook and finally opened. Phil stood there clothed in arrogance.

"Move that car. It's blocking my view and the footpath."

Had David been in a calm reflective state, his words might have been well chosen and delivered with good control, but he was beyond anything except the magnetic power of rage.

Phil stepped forward. "Fuck off! You aren't allowed on my property."

With both hands, David grabbed Phil by his shirtfront and swung him away from the door over the balcony railing. Then David leapt the railing as Phil rose to his feet. His fist crushed Phil's nose and David heard a pop. The second punch was headed for Phil's stomach when David was knocked off balance by an unexpected blow to his back. He stumbled and staggered forward. Though inside a dark haze, David knew he was fighting Phil and his mate. David spun to avoid the other man's fist. Phil's held his nose, attempting to stem the flow of blood. David charged at his mate. The man roared and reeled backwards. He gasped as he hit the balcony railing.

Breathing heavily, David swung his fist into the side of his head. He collapsed. David then went for Phil, who had crumpled to the grass. David felt nothing as he returned to his car, started the engine and accelerated onto the highway without looking to either side.

CHAPTER SEVENTEEN

By lunchtime, David dismissed the incident with Phil. The only troubling thing was how little what happened bothered him. What was going on? When did he mutate into someone who acted without thought? As he looked forward meeting Julia, the haziness subsided. Julia had sent him a coded text. She was house-sitting for a week and wanted to meet for lunch. Lunch was a delicious euphemism: more tantalizing than coffee. Imagining an explicit interlude, David drove to the rendezvous.

The apartment was quiet, the air heavy with conspiratorial silence. David imagined the ghosts of illicit affairs past floating in a welcoming dance. It was a bizarre thought. He didn't know anything about this place or its owners. He only knew he was crossing a line he shouldn't have had the courage to draw. His faithfulness to Lilijana was unquestionable. Unshakeable. He had no need for a line in the sand because there was no sand. Who sets boundaries when there's no need? Who builds walls when no one is trying to escape or invade? The safety and security, the 'until death us do part' of his marriage was secure and not under threat.

"Are you stuck?"

David looked at Julia and remembered why he was here. He didn't understand how he had stepped out of a small safe world into this jungle of lust and deceit. He couldn't see where he had gone wrong, then turn around and go back. He didn't want to go back. Guilt and doubt had vanished. How had he come to this place where he was prepared to risk everything for a thrill ride with Julia? That's all it was: escapism from a mundane and sometimes painful existence into the excitement of life. This affair was nothing but two people using each other for pleasure. That sounded horrible and cold. David shuddered at the thought.

"David? Are you all right?"

"Are you sure about this?"

Julia closed the distance between them and took his face in her hands. She kissed him hard then stepped back while holding his hands. Her eyes were burning bright. "Make love to me."

There it was. Weeks of dry-mouthed anticipation had reached their climax with those four words. Lack of opportunity had been the only hindrance since they'd settled on the rules. David had fantasized about having sex with Julia, but knowing it was going to happen made the imagining more intense. He thought he might have murdered his conscience because David didn't feel bad. He looked at Julia and enjoyed the blazing heat of her eyes.

"Would you like a written invitation?"

David smiled and pulled her close. "Can you feel my acceptance?"

Julia nodded then led David to the master bedroom. They stood at the foot of the bed and kissed until everything blurred. There was heavy breathing, buttons and zippers opening. It was wet and hot. It was soft. He was hard. They fell onto the bed and grappled, feeding on each other's flesh. There was moaning and sighing. Julia's hair swept his face followed by her breasts. She was on top of him, then underneath, then beside him. It was quick, hurried and desperate. She whispered his name. He shuddered and then it was over.

The ghosts of illicit affairs past laughed and nodded. He heard murmurs and thought the ghosts were trying to speak.

"Are you okay?"

Julia pressed her body against David's as they lay wrapped in post-coital bliss. "David? Are you all right?"

"I'm not sure 'all right' describes how good I feel right now."

Her arm was across David's chest. She squeezed him.

"Can we stay here forever?"

It was such a stupid question that David almost laughed. It was the kind of thing people say when they're happy and don't want the real world to intrude. When they don't want the pinprick of life to burst the balloon of escape. They could have been on a holiday. Work felt so distant. His friends and family so far away they might have been dead. David wanted to stay as well. It was so comfortable. Nobody knew where they were. Nobody was calling, clamoring for their attention, demanding that they act. This was freedom. This temporary bubble was heaven on earth and David wanted it to be as eternal.

"Sure, we can stay forever, or at least for another half hour."

As Julia's hand wandered past his stomach, she found him ready for a replay. He rolled on top of her and kissed her, savoring the taste of her lips and her tongue. It was slower this time, more deliberate and patient, but no less passionate.

***

"Is your friend a slob or are we responsible for this mess?"

Julia glanced around with half-hearted intent. "A bit of both probably."

"Should we tidy up a bit?"

"It's only going to get messed up again."

David was offended by the disorder and Julia's indifference to it. After he finished dressing, he started making the bed. He straightened the sheets and quilt, and then replaced the pillows.

"Your friend needs more pillows."

Julia pulled on her jeans and buttoned them. They looked custom made. With or without clothes, Julia looked terrific. Most people looked better dressed, when blemishes were hidden and flaws disguised. Sagging breasts could be supported by push-up bras and tight-fitting jeans could squeeze excess fat into eye-pleasing form. Un-tucked shirts obscured love handles, socks buried fungal toes, baggy jackets could add mass to a slight frame, black clothing diminished the appearance of a portly one.

"Those jeans look comfortable."

"They are."

Having fixed the bed, there wasn't actually much mess. David realized that nervous energy had compelled him to tidy up. It was what he did when agitated at home.

"How do you feel?"

"Good. How about you?"

"I feel a bit weird," said David, "and a bit hungry. I'm going to have to skip lunch."

"I'm sorry I wasn't enough for you."

There was no humor in her voice but he hoped she was joking. Surely, she couldn't be hurt by his hunger. Julia wouldn't meet his eyes, so pulled her tight against him. Her rigidity melted quickly in David's strong embrace.

"Maybe we could incorporate some food into our next meeting."

"Now that could really get messy."

'Never mind. I like cleaning. What about pizza? Anything that falls off the slice has to be retrieved by mouth."

"Kinky," said Julia as she playfully slapped David's chest.

"Seriously," said David, "that was great. Better than I expected, and I expected a lot. I've got a pretty good imagination."

"So I exceeded your expectations?"

David nodded.

"That's nice."

On their way to the front door, Julia had to stop to feed her friend's cat. David had seen no sign of a cat. Normally, resident felines appear instantaneously when humans enter their territory. Julia walked to the kitchen and extracted cat food from the fridge. The sound of the refrigerator door summoned the cat to dinner. It pranced into the kitchen and meowed its appreciation as Julia emptied the tin into a yellow bowl. She tossed the empty can in the bin then picked up the water bowl and dumped its contents into the sink.

"Do you like cats?" she asked as she refilled the bowl and placed it on the kitchen floor.

"No," said David. 'I'm a dog person."

"Me too. Do you have a dog?"

"I used to."

David and Julia stood in the foyer discussing their dogs. She had two: a Jack Russell terrier and a poodle. Both males. She wanted an Irish Wolfhound but couldn't afford to feed such a beast and her backyard was small. David said if he wanted a horse for a pet, he'd simply buy a horse. He didn't like them, however.

"How can you not like horses?" said Julia, like it was a criminal offense.

Unsure whether to answer with one of his childhood anecdotes, David became aware they were leaving together. A sense of alarm gripped him. "Shouldn't we get going?" said David. "What time do you have to be back?"

Julia looked at her watch and sighed. "Pretty soon."

"Do you think anyone saw us arrive together?"

"This is a question about busybody neighbors, isn't it?"

"Seriously, Julia. If someone did see us, they might know you, but who am I? What am I doing here for an hour in the middle of the day?"

"You're being paranoid."

David fixed Julia with an expression that said he was perfectly sane and she had better pay attention. Miraculously, it worked.

"Okay," said Julia holding her hands up in surrender. "I forgot something inside. I'll see you tomorrow. Same time. Just knock on the door when you come."

She leaned toward him and pecked his lips. "I don't like anchovies, by the way."

Smiling, David walked down the street to his car. As he unlocked the door and climbed in, he castigated himself over the lack of discretion they'd shown. This dangerous liaison needed to operate as clandestinely as possible. They couldn't be seen arriving and leaving together in the middle of the day. Neighbors couldn't be trusted, especially older ones, who had nothing to do but mind other people's business. Eyes. Hundred of eyes. Thousands of eyes. Watching him. His skin crawled at the thought of being observed from behind opaque curtains and peered at between the slats of Venetian blinds. His life on show. A fish in a fishbowl. A shiver rippled through him. How many amateur sleuths were watching him right now, studying his movements and piecing together his subterfuge? Whistleblowers in waiting. Private detectives amassing evidence and building a watertight case against him. The magistrate speaks in a thunderous tone proclaiming his guilt. Guilty of cheating on his wife. Of lying to her. Betraying her.

David started the car and cranked up the radio to blast away his terror. Julia had said he was paranoid. If only he believed her. He would have to live on the edge of his seat, ready to flee when the truth was uncovered: when his dark deeds were illuminated by unforgiving light.

He pulled out from the curb, and headed back to work. As he drove, he examined himself more deeply. His fears centered on being caught, not the impact that discovery would have on his family. Neither did David feel any guilt. The inevitability of a bad end to this affair was not enough to make him stop. He was gripped in the painful talons of an animal called lust. He didn't want to be released. To be free was to fall, and he didn't want to fall, he wanted to fly. The suffering was necessary. Unavoidable. To keep flying, he would have to endure the pain.

"I want the pain," he said. "Because it's worth it."

People deceive themselves all the time. They choose what to believe. They determine their own reality within the wider dimension where everyone else exists. They convince themselves of things because to accept the alternatives would welcome the blade that slices through flesh and releases torrents of blood. It would be to surrender. To lie on the ground and invite hopelessness. Though David lied to himself, only a small whimpering protest was left to challenge the lie because the lie was good. The lie was safe. This was rubbish, absolute bullshit. As David considered his life, he knew his existence was carried by faith. He was blinded to his destruction because he chose to be.

David watched the road signs. Parking restriction notices. Give Way and Stop signs. Speed limit signs and road work signs. The radio played Bryan Adam's classic rock song about adultery: *Run To You*. More signs. Information overload. Red lights. Green lights. Pedestrians crossing. Animals crossing. One way traffic. Wrong way. Go Back! David kept driving.

both of hers. 'No more rules.' CHAPTER EIGHTEEN

A familiar sight greeted David as he approached his driveway after work. Parked in front of 1008 was a police car with two officers inside. Either they had just arrived or were waiting for Phil to bust him for drugs. David had lost count of how many times the cops had visited. What did their other neighbors make of it? The biggest disturbance to their idyllic semi rural paradise had come from Kevin's Harley Davidson. Phil and Naydine were in a league of their own: a whole new category of unwelcome scum.

As David veered around the police car and lined up the entrance to his driveway through the narrow open gates, he saw Tomo's Subaru Impreza parked halfway down the drive. David's car could not fit behind it. He brought it to a stop with ten centimeters between his bumper and Tomo's. What a wanky car! He felt like driving right into it and blaming Tomo for the way he parked. He thought better of it with the police sitting there. In their minds, David was just as much trouble as Phil. He'd been mistaken to think they would take his side.

David drew a breath for courage. Anxiety squirmed in his gut over what had happened that morning, and what had gone on at lunchtime in that flat in Wollongong. It seemed likely the police were here to see him and not Phil, which meant he was in more trouble. To top it all off, Tomo was visiting. David's temples pounded as tension squeezed his head. He felt dizzy. Was the car spinning or just him?

A sharp rapping on the car window startled him. When his car crashed into Tomo's, he didn't understand how. He reefed on the handbrake then realized his foot must have slipped off the brake. He turned and saw the cute female officer who had visited once before. Paralysis gripped him as Tomo approached. He was swearing until he saw the police. David left the car and stood to face the music. There was, however, nothing harmonious or melodic about Tomo's words.

"The fuck Dave. What's your problem? Why'd you hit my car, motherfucker?"

Turning from Tomo to the police officers, David attempted a hangdog look. The cold grey of the female officer's eyes matched the set jaw of the male officer's, as though they wished they were the ones spraying verbal abuse. David felt the tirade was justified, so he remained quiet. Before too long, Lilijana joined them and added her dismay. It was chaotic and frightening. David wanted to run and hide. Could there possibly be a worse convergence of diabolic circumstances? He doubted it.

"Mrs. Lavender, could I ask you to be quiet please? You aren't helping."

"You better fucking help that bloke. He's lost his mind," replied Tomo.

"Excuse me sir," said the male officer, "What is your name?"

"Tomo."

"Okay, I'm going to ask you to calm down as well."

"But what are you going to do about this?" Tomo gestured at his damaged Impreza.

The female officer said, "Do you know this man?" with reference to David.

"No."

"Tomo!" cried Lilijana. "Of course you know him. Why did you say that?"

The female officer had moved to Lilijana's side and placed a restraining hand on her arm. Not at all mollified, Lilijana added, "Tomo is David's stepson. My son."

So far, David had not been called on to contribute. It was entirely his fault.

"Right," said the male officer as he felt for the right way to handle the situation.

"Tomo, the damage to your car is not our concern. A collision between private vehicles on private land where the involved parties know each other is for those involved parties to sort out by themselves."

Lilijana's stare forced Tomo to swallow his words of protest.

"We are here," continued the officer, "to speak with Mr. Lavender about a matter which doesn't concern you, so could you to please go inside and allow us to talk?"

Tomo moved but Lilijana didn't. The female officer asked her to leave as well. David looked at his wife and tried to project calm. After a grilling by the police, he would have to face her cross examination. That was assuming the police did not charge him with assault. Lilijana's face was impassive: a mask she wore when she was irate. He was fearful of her response. She looked like she wanted to kill him. Was she capable of that? What if she found out about Julia? Would she transform into Lorena Bobbitt? David gulped. A cough escaped his dry throat.

When Lilijana left, the police focused on David who hadn't uttered a word. He should have apologized to Tomo. That was an accident. Lilijana's wrath was more bewildering/ Something was definitely wrong. Did she know about his tryst? Already? Maybe she knew one of those nosy fucking neighbors.

"Mr. Lavender?"

David tuned out often these days. People spoke to him, but he was somewhere else. "Yes, officer?"

The female officer spoke. "Mr. Lavender, we are here to talk to you about an incident that occurred between you and John Valentine this morning."

"Who?"

The male officer said less patiently, "You and you next door neighbor."

"Uh-huh."

"Mr. Valentine alleges that you assaulted him and his guest. What do you have to say?"

Hoping the ground would spout a convincing lie, David stared at it. He couldn't deny it happened. There were three witnesses, and David's presence on their property was a breach of the Apprehended Violence Order. If Phil said David had clobbered him and his mate, and Naydine backed his story, David was stuffed. What could he say? That he was provoked by the Commodore blocking his view of traffic?

"I lost my temper. Sorry about that."

"You lost your temper and you're sorry about it?"

"Uh-huh."

"Mr. Lavender," said the male police officer, "you will need to come with us to the station where you will make a formal statement and subsequently be charged with assault. We will arrest and handcuff you unless you come of your own accord."

"Charged with assault? Why?"

"Mr. Valentine wants you prosecuted."

The fact that Phil had laid formal charges, to which he had just admitted, left David stunned. His knees trembled and he began to fall. A strong hand held him up.

"Are you all right, Mr. Lavender? Do you understand that you have to come with us?"

"Uh-huh."

"Please inform your wife. She may wish to meet you at the station to arrange legal representation if that is what you want."

David took two cautious steps to test the strength of his legs. The police carried him through his front door, where he found Lilijana in the hall.

"What's going on, David?"

"I had a disagreement with Phil and the police want to talk to at the station. They're charging me with assault."

"How does a disagreement end up in assault? Did you hurt him?"

"He's overreacting as usual. I told you he's trouble."

David was leaving when Lilijana's next question brought him to a halt.

"Are you lying to me?"

He knew better than to ask what she thought he was lying about. "No, it's nothing."

"It's not nothing. I'm coming with you."

"Don't worry about him, Mum."

"Shut up, Tomo and go home," Lilijana said harshly. She must have regretted it because she immediately softened her words. "Please just go home, Tomo. Okay, love?"

"Let's go." David left with the police, who were both frowning at him.

In the back of the police car he felt inexplicably safe and relaxed. His tension uncoiled and his heart rate slowed. He knew this matter with police was not related to Julia nor was Lilijana's attack on his honesty. It also had nothing to do with Tomo. David was glad to have smashed his little buzz box car. There was, however, some relevance between his battle with Phil and his marital discontent. With each day he felt further away from Lilijana. The chasm of disconnectedness widened. His feud with Phil had a deleterious effect. Ruling out non-related matters cleared the fog from David's mind. He was going to be charged with assault because he had lost his temper. Phil was a prick and he deserved the beating he got, but Phil wasn't to blame. David didn't feel contrite. If he had to apologize to Phil, he would choke to death on the words.

Neighbors could be great when you needed someone to watch your place, feed your animals, or collect your mail. They could be good to chat with about mutually displeasing neighbors, like those who had parties every Saturday night, or didn't maintain their properties. They shared tip and tools.

Phil and Naydine weren't that type.

They arrived at Wollongong Local Area Command Headquarters and David was escorted inside. He might have been a spectator for all the anxiety he felt. He didn't know how much detail would be expected in his statement or how honest he was going to be. He didn't know what processes he would be put through, or who he would deal with. He didn't know if he would be allowed to go home, or if Lilijana would want him there. Would he need to ask Matt for the use of his couch? Would he feel guilt or sorrow at some stage? Would his anxiety return with a vengeance and hospitalize him again?

He was ushered into a room with a table and three chairs. The video camera in the corner might be recording him or not. When the door opened, he kept his eyes fixed on the wall rather than the police. They were not the same pair who brought him here.

"Thanks for coming down, Mr. Lavender," said one officer, as he took a seat opposite David.

"Thanks for having me," quipped David.

The second officer remained standing in the corner underneath the camera. Neither man smiled at David's joke.

"Tell us what happened at 1010 Princes Hwy, Chinaman's Hollow, this morning, Mr. Lavender."

"I was running late for work, which was made worse by the car parked on the footpath at the front of 1008. That's an offense, isn't it? To park on the footpath?"

The officers' faces showed serious interest.

"The white Holden Commodore belonging to Mark Micovski, who was a guest of Mr.Valentine?"

"I don't his name but, yes, that's the car."

"Continue."

"I'd asked Phil many times to tell his visitors not to park there. Not only does it make it hard to pull out of the driveway, it's also dangerous for pedestrians because they have to step onto the road."

"So you got frustrated. Then what?"

David was impressed. These guys were deadly. They weren't buying into anything which failed to address the issue. They knew what they wanted to hear and that's what they listened for.

"I got out of the car and went to knock on the door—"

"In violation of the AVO against you," interjected the standing officer. It was the first time he spoke.

"I wasn't thinking about that. I was pissed off."

"Which is the reason Mr.Valentine took out the AVO in the first place."

"Please continue, Mr. Lavender," said sitting officer.

David wished they would stop calling him Mr. Valentine. It made Phil sound like a pillar of the community when he was, in fact, a dick and a menace to society.

"I knocked on the door. Phil answered."

"Who's Phil?" asked standing cop, who was getting on David's nerves.

"My neighbor. I call him Phil because he's not good enough to be John."

"So you knocked on the door and Mr. Valentine answered. Then what?"

"I asked him to move the car. He refused and reminded me about the AVO. I threw him over the balcony railing. Then we fought. His mate joined in but I kicked both their arses, and went to work."

"Mr.Valentine says his wife answered the door and you made a lewd comment about what she was wearing, which you followed with an offer of sex."

David looked from one officer to the other and then up at the camera. This was a turning point in the interview, although he couldn't pinpoint why. Apart from being repulsed by the idea of sex with Naydine, he was astounded by Phil's lie. The man was in the right and David was in the wrong. So why would he lie about the details of the assault? Maybe he was being baited. Perhaps Lilijana watched him from behind a one way mirror or on the video feed from the camera. The police glared.

The truth would be David's savior. In his eagerness to destroy him, Phil had miscalculated. Naydine's brutally unalluring exterior could be seen by any sober person with eyes. Why would he play with the neighbor's dog when he already had a beautiful wife? They didn't have any idea how sour his marriage was, or that he was having an affair. Phil's accusation was nonsensical. It wasn't believable.

"Have you met my wife?"

Sitting officer seemed surprised. Standing officer remained impassive.

David felt he was gaining control. "She's beautiful, intelligent and caring. a real sweetheart." He paused for effect. "Naydine, on the other hand, is not exactly...." He waved his hand as though reluctant to say the words. "I don't want to sound unkind. I think you know what I mean. Why would I go after her?"

"Who knows what sort of sick fantasies you enjoy in your twisted mind," said sitting cop, reclaiming the upper hand. "Maybe you can't get enough from your wife so you'll take it anywhere you can."

"Maybe you're not getting any action at all from your wife," added standing cop.

"Maybe it's just about power and getting one over on Mr. Valentine. Throw your leg over his bitch then stomp on his angry red face."

Their language was a bit over the top. And Naydine? Why the focus on sex? He was here for alleged assault. David thought of Julia and then Lilijana. He must have been silent for some time.

"Mr. Lavender," said sitting cop, "I don't think you realize the seriousness of your predicament. Sitting mute isn't going to help. Tell us exactly what happened and then write it down. We're looking for honest answers. Is that too much to ask?"

Glancing from sitting cop to standing cop, David said, "You're trying to make me confess to something I didn't do."

"Do you deny assaulting Mr. Valentine?"

"I want to speak to my lawyer."

"That's your right," said sitting cop, "but it's going to make this more complicated."

David folded his arms across his chest. "Lawyer. Now."

CHAPTER NINETEEN

David told Lilijana nothing, apart from the allegation of coming on to Naydine. Lilijana had not witnessed or heard his interview, and was not legally entitled to details. This made her even angrier. Lilijana's anger was a concealed exploding device, innocuous until activated by an unsuspecting footstep. Not a volcanic eruption which built underground for months and finally burst through the earth, but a sudden detonation of noise that normally ended quickly. However, Lilijana was seething.

David couldn't see the point in confiding. How would more detail ameliorate her wrath? His life had been bouncing along the tracks and finally run off the rails. David only blame himself. Yet he also resented Lilijana. Everything had unraveled when she withdrew. He could feel her hostility, but his dominant emotion was sadness. Although she drove the car he rode in, they were not, in any sense, close.

The lawyer had been an old school friend of Matt's, a small claims specialist with some experience in criminal law. Kelvin Woo had argued for a full confession. Then he'd floated the idea of attacking the neighbors' character. Even though there were three witnesses to support any lie, David had moral superiority, according to Kelvin Woo. There was a precedent in a case Kelvin had successfully prosecuted, where a man had a genuine claim but the judge ruled against him because the man had a criminal record. A previous incident of neighborhood contention had resulted in the man being fined. History and the man's character worked against him even though he was in the right.

"I breached an AVO to go deck this guy and his friend upon his lawn. How can we defend that?"

"Deny it."

"Are you serious? There were three witnesses."

"Independent witnesses?'

David and Kelvin shared a smile as the penny dropped. David shook his head, and said, "Phil, his wife, and his mate: this Micovski character, whose car I ran into."

Kelvin raised his eyebrows. "What happened?"

"It was an accident. I rear-ended him on the way to church."

"He was going to church or you were?"

David laughed. "I was."

Kelvin scribbled on the pad in front of him. "Was anyone else in the car?"

"Phil was in Micovski's car. Lilijana and the children were with me."

"What was the outcome?"

"Micovski yelled at me, questioned my eyesight and my right to hold a license. I apologized. We exchanged details then went our separate ways."

"Has there been any follow up?" asked Kelvin. "From Micovski or his insurance company?"

David laughed again. "You reckon these types of people insure anything? They're more like the reasons the rest of us have insurance." This sounded so snobby that David coughed as he finished saying it. Talk about tarring everyone with the same brush.

"You know Phil's claim that you," Kelvin searched for the right word, "propositioned Naydine? It sounds like payback, don't you think?"

It was easy to see Kelvin's line of reasoning. David had called the police to 1008 several times, which meant Phil and Naydine had to answer awkward questions and promise to behave. Then David had rear-ended the car belonging to Phil's mate. David had become a nuisance and they were clearly looking to get him.

"You may not have hit anyone," suggested Kelvin. "You went next door to ask that a car be moved because it was parked illegally and dangerously. The residents at 1008 started the fight and you were simply defending yourself. You didn't want any violence. You aren't a violent person. You're a God-fearing man, a law abiding, church-going citizen whose only crime against his neighbors was concern for the escalation of arguments in their home. You called the police because you were worried about their safety. And the car crash was an accident. You apologized and were willing to pay for damages."

Kelvin paused. David was impressed.

"The sexual harassment allegations are ludicrous. Look at your wife. Why would you bother with a scrubber like Naydine?"

"You're not going to call her that in court, are you?"

Kelvin put his pen down and stared at his notes. "You're going to plead not guilty to both charges. Phil and Naydine will look like vindictive, dishonest trash, who conspired to get you out of their lives."

David smiled, "Yes, sir."

***

Back in the car, Lilijana broke the silence. "Are you going to say anything?"

"Kelvin says I'm a model citizen. He'll have both of the charges dismissed."

"Dismissed. You're going to say you didn't do it?"

"I didn't try to crack onto Naydine."

She stared. David was about to tell her to watch the road when she turned away and said, "But you thought about it, didn't you?"

"What?"

Had things becoming so appalling that she thought he would duck next door and hit on the neighbor's wife? Maybe if the woman had been an irresistible stunner, but Naydine? It was preposterous. Although laughter was inappropriate, he couldn't stop himself. Lilijana failed to see the humor and barked at him.

"Who is it then?"

"David feigned ignorance. "Who is what then?"

"Who are you sleeping with?"

Lilijana was serious. David had thought she was uninterested, disengaged from his life. Had she been on his case the whole time? Did she know about Julia? Or was she reacting to the stress?

"I sleep with you each night, honey," he said sweetly, hoping to strike the right chord.

Lilijana turned to glare at him again. "You've got a funny joke for everything, don't you David? Always with the jokes. Well, I'm not laughing. Look at me."

Their eyes met. He felt his pupils melting from the withering heat of her glare.

"It's not a joke, David. I'm sick of your jokes."

In troubled times, men look for refuge or escape. When they're being battered by life's storms, they search for allies or solutions. They will fight alone if necessary, and to the bitter end if they must, but not as a matter of preference. Men choose friends and partners for what they can get, as well as give. It's a balance between satisfying the self and satisfying others: an equilibrium worth fighting for.

The appearance of the family home should have been a source of relief. The lights were off. Lilijana had delivered the children to Amy, a friend of hers down the road. She seemed to have forgotten them temporarily. Four hours had passed since the police car took him away following the minor collision with Tomo's Subaru. It was hard to believe so much had happened in one day.

"What a day, huh?"

David's icebreaker failed to cut through the chill. Lilijana looked calm but she wasn't calm. She was sub zero hostility personified.

"I'm going to get the children," she said flatly. "Do you have a key to get in?" She reefed on the handbrake and threw the lever into park, before switching off the engine and wrenching the keys from the ignition.

"Uh-huh."

"There's some leftovers in the fridge if you're hungry." Her words were clipped by the slamming door.

David looked at the house and then Lilijana's back. She was stomping, which accentuated the movement of her well-rounded buttocks. He felt a stirring of desire for which there would be no outlet. Not with Lilijana. He left the car and went inside.

Why did he think of inappropriate things at inappropriate times? Why did he have such crazy thoughts? David knew as much about schizophrenia as the next bloke. Without any direct experience, he'd gleaned his understanding of mental disorders via television news, documentaries and Hollywood. He knew the prevalence of mental problems in the community was high. Every second person charged with a crime blamed it on a mental illness. Violent assaults and murders were attributed to voices or past traumas which had obliterated rational thought and morality. Responsibility was shifted from the perpetrators to their illnesses. Their defense lawyers proved with the help of medical experts that their clients could not be held responsible because they were sick. Whether whispering voices of carnage and evil directed their actions or not, whether they were compelled and really had no choice or not, David felt they should still be held responsible.

Noticing the flashing light on the answering machine, David pressed play to hear the messages. Nobody had found the time to set the time and date, so unless they checked their messages daily, they had no idea when the caller had rung. The mechanical voice announced there was one new message.

"David, it's your father. I need some help around the house this Saturday. See you then."

That was dad. No please or thank you. No consideration for other's schedules. David would have to go and help. Partly because the message was worded like a command, and partly because David worried his father would hurt himself attempting jobs around the house. Certain tasks which involved climbing ladders, for example, were becoming physically dangerous. The thought of his dad stretching at perilous heights filled David with dread.

Staring inside the refrigerator, David determined his hunger level. He glanced at the clock on the wall. Its glass cover had been smashed by a careless guest soon after they moved in. Lilijana had wanted to throw the clock away. David had donned mock passion as he pleaded for the right of the timepiece to be allowed to continue its work. Lilijana had feigned outrage that David should care so much. It was a gift from a former girlfriend. The clock had never been taken down, other than to change the battery. It still kept accurate time.

David selected a small container packed of spaghetti bolognaise and placed it in the microwave.

Schizophrenia must be awful: to hear actual voices speaking to you, nagging you, criticizing you. The quiet voice David heard when he was talking to himself was, in fact, his own voice. Any compulsion to do its bidding was only as strong as he allowed. He could tell himself to shut up without causing offense. The prompting he received during his pursuit of Julia was never irresistible. David could be as fearless or fragile as he wished.

The microwave beeped. As David retrieved the steaming spaghetti, he heard the front door open. The house received a much-needed injection of life from his children. He greeted Alen and Danijela as they entered the kitchen to chat about everything and nothing, obviously pleased to see him.

They had eaten ice cream at Amy's house and wanted a warm Milo before bed. They wanted to know if everything was okay with the police and Tomo. They wanted to know what was wrong with mum.

"She's angry with me," said David as he prepared two Milo nightcaps. "She'll be all right tomorrow."

"What's she mad about?" asked Alen.

"I did something pretty silly."

"Very stupid," said Lilijana who joined them. "Pretty silly is forgetting to wear sunscreen at the beach, or packing you sandwich loosely at the bottom of your school bag."

David had lost count of how many times he'd extracted disgusting food in stages of putrid decomposition from his son's school bag. He looked at Lilijana with what he hoped was a conciliatory façade.

"Yes," he said emphatically, "Mum's right. Those things are silly. What I did was stupid and I'm sorry I did it."

"What did you do?" asked his son.

"I got into a fight with Phil next door."

"What'd you fight about?"

"I asked him to move the car off the footpath and he got mad at me, so I got mad at him and we fought for a bit."

"Did you win?"

David missed the question while considering the lies he had just told. An invisible hand smeared him with a greasy paste of guilt.

"No," Lilijana said. "He lost and has to go to court to face the judge."

"Never mind, Dad," said Danijela. "Maybe next time you'll win. If you try as hard as you can."

A massive lump of emotion swelled in his throat, forcing him to cough so he could draw another breath. His little girl had used his own words against him. Her innocence blasted him, and he was sure he was going to cry. Lilijana ordered the children to finish their drinks in the living room with a piggyback admonition to leave the television off.

David mumbled a sincere thank you.

"They think you're great," said Lilijana. "They shouldn't see you cry about nothing."

"It's not nothing."

She stepped closer and lowered her voice. "You're right. It's not nothing. You just lied to them. Twice. You're not sorry about what you did, and every time you open your mouth you only make it worse."

A wall of vehemence stood between them. He didn't know how to break through it. She stared at him, as though trying to telepathically suck answers from his mind.

"I lost my head and I am sorry about that."

"But you're not sorry you beat up John and his friend, are you?"

The split second pause was too long. The fight had started the way he said. Yes, he had been the aggressor and, yes, he had breached an AVO on his way to committing assault, but the fight had begun the way he told his children. Was there any point in telling Lilijana that? He turned away from her.

"Are you happy?" she asked.

David was taken off guard. It heralded a whole new direction: one that did not involve him fending off Lilijana as he backpedaled away. David was transported back to their previous conversation when he'd almost confessed to his romp with Mel. Lilijana had been willing to talk and, more importantly, to listen. An ill-timed phone call had murdered the moment. Had he confessed, life would have been altered. It might have been so much better.

"David?"

Taking a deep breath, David slowly faced Lilijana. This was another watershed: a crucial, pivotal moment. He was being given an opportunity to address his discontent and the root of all his troubles. "No."

Lilijana's mouth opened. She narrowed her eyes then raised her eyebrows. "You're not happy with me? With us? With your life?" Her voice trembled.

David was amazed at how quickly she crumbled. Her dissolution confused him. Instinctively, he reached for her, but she did not respond to his touch. Although it seemed cruel to offer truth rather than comfort, David seized his chance. It was too important for timidity to quash it.

"I feel like you don't care about me or any of the things I need. It's as if you're far away and our marriage has gone stale. The only reason it isn't rotting is because you're cold."

David allowed his words to penetrate like butter melts into hot toast. He felt the urgent need to make her understand, but had to tread lightly. He had to be diplomatic and sensitive. He had to push hard enough to break her shell, yet not enough to crush her. Despite everything, he loved her.

They stood clothed in unspoken thoughts and powerful emotions.

"I don't know what to say," Lilijana said finally. "I'm shocked. I didn't know you felt that way."

Lilijana had not cared to delve beyond his aberrant behavior to search for deeper causes, nor investigate his malaise. She hadn't been willing to invest in their relationship. It was a damning report card. She should be saying the same to herself. She should be accepting the blame.

When Lilijana moved away, David expected an apology.

"I'm sorry," she said, then turned and walked away.

"You're sorry? That's it?"

She stopped and turned to face him, her cheeks stained with tears, her eyes red and puffy. David felt a pang of guilt for not simply accepting her apology. It was obviously genuine, albeit insufficient.

"What do you want me to say, David?"

A list formed in his mind. I'm sorry I've been treating you like shit. From now on, I'll treat you like a king. I'm sorry I'm a failure as a wife, and I promise to do better. Much better. I'm sorry I don't listen to you, and I swear I will be more attentive. I will be less judgmental and more tolerant. I'm also really sorry I've made you sexually frustrated by withholding your conjugal right. From now on you can make love to me as often as you want, wherever you want.

Lilijana stared at him, waiting for an answer. She'd reassumed control.

"Nothing,' said David meekly. "Thank you." He allowed Lilijana to emasculate him, just as she always did. Then he turned his attention to the spaghetti bolognaise.

CHAPTER TWENTY

"That's a shame," said David. "This has been perfect for us."

He leaned over Julia's bare stomach and nibbled at a pizza crumb which had fallen near her navel. She giggled, making her stomach bounce. David began to kiss her, moving upwards from her stomach to her breasts. She sighed as he gently sucked her nipple.

"I guess we'll have to find another love nest."

"Do you have any more friends who need house-sitting?"

Julia ruffled his hair as he continued to pleasure her. "Unfortunately not. What about you?"

He mumbled a response and she laughed. "You sound like you've got something in your mouth."

This was the kind of enchanted moment David wished he could bottle. In this erotic and electric here and now, there was no trouble, no pressure, no pain and no demands. He felt free. Having abandoned any pretense of guilt, David floated in a tropical sea of sensuality. The suggestion it might have to end, albeit temporarily, caused an enormous dark cloud to pass in front of the sun. Even as he moved onto Julia and eased her thighs apart, he felt his tumescence wilting. He paused.

"What's wrong?"

David rolled off Julia and glanced at the clock on the bedside table. There was still time but the fire had been quenched.

"Would your friend let us use her place anyway? You know, at lunchtime?"

"I don't want to put her in a compromising position. She works with my husband. If I told her about us, and asked if we could carry on in her bed, don't you think it would be awkward?"

"It would be extremely awkward."

"Anyway, I don't want to tell her about us."

Julia snuggled into David's side and placed her hand on his chest as he lay staring at the ceiling.

"Just knowing I was cheating would make it hard enough for her."

"Have you told anyone?"

"Just one close friend. It's not something I could have kept totally to myself."

David stroked Julia's hand and leaned in to inhale her fragrance. Her delicate fruity perfume mingled with her natural scent. He felt himself stirring once more.

"What does this friend of yours think about the affair?"

"She thinks I'm an idiot."

"That sounds familiar."

Julia kissed him. They were both idiots and happy to be enmeshed in folly. He kissed her back, but for the first time since their relationship had slid into intimacy, David thought he might have had enough.

"What are we going to do? We can't go to your place or my place. We don't have any willing accomplices who will offer us a love nest. We can't even..."

She pressed her mouth to his with force. "Let's work it out later. Time's a wasting and I'm still peckish."

In the strange land between immersion in good feeling and the precognitive sense of loss you know will come when it ends, there's a tension between what is and what will be. There's a tug of war between one pleasurable reality and the far less pleasurable one to follow. It could be difficult to live in the moment. David's body responded to Julia's automatically. He was rarely switched off in her presence. One touch, one look, was all he needed.

His mind wandered as they made love. In his mind's eye, he watched Lilijana reading. She lay her book on the coffee table, and turned to him with a smile.

David felt angry that she'd entered his private space. He thrust into Julia with increasing force and alacrity. She gasped each time he penetrated her to the full length of his penis. He hurried to his climax like a greyhound chasing a rabbit. The orgasm left him shuddering and his right leg shook spasmodically. He opened his eyes and found Julia staring.

"That was different."

"Sorry," said David softly. "Are you okay?"

She kissed him and said, "We'd better get back to work."

Drenched in shame, David dressed. He'd never made love so selfishly, not to anyone. He finished dressing in silence in which Julia participated. Someone would have to break the distance, reopen the door of communication. All he could think of was to apologize again, and...shockingly, he thought of ending the affair.

Julia fixed her hair, looking into the mirror. "I'm okay with motels and we can split the bill. It will have to be different motels, though, and we can't meet every day. We'll have to keep it to a weekly thing."

"A weekly thing," mumbled David. He didn't like Julia's tone, nor the attitude she displayed to press on with the affair. She didn't seem bothered by his angry and violent love making.

"I know what you're thinking," said Julia, light and unflappable, "but maybe it will be better."

When he'd finished tying his shoelaces, David stood up, walked over to Julia and placed his hands on her shoulders. He squeezed them softly. "I'm sorry about that."

They looked at each other in the mirror. David marveled as Julia smiled. Her eyes sparkled. Damn, she was beautiful.

"Stop apologizing," she said. "I liked it."

"See you tomorrow," said David before kissing Julia's cheek.

As he left the apartment, David was conflicted like never before. He didn't want Julia to like the way he had hammered into her as though she was just an orifice. That was wrong. He shuddered involuntarily. He loved and respected her. His violence had negated that. Sure, he apologized but it takes a better man not to do anything wrong in the first place. Something was happening to him. He was losing himself. The affair with Julia. The beating he gave Phil. These were the behaviors of someone driven by narcissism and hubris. Was this the new David Lavender?

On the street, the sun assaulted his skin and eyes. He felt himself shriveling. An eerie discomfort descended as he hurried to escape the light. Darkness was calling, urging him to come where it was cool and his secrets were safe. David walked faster to his car, unlocked it remotely and scrambled inside. The heat was suffocating. He lowered the windows, turned on the ignition and with the tweak of a dial had cold air blasting his face. He realized how hot he was, how sweaty, and how dizzy. He needed to calm down.

His phone rang and startled him.

"David, are you all right?" Julia asked.

David managed to croak out a yes.

"What's wrong?"

"Bit hot that's all. I just switched on the air, so I'll cool down in a tick."

"Isn't your court case tomorrow?"

"Shit!"

"Is that what's worrying you?"

The bloody court case. He should have appeared before the magistrate the day after his arrest, but the local courts were choked. The fact that bail had been waived, and the whole matter was dealt with expediently gave David the impression his assault was an indiscretion, or even a community service.

"Actually, I'm pretty confident of getting off."

"What about the breach of AVO?"

David jerked at his seatbelt. It locked and he swore.

"David?"

This was beginning to resemble a husband wife conversation. Julia's voice was taking on Lilijana-like qualities. He pulled the seatbelt again and it locked a second time.

"Fucking thing!"

"David, what's wrong?"

"The seatbelt keeps locking."

"Okay. Try pulling it slowly across your chest, and I'll talk to you later. Good luck tomorrow.'

Julia handled him exactly like Lilijana did when he was throwing a bit of a tantrum. She spoke to him seriously and gently as to how to resolve his problem. Then she ended the conversation. With images of Julia morphing into Lilijana and back again, David fastened his seatbelt and drove off.

As the frosty air washed over him, his anxiety and rage abated. Nearly two weeks had passed since he'd been charged with assaulting Phil. Twelve days since that ride home from the police station with a furious Lilijana. Then their conversation about his state of mind. Her apology had made him feel guilty. Somehow, she'd managed to bury him instead of resurrecting their marriage. That was what he wanted. Fucking around with Julia was just to make him feel good. It was a substitute life, and Julia was his substitute wife. How pathetic!

Lilijana went to work, looked after the children, and did the housework. She didn't neglect David and was unfailingly polite, but she had lost her enjoyment. She was a robot by choice, a shadow of her former self. He longed to be anywhere but with her, yet he pined for her and lamented her disintegration.

He and Kelvin had held several meetings about his upcoming court case. He'd been to the pub a few times with Matt, argued with Tomo about his Impreza, and given his dad the help he requested.

Despite asking for David's assistance, he still tried to get things done. David had found him halfway up a ladder, fiddling with a fly screen. After a typical businesslike greeting, he'd voiced a litany of complaints about the place falling down. David's mother wasn't there to help him with the maintenance. She'd died from bowel cancer five years ago. David had given up on offering consolation. His dad didn't want to be comforted. He hadn't recovered from the loss and never would. Life seemed pointless without her, which was why he obsessed over the house and kept as busy as possible. He was both envious of the dead and afraid of the painful fade that led to death. David reflected on the morbidity of dying whenever he visited his dad. As long as David recognized his junior role, they worked well together. Other times, David enjoyed his company, like when they watched cricket or footy and had a few beers together. Bill Lavender had played in representative teams for both cricket and rugby league. He loved his sports and at least they had that in common.

David knew he should visit more often. The only thing preventing him was laziness. Despite the compulsion to do the right thing, David sometimes resisted by demanding time for himself. It was self indulgent, and he knew it. There was a connection between this and his descent into violence and adultery.

What kept David going through the miserable winter of Lilijana's cold hostility and the potential doom of his court case was Julia. Every lunch time they shared was like sunshine with a soft breeze. Now, however, these munch and hump sessions were going to end or drop dramatically in frequency. Could he handle only having her once a week? It was still more often than he and Lilijana had sex. Only in the first year of marriage had they made love once a day, sometimes twice. Before life swallowed them and chewed them up, before children came along, before ambition ignited in Lilijana and diminished in David. He was sure once a week would be okay. It might even be better.

The phone rang and again made him jump.

"Just wanted to make sure you were okay and that you sorted out your seatbelt," said Julia.

David laughed. "I was just thinking about you. What day are we going to get together?"

"It might be a good idea to change the days."

"Why? Then I might have to wait longer than a week."

"Sometimes less than a week."

"Thanks for making me happy, Julia."

Her pause made David think she hadn't heard him. Finally she said, "You're welcome. See ya."

David had wanted her to say he made her happy, too. Sometimes he wondered. If she was not enjoying it, common sense said she'd break it off. Until today, David had given no thought to breaking it off. The farther he fell away from Lilijana, the deeper he plunged into Julia.

The phone was still in David's hand when it rang again.

"Mr. David Lavender?"

"Speaking."

"You are Bill Lavender's son?"

David gripped the phone tightly. He quickly forced a gap in the traffic and pulled to the side of the road. "What's wrong?"

"I'm sorry to have to tell you, but your father's had a nasty accident. He's been taken to Wollongong Hospital in critical condition."

"I'm on my way," said David flatly.

CHAPTER TWENTY-ONE

"Can you drive? I want to drink a lot."

Lilijana stared as though there was something wrong with his face. Thoughts seemed to fester inside her mind and jostle for space on her tongue.

"You've already been drinking a lot."

Even though the ice had not thawed, David remained hopeful. A hopeless fool was what he was. There was no empathy in her voice, no sympathy. Just officiousness. Business. Do what must be done. Did the woman have no heart? If she did still have a heart beneath the snow of her angry indifference, surely she could open up. Especially under the circumstances. By the time he'd arrived at the hospital, Bill Lavender had died. It was too late to say goodbye. A neighbor had found him on the ground by a ladder. His head has been bleeding profusely. Although the ambulance was prompt, the doctors could not do enough. A man farewells his father and he's not allowed to drink? Lilijana was heartless.

"So," said David, trying to avoid conflict. "You'll be okay to drive then?"

Lilijana frowned and snatched the keys from his hand.

She called to the children and left, leaving David wondering how insufferably long the next lecture would be. Since breakfast, he'd downed several Vodka Mules. This was no way to handle his father's funeral. The alcohol in his bloodstream prevented him from following Lilijana. It was as though he'd forgotten how to walk.

Alen bustled past him. "Come on Dad," he said cheerfully, as if they were off to the footy. "Let's go!"

How was he going to make it through the day? David would have to greet people at the chapel, and nod gravely as he received their condolences. There would be serious, firm handshakes, along with hugs and kisses. David would sit in the front with his family. The service would begin. The minister would speak in soft, reverent tones before inviting David to deliver his eulogy: the one he had not prepared. He would choke up but not lose control. Others would speak. The congregation would sing. The minister would say a few more words with artificial sincerity. Then he'd send the box containing Bill Lavender into a furnace not unlike the hell where some

Christians believed non-Christians would spend eternity. Eternity was such a long time. Could any God be so cruel?

The sound of the horn snapped David out of his melancholy. He left the house and closed the door.

Silence accompanied them all the way to the crematorium. David shuddered as they entered between wrought iron gates hung on sandstone pillars. Hospitals and cemeteries made him uneasy. He wanted this day to be over.

***

Bill Lavender had made no arrangements for his departure. No funeral plans. No will. Not a single thought for those he would leave behind. David was left to sort things out. To plan, to organize, to sort, to pay. To grieve? No, there hadn't been time. Sadness was alien. What David felt was shock. He'd thought of his dad as bulletproof. A knot burned in his throat. David slammed his hand against the inside of the car. No one said anything. He wanted them to ask if he was all right, so he could say he was definitely not. He felt anger instead of grief. It was undisciplined, and he wanted to keep it together so he could say goodbye properly. He wanted to play the dutiful son. No, that was wrong; he didn't want to play anything. Bill Lavender would have detested pretense.

Lilijana had helped with the arrangements and done most of the work. She had consulted him, but his part was reduced to agreeing. That was easy. David liked easy.

The service would be simple and straightforward with as little bullshit as possible, in deference to his father. The minister was a concession to Lilijana, as Bill did not believe in God. He made a point of explaining this to David during his religious phase. He seemed to feel that life was purposeless. David should find what meaning he could and enjoy it while it lasted. Arguments exploded over the issue as hard cynicism collided with passionate hope. David refused to accept that life was an accident. He didn't understand its meaning, but he knew there was purpose. There was a point to life. There *must* be a point, otherwise what *was* the point?

At the chapel, he began consoling the mourners, just as he had imagined. Those he embraced inhaled alcohol fumes and did their best to ignore it. Compassion rules at funerals. Everyone is sorry. Everyone walks on eggshells, chooses their words carefully, feigns interest to cover boredom and whitewashes judgment with mercy. Everyone is concerned. The alcohol was losing its grip and so was David.

Inside the chapel, David made his way to the front, where he sat down gently. The religious tone was understated, and dim light mirrored the mood of those who marked the occasion. A barren cross hung above the lectern. Lilijana scorned the Roman Catholics and their symbol of Christ on the cross.

The coffin lay on the catafalque, covered with dark green cloth. A photograph in a plain wooden frame stood on it like a sentinel. A low murmur of discreet conversation deepened the somber mood. David looked at the wooden box containing his father's body. He stared until his eyes blurred. Another Mule was what he wanted, but it was too late to get one. Too late to leave. Too late for anything.

When the minister raised his hands to lower the muffled voices, hot tears burned David's eyes. He felt what he'd long anticipated: deep, cutting sorrow. Wishing his grief had visited him earlier, or even after the service, David tried to regain his balance. His world was a ship taking on water through a hole ripped in its side. He felt himself sliding. Then the minister called his name and he slowly rose to his feet.

"Sorry," said David to no one in particular.

Gripping the lectern in both hands, David stared at it. How to begin? What to say? He regretted not preparing the eulogy. He would have to speak off the cuff, candidly, from the heart. That would have suited his father's style. Maybe it was for the best.

"Thanks for coming," said David. "I didn't know Dad knew so many people, but there are a lot of things I don't know about him."

Strangely, David thought about proper grammar and whether anyone would notice. He also wondered if anyone was interested in his speech. Like so many others, he detested public speaking, and also hated this situation. Of course people were listening. Who attends a funeral and ignores the eulogy, especially when delivered by – by anyone, really. His thoughts were rambling, which meant his eulogy was probably meaningless.

"I'm hoping to chat with as many of you as I can after the service. At the wake. Maybe you can fill in the blanks. You see, I really only knew Bill Lavender as a father. We had some good years where we managed to communicate rather than talk at, or over, each other, but he's always been a bit of a mystery. Maybe I was a mystery, too. I don't know."

Stealing a glance at Lilijana, David regretted repeating the phrase, 'I don't know.' He needed to talk about his dad more positively. Lilijana wore a poker face while David drew blanks on good things to say. He swallowed and took a breath.

"My dad was good with his hands. He could build and fix stuff. He was creative that way. He made me a cricket bat and a set of stumps with bails. We couldn't afford the real deal but what he made was just as good. I remembering being skeptical - I was eight or nine at the time. But if something depended on Dad, it would happen just as he said. He was determined like that. Pig-headed, you might say."

He tried to focus on familiar faces, searching for an encouraging smile, an affirming nod. They all wore impenetrable masks. Among them were strangers, and Julia. What was she doing here? He fought down panic, and felt a new wave of misery as his gaze found his children. When it was his turn to go, would they tell their friends and family how little they knew their dad? It was true. What a depressing thought. He smiled weakly, wishing he could spew sunlight over them. He'd let them down. He was a failure. Danijela smiled and infused him with hope like oxygen under water. He could breathe again.

"My dad was physically and mentally strong, and he taught me to be unbending: uncompromising. Hard as nails, he was. I'm a bit softer than him sometimes. I suppose that's why... we clashed a bit. That's actually a massive understatement. We really went hammer and tongs. What does that mean? Hammer and tongs? Anyway, we went hard. I reckon he was always pissed off after losing mum. Well, he loved her, so you can understand. But he could have acknowledged my loss as well. Been sensitive to my pain. The pain I still feel. But he wanted me to toughen up and stop crying. 'Don't be a fucking pussy.' That's what he would say. Direct quote. Pardon my French."

After David dropped the 'f' bomb, he saw the mourners' collective gasp reflected in Lilijana's white face. He supposed he had gone overboard. That's what happens when you shoot from the hip. No point bullshitting. His father wasn't here to defend himself, but appreciated straight talk.

"I never told dad I loved him, and he never told me he loved me. I wonder if he did. Or if his heart shriveled up when mum died and he lost the capacity. Anyway, he stopped caring.

"Dad," said David, turning theatrically towards the coffin, "I know you can't hear me, but I want to tell you I love you. Thank you for contributing to my life."

David congratulated himself as he left the podium with nothing left to say. Lilijana glared as he resumed his seat. He didn't look at her because he was afraid. In the background of the blood rushing in his head, David heard the minister thank him, and invite everyone to stand for the singing of hymn number five hundred forty eight. David found it in the hymnal then mumbled absent-mindedly to match the cadence of the old tune. All the while, Lilijana melted the flesh off his face. Deservedly so. For David had just delivered, if not the worst eulogy in history, then at least a top ten candidate. If anyone had recorded it, it would be popular on You Tube. It would go viral. Those who thought such appalling outbursts only happened in movies, were proved wrong in ten minutes. His bitterness had been thinly disguised with humor. He didn't know what would happen next. Emotionally, David was tip toeing-on a precipice. God, he thought, can I please have another Mule, or maybe Vodka straight up? David waited for God to answer but wasn't disappointed when he didn't. God didn't show him favor. God had fucked up his life by giving him a dad like Bill Lavender.

Despite David's turmoil, the service proceeded. Attendants removed the photograph and the dark cloth from the coffin before signaling the minister.

The naked coffin descended slowly as the minister pronounced the final prayers, committing Bill Lavender to his maker. The cremation would take place after, out of the sight of the mourners, in the committal room where they addressed legal formalities.

The following condolence ritual had to take place without David because Lilijana rushed him away. Quickly arranging for someone to take the children, she dragged him to their car and pushed him into the passenger seat. He began to speak, but she fired the engine and ordered him to buckle his seatbelt.

"What was that?" she demanded. "You made a complete fool of yourself. Why?"

David considered his response. Attack? Defend? Retreat? Apologize?

"I'm sorry, I shouldn't have had those Mules. I should have written a speech and I–"

"I can't believe what just happened. You can blame it on booze if you want to but I'm not buying that. You can handle alcohol. God knows you've had enough practice."

That sounded like a compliment but David said nothing.

"How do you feel?"

The question surprised him. Lilijana had a PhD in self-righteous lecturing, and it was now completely justified.

"About what?"

"About what you just did? What you said? The way you said it? About the fact that your dad is dead?"

"I feel like shit!"

"Eloquent as ever," said Lilijana without the usual venom associated with sarcasm. 'If you could express your feelings more clearly, you might not have these thoughtless explosions. Are you going to behave at the wake or should I just drop you at the local where you can finish writing yourself off?"

That was a good question for which David had no answer. Lilijana told him to behave himself or else. No need to ask what that meant. It could have referred to a host of punishments, and he did not want to walk to the gallows. They passed through the gates of the cemetery. Silence was her weapon and his defense. Thirst dominated his thoughts and was soon joined by hunger. He tried to remember what goodies Lilijana had arranged for the wake but satisfied himself they would be a cut above average. His reverie in anticipation of food was interrupted by another question.

"Who was that woman in the back row? The youngish attractive one, wearing a grey blouse?"

"I don't know," said David, hoping it was not too quick. "I saw a few unfamiliar faces."

"Strange, she was alone. Quite attractive. I wonder if she'll be at the wake?"

David recognized the trap. She wanted him to say he didn't care whether she went to the party or not. David knew why she was alone, and agreed she was quite attractive. Hot would describe her better.

"I have no idea if she'll go to the wake."

He desperately hoped she wouldn't. The sparks between him and Julia would set the house ablaze. She would probably feign detachment while spinning some yarn about how she worked for Bill, or her father worked with him. Lilijana would buy it, unless she saw David and Julia together, and then she would be Sherlock Holmes with ESP. David wished Julia hadn't come, but was so happy to see her that if Lilijana had not dragged him away, he would have made a bee line straight for her. So far, this important day in his life had been a disaster. Julia's presence at the wake would make it catastrophic. If he tried to text her, Lilijana would want to know who he was messaging. If she showed up, he would have to deal with the fallout. David spent the rest of the trip strategizing, manufacturing lies and other alibis, and daydreaming about an endless supply of Vodka Mules.

CHAPTER TWENTY-TWO

"I know the timing isn't great but I..." Lilijana averted her gaze as her statement of intent petered out. It had begun with the typical resolute tone that David expected to hear when his wife had made up her mind. This time was different. When the pause grew too long, he spoke, knowing she hated him completing her sentences.

"Don't really care about you and I'm sick of your childishness?"

She spoke sharply. "No, and acting so petulantly isn't helpful. This is hard for me."

"Is it?"

Lilijana explained she was having a difficult time understanding David's behavior. She knew something was terribly wrong with him and their marriage, but she couldn't figure out what to do. She prefaced her comments by referencing David's confession, the night after he'd been arrested. With the avalanche of misfortune that had crashed down upon them, Lilijana was emotionally exhausted. His behavior at his father's funeral and the wake were the final straws. She needed to get away.

"I don't know what to say," said Lilijana, her voice beginning to waver. 'I'm not even sure how I feel. There's so much I don't understand, and I can't even express what's going on inside here." She pointed to her heart. "And here." She pointed to her head. Tears followed like thunder after lightning.

Anger erupted inside David. Lilijana was running away to try to solve her problems, of which he was the biggest. He was going to be left behind with the children until she was ready to return. What if she didn't come back?

"So you're upset and your solution is to fuck off and leave me."

"I'm not leaving you, David. Don't blow this out of proportion. I've been sitting on this invitation to a weekend away for over a month. I wasn't going to go but now I think it's a good idea."

"Already, we're down to 'it's a good idea,'" said David, trying to suppress his rage. He sucked at controlling himself. Lilijana would have seen it in his eyes even if she hadn't heard it in his voice. "If we keep talking, maybe I can argue you into not going."

"I'm going," she said flatly. 'I already spoke with Amy, and she'll be able to give you a hand getting the kids to and from school."

"Nice of you to make arrangements without consulting me."

"Stop it, David," said Lilijana. Her voice rose and sharpened. "This is exactly why I need some time. Why we need some time. It's only for the weekend. I'm leaving Friday night. Jennifer is going to pick me up and then I'll be home on Sunday."

David wanted to hit something or to swear. Most of his wrath was directed at himself because Lilijana spoke the truth. He was overreacting. He felt tired. The emotional rollercoaster he'd ridden all day was coming to a stop and he felt drained of life and energy. He might have been an orange, juiced with indifferent violence. His behavior at the funeral had been bad, but at home he'd continued drinking. As Lilijana walked away, he catalogued his indiscretions.

Old Aunty Mildred, his father's older sister, had commented about David's lack of respect for her brother. David had reminded her that for the past fifty years she had shown no respect for Bill, and should have stayed away today. She had shunned Bill when he married David's mother because she wasn't good enough, and Mildred was a twisted bitch. For the first few years of his marriage, Bill had tried to reach out to Mildred. He wanted to be reconciled. When David was born, Bill felt sure she'd want to meet her nephew. David's arrival, together with the passing years, should have softened her heart. Mildred said she had come to the funeral because Bill was her brother. David had called her a fucking hypocrite and ordered her to leave. Lilijana had been able to mollify Mildred, despite her frigid rage and shock.

Later, David chatted with an unknown lady out of alcohol and grief-fuelled lust due to her extraordinary beauty and short tight-fitting skirt. He flirted and stood too close as she backed into the wall. Then he pressed himself against her. With her breasts squashed against his chest, he suggested talk somewhere private. Matt had guided David away, and then placated the woman. Red-faced, she'd attempted a smile but was obviously horrified.

In the kitchen, David had found people talking and laughing. He had asked what was so fucking funny, and told them to go home and watch Seinfeld if they wanted to giggle. He then proceeded to talk about Bill Lavender's favorite television show. The small crowd behaved with impeccable sensitivity and stayed to listen. He told them how much his dad had loved MASH, and then began to recite classic one-liners from Hawkeye and Trapper. He denied that the show was going downhill with the departure of Colonel Henry Blake and the lovably incompetent Major Frank Burns. He insisted it was still funny. Everyone had to agree it was the funniest show ever. He told them his Dad had loved *The Godfather*. Quotes followed, then discussions of the best scenes and favorite characters. Some dope proposed that *Terminator: Judgment Day* was better. David threw a Vodka Mule into his face. He called the man an arsehole, and ordered him to replace the drink he'd been forced to waste on his face. Matt had intervened again.

***

"Someone's at the door," called Lilijana from the other room.

Having drunk himself into oblivion, David had continued into stunned inebriation. The effects of the alcohol were weakened by sober reflection and the news Lilijana was leaving, albeit only for the weekend.

"I'll answer it then, will I?"

Matt stood there grinning when he opened the door. "I think I left my wallet here, mate."

"You'd better come in and look for it then."

With a firm hand on David's shoulder, Matt asked, "Are you all right now?"

"Thanks for helping me out before. I was running off the rails a bit."

"You were a fucking train wreck!"

"Do you have time for a drink? I need to talk."

"I've got time to talk and I'll have a coffee if that's what you're having."

David looked at him sideways. "All right smart arse. I'll have a coffee after I finish this one." He lifted a bottle of Mule.

"How much of that shit did you drink today?"

"I dunno. I lost count after I asked Aunt Mildred to leave."

"Sounds like you're rewriting history there, buddy."

"Whatever, I really need to talk."

They went into the kitchen where David switched the kettle on and grabbed a mug from the cupboard. He added a teaspoon of coffee and two of sugar before turning to face Matt. "I really stuffed up today."

"Yep."

The water in the kettle roared as it came to the boil. David poured the water into the mug. "Grab some milk from the fridge, will ya? Who was that woman I got overly-friendly with?"

"No idea," said Matt as he handed the bottle of milk to David. David opened it and added a dash to the coffee. "But you'll never see her again if she has any say."

"Come and sit down," said David, leading Matt to the lounge room. The children were in their bedrooms and Lilijana had disappeared, no doubt trying to avoid him.

Once comfortably seated, David said, "My life is so shit at the moment, and I'm making it that way. Well, most of it's my fault."

Matt was watching David, inviting him to speak.

"I could be forgiven for being upset about my dad dying, even angry. If I lost my cool and said or did something really inappropriate on just one occasion, then people would shake their heads, make tutting noises and say I was a poor grieving son. That would be reasonable, wouldn't it?"

"But that's not what you did," said Matt.

"Right," agreed David. "I acted like a complete bastard and didn't even try to restrain myself. I made the dumbass decision to start drinking Vodka Mules at nine o'clock in the morning and to keep drinking them. I should have prepared a eulogy instead of shooting from the hip and shooting myself in the foot."

"So you had a bad day."

"I always said you should be awarded a PhD in understatement."

"And you should get one for hyperbole."

"You think I'm exaggerating the extent of my stuff ups today? You witnessed most of them."

"All right," said Matt, "You had a truly shit day. What else is going on?"

David finished the rest of his mule then took a mouthful of coffee. "Lilijana is going away for the weekend. I'm worried she's going to leave me. The other night I told her she wasn't making me happy."

Putting his coffee mug on the table, Matt leaned forward and glared at David. "What the hell did you do that for?" His voice was high with incredulity.

"She asked me and I felt I should be straight."

"Honesty is not always the best policy."

"She never talks to me and the one time I tried to share what was going on, we got interrupted. Those moments when she's willing to listen are so few and far between that I just had to seize that one."

"What did she say?"

"That she was sorry I felt that way."

"What sort of reaction were you expecting?"

"I expected her to say she was sorry she made me feel that way," said David. "Do you see the difference?"

Before Matt could answer Danijela appeared and said, "We're ready for lights out, Dad."

"Where's Mum?"

"I don't know. Can you come?"

David excused himself and followed his daughter to the bedroom where he tucked her and Alen in, kissed them both on the forehead, wished them a good night's sleep and turned the light off. He had performed this ritual every night when the children, including Tomo, were younger, but as the year's rolled by he had found reasons to avoid it. Lilijana had taken up the mantle. Sometimes he had blamed tiredness, other times busyness. Mostly he had chosen to watch television and did not want to be disturbed. He felt ashamed as he stood in the dark and looked at his children. Tears welled in his eyes.

"What's wrong Dad?" asked Alen.

"Nothing," lied David. "Go to sleep. I love you guys."

"Love you too," they chorused as he turned and left.

When he reached the lounge room he started talking again, assuming that Matt was listening. "My children have grown up and I don't even know them. I don't know what they like. I don't talk to them about school. I don't know their teacher's names. I don't know anything. I've ignored them. Why did I do that? I could blame Tomo, I suppose."

"Okay," said Matt slowly and skeptically, "that seems like a long shot but I'm listening."

"Tomo and me used to get on great. I loved him and being a father to him, but when Alen was born I felt a different kind of love. The emotional connection to my own flesh and blood diminished my feelings for Tomo. Not consciously, but it happened and when Danijela came along, I stole more from Tomo. Stole makes it sound deliberate. It wasn't like that. It just happened. My love for my own children was stronger than my love for Tomo, and he sensed that. He was jealous and the seeds of rebellion festered. The competition between Tom and Alen caused a shit load of trouble. There was a time when Lilijana and I felt we were losing control. The children fought. We fought. It was a bloody war zone for a while. And I don't need to tell you how little Lilijana needed another war zone.'

"I remember you telling me about it," said Matt.

"Anyway, my focus was on sorting out Tomo. As his behavior worsened, more time and energy was demanded. Alen and Danijela were left out. Not by Lilijana. She was awesome. Mothers can be bloody legends. Not me, I couldn't find enough..."

A sudden gust of guilt whooshed into his mind and blew away his words. Hadn't he found more for Julia and kept on loving Lilijana? Why hadn't he tried harder with his own children? Here he was making pathetic excuses for his failures as a father, just as he blamed Bill for doing a lousy job with him. Maybe that's what today was about: anger at his father and for following in his footsteps. There was no deliberate decision to do it. The opposite was true, but David was a prisoner of his past.

Matt pressed David to continue. "Enough what?"

"I never wanted to be like my dad, Matt. I tried so hard but I failed. I am him."

"Take it easy, Dave."

"What am I doing? My marriage is going to shit. I barely know my own children. Chalkie won't talk to me anymore. I've been arrested for breaching an AVO taken out by my neighbor, whom I've been waging some dumbass war against just because he used a chainsaw with what I thought was malicious intent. And," continued David lowering his voice, "I'm having a fucking affair."

Matt finished his coffee and laid the mug on the table. He kept silent, and that's what David needed: time to put it together. He excelled at making bad choices. His friends at school gave him an early taste of everything his mother would have dreaded. His choice of girlfriend exposed him to the manipulative and selfish attributes of sex. He chose to pursue alcoholic escapades rather than study. His first car was an absolute lemon. David held a succession of jobs which neither suited not satisfied him. He walked away from a stable long-term relationship with a woman who was devoted to him. His choice was to seek solace from the burning intoxication of whiskey.

"Are you okay?"

"No," replied David. "I was thinking of all the shit choices I've made. It's all my fault."

"It's not all your fault. You've made good choices as well. You just can't see then now because you're miserable and drunk."

Matt's words held no criticism or judgment. He could always expect his honesty. He'd given David a gobful when he deserved it, but Matt's lines were drawn further out than most people's. He could overlook a lot, ignore a lot and forgive a lot. Was it true that David had made good choices? He couldn't think of any.

"Good choices?"

"I'll give you three quick ones. Friendship with me, buying this house and marrying Lilijana."

David dropped his head in his hands. "You found me, and so did Lilijana. It was her idea to buy the house, because I wanted to keep renting in Sydney."

"You're just being fucking difficult. If this is a pity party, I've got an urgent prior engagement. Did I hold a gun to your head to make you hang out with me? Did Lilijana drag you to the altar in chains and hold a knife to your throat?"

"Point taken," said David.

"How about we discuss solutions? Nothing shits me more than a whinge fest. Identify the problems and find some solutions. Ready to make the world a better place?"

"No."

"Let's talk about today," said Matt enthusiastically as he sat forward.

"I thought we already did."

"Your dad died and you got drunk at his funeral. Do you reckon that's ever happened before in the history of man? In Finland, they say the only difference between a funeral and a wedding is that there's one less drunk at a funeral."

Despite the poor taste of Matt's comment, David laughed. "Where do you get this shit?"

"Internet. Anyway, my point is that getting drunk and being obnoxious is not a capital offense, even at your own father's funeral. It's not the unforgivable sin. Apart from the young lady you assaulted, I think everyone will cut you some slack."

"Aunt Mildred won't forgive me, and I didn't assault anyone."

"Tell the judge. As for Chalkie, you've thrown him a pretty big curve bowl. He's a righteous dude with religious sensibilities. It's not just that you offended him; he's worried. He doesn't know what to say to you."

"You've spoken to him about me?"

"Uh-huh."

David didn't mind this, nor could he think why he should mind.

"Give him time," said Matt, "He'll come around. He was there at the funeral. Did you see him? I reckon he should get off his high horse, and told him so. But don't forget he's dealing with a past he's not proud of. That impacts how he relates to people."

"Fair enough," said David. "Mate, you're good at this. Why don't you do it professionally?"

Matt laughed derisively. "I can't be bothered helping people I don't like. I just don't care enough."

"That's two down. What about my marriage?"

"I left that one for last because the other situation you're in is having a negative impact on your marriage."

"How so?"

Shaking his head in exasperation, Matt said, "You can't fix your marriage by having an affair. Every time you fuck Julia, you fuck your marriage a little bit more."

This was true, but David ignored it. It was like a pair of Jehovah's Witnesses coming to his home. Though he could see them through the window, there was no way he would answer the door. They would keep coming back until they could press a copy of the Watchtower into his hands, because that's how they earned their salvation, but David wouldn't help them get to Heaven. Their truth was not welcome, neither was the one Matt just uttered.

"Okay," said David cautiously, "what about my marriage then. Lilijana's leaving for a weekend away and she might not come back."

Matt placed a hand on David's shoulder. Fixing him with an earnest look that made David dizzy, Matt said, "Stop fucking Julia, and then we'll talk about getting Lilijana to stay. That's if you're not being paranoid about her going."

David had heard enough. "What was it you left here? I'll help you find it."

"Nothing," said Matt as he stood up. "I just thought you might like to talk."

David smiled and Matt said, "Think about what I said."

CHAPTER TWENTY-THREE

Sometimes the nicest people can say the nastiest things. The wisest people: the most foolish, the sweetest, the most bitter. David was capable of good decisions, but he collapsed to his default position: the king of folly. His reaction to Matt's warning was to pretend he hadn't heard it.

There was some good news amongst the gloom of Matt's rebuke. He had predicted that Chalkie would come around and reestablish contact. This was a monolithic beacon of hope onto which David fixated with passion. He wanted the three of them back at the pub talking shit with a dash of philosophy. Chalkie's absence was a gaping hole. If any more pieces were ripped away from David's life, he'd probably bleed to death.

On Sunday, David decided to forego church in favor of mowing the lawn. He could take or leave his weekly visit to God's house. Lilijana would invariably force him to go, either by telling him he had to, or suggesting it would be good for him. She was mostly right, too. He usually did find church pleasant. As light and fluffy as the conversation tended to be, and as counterfeit as the joy appeared, it was nonetheless energizing to be surrounded by happy, enthusiastic people. He also enjoyed the music, although the mysteries of hand clapping remained beyond his understanding. The sermon usually contained amusing anecdotes, and some very insightful commentary regarding the human condition. David especially liked it when the message from the preacher seemed to have been for him. Even when the content made him squirm, it still made him feel special. The more he thought about it, the more he felt like going but standing with his hand on the starter cord of his Victa, he opted to cut the grass.

The mower roared to life and David lowered the blade to his preferred cutting height. As the backyard was small, he soon finished. David pushed the mower along the side path to the front yard.

"You're not gonna do the front, are you?"

Phil stood at the edge of his property with his arm folded across his chest. It was stupid question that deserved a stupid answer.

"I thought I'd take the mower to the beach, and leave the front yard until next week."

"Smart arse."

Choosing to ignore the insult because he knew it was warranted, David reached down to the mower and primed the engine.

"I'm trying to sleep," said Phil.

"I'm trying to cut the grass."

"It's kind of early, isn't it?"

"Wakey-wakey it's nearly ten o'clock."

"I like to sleep in after a big night."

You like to sleep all the time because you're a lazy prick, thought David. What he said was, "Busy in the drug lab all night, huh?"

David could feel Phil's hackles rise. The goading was unnecessary but David enjoyed it. He wondered where the fear had gone. His frightened mistrust had been replaced by seething hatred and a feeling of superiority. David was twice the man Phil was. Maybe even three times. He laughed when he remembered how afraid and worried he'd been. He relived the thrill of tossing Phil off his verandah, delighted in the memory of his in-and-out appearance before the magistrate on assault charges. Kelvin Woo had been right on the money. Case dismissed. When the magistrate said he didn't believe Phil's testimony, David had nearly laughed.

Phil stepped over the boundary that separated their properties and walked quickly toward David.

"I think you'd be better off staying back where you were."

"Is that a threat?"

By the time David noticed that Phil was holding something, his neighbor had covered the distance between them and was waving a knife in his face.

"I'm getting sick of you," said Phil as he stared into David's eyes. "That dickhead judge should've thrown the book at you!"

Recognizing fear-based false bravado, David held his ground. Somehow he knew that nothing would happen. Phil was posturing, attempting to frighten David.

"I've got a feeling it's illegal to threaten someone with a knife," suggested David.

"Fuck the law!"

"I thought you might feel that way," said David, trying to keep his voice even. "I'll let the police know when I call them."

"Do it and I'll tell them what a prick you are, and how you're threatening me and Naydine. They'll haul your arse back to the cop shop."

Phil sounded pathetic. "Being a prick isn't against the law, and the best way for you to be left alone would be for you and your boyfriend, and your mother to piss off out of that house. Preferably out of the suburb."

The two men stared at each other. David had tried to provoke him by saying Naydine was his mother and the driver of the Commodore was his boyfriend. Phil didn't take the bait. Either he was too dim-witted or drug-stupefied to understand the insults, or couldn't think of a comeback.

"If you don't mind, I'd like to get back to the lawn," said David, and when Phil didn't move he added, "Fuck off arsehole!"

As Phil walked away, David restarted the Victa. A trickle of uncertainty rolled down his back. Was he pushing Phil too hard? Asking for more trouble than he could handle? What if Phil really was as dangerous as David's first impressions suggested? What if his gut instinct had been right all along?

He finished the lawn with a creeping sense of dread. His high and mighty position, from which David had achieved moral and tactical superiority in his war against the neighbors, suddenly made him sick. He struggled to put away the mower and sweep the paths and driveway. Strength deserted him, as did his resolve and confidence. It had only taken a sharp blade being swished in front of his eyes to steal it. Robbed of his peace of mind, David was also swamped by waters of doubt in relation to Lilijana. When would she return? Would she come back at all? Would she stay? Somehow David finished his work, and stumbled into the kitchen, where he grabbed a Victoria Bitter.

The beer was deliciously cold in his mouth and throat. He drank until the bottle was empty. He took a second stubbie from the fridge, ignoring the Vodka Mule beside it. Since his father's funeral, he'd developed an overwhelming aversion to it. He'd created a slogan for them: 'Drink Vodka Mules and make an arse of yourself!' David took his second beer to the lounge where he sat down and drank it in a leisurely fashion. He switched on the television and found an old movie called *Solomon and the Queen of Sheba*, with Yul Brynner. He felt much better.

When Danijela came in and asked him to play Uno he only agreed after she explained that Alen was playing Xbox. She was bored. During the game, David was reminded of how little time he'd spent with his children. Had they ever been babies, toddlers, pre-schoolers? He could not imagine them that young. Had he watched them all those years but failed to record it in his memory? It would have been nice to go to Network video and hire a DVD of highlights. Those years were gone. Danijela was delighted when she was able to go out and win the hand. For the rest of his life, David determined to pay closer attention.

***

As the weekend drew to a close, Lilijana returned from her trip. David had been wondering how to reignite his marriage, while pretending Matt had not suggested that he end his affair with Julia. During moments of inert melancholy, he pondered what Lilijana might have been thinking. Naturally, he imagined the worst. She was going to walk through that door, lavish affection on Alen and Danijela, and greet David with a forced smile. Once the children had been put to bed, she would deliver the bad news. In conclusion, David heard the word divorce and it landed on his head like a piano.

David had a long history of imaging the worst, though disaster had never happened. He knew he was just lucky, and had been fortunate to avoid catastrophe. Troubles were intrinsic, not just to growing up but to life in general, and David had his share. Serious misadventure had never visited him though. Until now. The thirty-ninth year of his existence was proving to be his annus horribilis.

His positive fantasies had not come true either. He had never imagined himself as the winner of the Lotto, or in the driver's seat of the FPV Falcon for which he'd bought raffle tickets. All his wishful thinking had not saved his marriage nor had the good thoughts prevented his father from falling off a ladder. David was at the mercy of an unseen force which did listen to his concerns. Thirty eight years had made him wiser and bleached the naiveté from his system. Fate was faceless and merciless.

It was during another emotional trough that Lilijana arrived home. The impossible wait had stretched his perception of time. He was watching television when she opened the door and walked in. He wanted to quickly hug her so anything negative she might say could be squeezed into oblivion. Fear paralyzed him. He didn't want to get up and see her wearing an indifferent expression.

"Hi, I'm back."

Her voice was soft and sweet. It smashed through his inertia like a bowling bowl.

"I've missed you," she said as she came over.

David ordered himself to stand and take her in his arms. When he finally rose, however, Danijela came rushing to greet her. Her unreserved excitement made David feel ashamed. He had it all wrong. Surely, she was going to stay, or was this all an act? Was there a big 'but' at the end of that sentence which began, 'I missed you?' I missed you but realized I don't love you. I missed you but being away made me see I'm happier without you. David's stomach churned. I missed you but I can't stay with you. He felt sick.

"Are you going to stay, baby?" blurted David before he could stop himself. "I need to know if you're gonna stay."

Lilijana blessed him with a smile he had never seen on her face. On other faces, he'd always found it mind-blowingly nice and hard to describe. What did it mean? David was sick to death of trying to figure things out from vague symbolic acts and ambivalent expressions. He was desperate for straight talk. No more guessing games. No bullshit.

"Can we talk later?" said Lilijana apologetically. "After the children have gone to bed? I have a lot to say and I don't want to be interrupted. Okay?"

Bile burned the back of his throat. Her words could only mean one thing. Despite his morbid anxiety, he could not refuse her request. She had asked so nicely. It wasn't like her at all. She was buttering him up, treading lightly and softly, as she led him to a vulnerable place where she was going to kick the shit out of him and tear his life apart. David nodded mutely, and Lilijana smiled before kissing him on the cheek. He resisted the urge to wipe off that Judas kiss. Diving into a pool of self pity, David conveniently forgot that he'd betrayed her before this crisis.

With a blurry quality like the effects of drinking binges, David robotted through the evening. Dinner. Clean up. Children's showers. Bedtime stories. Ironing for the coming working week. Television. Sporadic conversation. Automatic and cold.

David was staring into the sink. Lilijana asked him to make her coffee. When it was ready, along with a tea for himself, he carried the mugs into the lounge room. He walked slowly, not wanting this conversation but seeing the necessity of it. It was like the walks he took at school, from his classroom or the playground to the principal's office, where he would be punished for indiscretion. He knew the cane would sting his hands and the pain would stick with him for hours. He didn't want to suffer, but he'd done wrong and had to be punished. He understood. It was fair. That didn't mean he had to like it.

"Ever since Petar went missing and I found out he was killed in action, I've been living a different life from the one I signed up for."

Lilijana looked at David for permission to continue. He thought it was an unorthodox way to tell him their marriage was over but he nodded.

"I thought life was going to be a certain way, and up until Petar's death, it was. To be honest, I don't think I have ever been that happy."

David heard the words and felt them like a slap in the face. Had he failed to make her happy?

"Leaving Croatia was the only thing I could do. My life was destroyed, my family ripped apart, and my country suffered terrible wounds. I knew I had to take Tomo away and begin again. Maybe, I reasoned, God would have mercy on me, and let me have another life. I have only just realized that I blamed God for wrecking my life, even though I asked for His help and threw myself on His mercy, I was angry at Him. Does that make sense?"

David found this hard to answer because he didn't really believe in God. He liked that other people did. It often made them decent and generous. He was glad Lilijana had faith, although at times, he's sensed a disconnect between her words and actions. But people who called themselves Christians and claimed allegiance to an invisible savior were not automatically perfect people. There were no perfect people. Lilijana's question confused him because he didn't know how to answer. Fortunately, it appeared to be rhetoric.

"That was twelve years ago, and I have only just worked out that I've been angry with God the whole time. Even when I praised Him and prayed to Him, I was mad. It seems crazy now."

For the first time, Lilijana sipped her coffee. She appeared to have finished speaking. David placed his mug on the table. Lilijana was making a startling confession and he was gripped by tense emotion.

"How did you find out?" asked David tentatively.

"Revelation. I was listening to this woman speak about the servant heart of a wife, and she was saying it was okay to take time for ourselves. We couldn't be expected to perform at our best for our husbands and children if we didn't look after ourselves. I was thinking how great it was, and how I would schedule some me time to freshen myself up so I could be a better wife and mother. Then the speaker stopped and made an elaborate pantomime of rewinding invisible tape. She asked if we heard what she said, and we all said we did, but she asked again. When we answered with more certainty, she said that what we heard was wrong in two ways. We should never use the word 'perform' in relation to our home duties. She was noticeably reluctant to even use the word 'duty.' She told us we should love our families not perform for them. Then she elaborated more and I thought, okay that's good, I get it."

In the last twelve months, David had not heard her speak this many words. Whether she was pissed off or over the moon, she never gave this much expression. David was both astounded and further troubled. Something was definitely wrong with his wife.

Lilijana sipped her coffee and continued, "She said that most of us didn't even know ourselves or how to look after ourselves. Some of us had so much pain buried deep in our hearts that we were afraid to stop and think. We were so broken that if we ceased our whirlwind lifestyle, our outward and impressive busyness, we would collapse. Have you ever felt that the pastor at church was speaking only to you?"

David smiled. "Yes."

"I was stung by those words, they knocked the wind out of me, but I went on the defensive and thought, I'm not broken. Then a voice said I was broken and at the same time I saw Petar. Then I lost it."

"The image of Petar?"

"I lost control and started to cry. I felt Jennifer's arm around my shoulders and when I turned, she was crying too. I found out later that women all over the auditorium started sobbing. It was unbelievable, but at the time I was only thinking about myself and that was the point. I needed to think about myself, and I knew I was broken and angry. Well, I couldn't stop crying."

David was left speechless. For Lilijana to show weakness was unheard of. He had never seen her cry. He started to speak then stopped when he saw her face. She was crying now. Still not knowing what this had to do with him and their marriage, David moved closer to Lilijana and put his arm around her shoulders. She pressed her face against his chest and sobbed, her body shaking, her breaths short and sharp. He felt the electric heat of her sorrow, so he held her more tightly and breathed in the smell of her hair. His eyes burned and the knot in his throat was suffocating, but he held onto her and himself. He tried to remember the last time he'd felt so close to her. This ecstatic intimacy was unsurpassed. It was arguably the most poignant moment of their eleven year relationship.

CHAPTER TWENTY-FOUR

"She opened up," said David. "Really opened up for the first time in years."

"That's good, mate," said Chalkie.

David looked at his friend, still amazed to be having this conversation with him: to be having any conversation. They were sitting in the Illawarra Hotel. It was around knock off time for the blue collar workers so the joint was pretty full. Chalkie worked for Barnetts couriers, and the depot was close to the town centre where the Illawarra was located on the corner of Keira and Market. Although Chalkie had contacted him and said he wanted to talk, the conversation so far had been pretty one sided. Chalkie seemed content to listen.

"She told me she had been angry ever since her husband was killed in the war in Croatia."

"She never seemed like an angry person apart from when she got justifiably mad at you."

David took a mouthful of Victoria Bitter from the schooner in his hand. "I don't remember giving Lilijana any cause to be mad at me."

"Who was she angry at?" asked Chalkie, ignoring the disingenuous remark.

"At God to start with. After a while she transferred it to me because she couldn't see God and got no response from him. I was a visible and ever present soft target. As the years rolled on, it got worse. She became more bitter and the only outlet she had was me. She didn't understand what was happening. It's only now, after this revelation, that she can see what was going on."

"It makes sense."

David nodded. "It does, doesn't it?"

Across the room, David caught sight of Tomo strolling in through the doors. He was with a couple of his moron mates. David hoped he would stay at the other end of the bar and not notice him. If he did see him, Tomo would have to say something. He always did. He was such a shit stirrer: forever saying something provocative, spoiling for a fight. He liked trouble, courted it and reveled in it. Chalkie followed David's gaze to where Tomo stood at the bar.

"You two getting on any better these days?"

"The day I got arrested—you know all about that, don't you?"

"Matt kept me up to speed."

"Did he tell you I accidentally hit Tomo's Subaru in front of the cops?"

"No."

"Tomo came out to see how badly his baby had been injured, and I suppose I inflamed things by not apologizing. He started going off at me and had to be restrained by the police. Then Lilijana joined us to see what the fuss was about and Tomo disowned me. The cops asked if he knew me and he said no. I was so shocked I couldn't speak. After all I've done for him and Lilijana, that little fucker was throwing me to the wolves. Every time he comes around, I have very evil thoughts. I'm having similar thoughts right now."

Chalkie smiled after finishing his beer. "Do you want another?"

Chalkie suggested he stop staring at Tomo if he wanted to avoid detection. David was thinking how nice it would be to confront Tomo. He pictured himself walking over and asking how his girly buzzbox Subaru was going. In his mind's eye, he saw Tomo's rage ignite like a lit match tossed in petrol. His own anger was boiling. He really wanted to hit Tomo and not just once but a few times, maybe more.

"I thought I told you to stop staring," said Chalkie as he returned with two more schooners. "Don't you know people can tell when they're being stared at?"

"Why is that? Is it a sixth sense or something?"

"I dunno."

"The number of times I've been admiring a lovely lady and she's turned to look at me is amazing. I have to quickly look away but I what I want to do is smile. That way I would appear friendly rather than creepy. There's a big difference between admiring and perving, you know. Between appreciation and lust."

Chalkie shook his head. "Not such a big difference. It's more like a fine line."

David drank more beer and looked at his friend.

"That's better," said Chalkie cheerily. "Now I feel like you're really talking instead of role playing in a dialogue of no interest."

"Sorry, mate."

"You know one of the things that makes women so attractive?"

David nearly choked on his beer. "What kind of question is that?"

If he was joking then Chalkie deserved an Academy Award for his poker-faced reply. "A serious one."

Dread grabbed David's throat and shook him. This was what Chalkie had come to talk about. He was preparing another hellfire sermon on the wickedness of adultery and how David needed to repent or be damned. This was exactly why he and Chalkie hadn't talked for a month. He tried to think of a way to change the subject or some smart arse remark to derail the freight train motoring towards him.

"One of the things that makes women so attractive is their unavailability."

Thankful that Chalkie answered his own question, David remained quiet. This was definitely heading where he suspected. Should he cut Chalkie off? No more sermons thanks. I'm all lectured out if you don't mind. Should he just leave? He listened.

"They are mysterious strangers who look nice and we imagine they must be beautiful on the inside as well. It's pleasurable to think about being with them. Not sexually necessarily, though that's usually the point. Look, she's so well groomed. She probably cares about details and presentation. She'd care about me. She'd look after me well.'

David had heard enough. "What the hell are you going on about, mate?"

"You know what I'm saying. You've had these thoughts. Sometimes it happens when you're talking to a lovely young lady and she's friendly and polite. You imagine she'd always talk to you that way. That she'd never get mad at you, or depressed, or criticize you. She'd be nice to you and more than that, she'd pamper you. You tell yourself you deserve to be pampered."

"I don't mean to rush you but Christmas is coming, and I'm wondering where the point is. What are you trying to say?"

"I understand why you ran to Julia."

"Oh shit," said David. "Here we go."

"Forget Julia," said Chalkie to defuse David's anger. "I didn't come to talk about Julia. I came to talk about you and me. I want to apologize."

"What for?"

"Hello, Dave. What are you doing in the Illawarra?"

David and Chalkie turned simultaneously to face Tomo, who had unfortunately found them.

"Same thing as every else here, Tomo," said David. "Now if you don't mind, we were having a private conversation."

Tomo pulled out a vacant chair and sat down. "When are you going to cough up for the damage to my Impreza?"

"When are you going to drive that shit box off a cliff?"

Tomo looked at Chalkie, then directly at David. "Why would I do that?"

"Because it belongs at the bottom of a hill wrapped around a tree."

"I'm going to sue you for the damages," said Tomo in a growl. He jabbed his finger into David's arm. "And then I'm going to kick your arse."

David swatted Tomo's finger away and reached out to grab his shirt front. He leaned close. "Don't touch me."

Tomo tried to knock away his hand but David held firm. Tomo snatched a fistful of David's shirt.

"Knock it off!" said Chalkie. "Let go of each other and walk away, Tomo."

Suddenly, he and Tomo were on their feet, their chests heaving from the exertion of trying to free the other's grip. They were equally matched and locked in a stalemate. Chalkie stood beside them, and soon others joined the scene. There was an excited buzz in the air. No one had come expecting entertainment but that's what they were getting.

David relaxed his grip and when Tomo followed, David pulled him forward and down. Tomo crashed to the floor then scrambled to his feet. David was lining up a knuckle sandwich when security intervened. His arm was twisted behind his back. Before he knew what was happening, David was being frog-marched out the door. On the street, he stumbled as he was released by the guard. He was furious, fired up with animosity and burning with hatred for Tomo: the boy he'd helped raise. He spun to head back inside. The mountainous security guy guarded the door. His face sent a threatening message.

Before long, Chalkie joined David on the footpath.

"How did I get made as the aggressor in there?"

"Come on," said Chalkie. "We weren't finished talking. Let's walk to the next joint, okay?"

As his rage dissipated, David's pace slowed and he was able to collect his thoughts. He admired Chalkie's way of not answering questions. It could be bloody annoying, but David could see some sense in it, with the benefit of hindsight. His friend was a wise man and a diplomat. The answers to some questions were too obvious to utter; the answers to others, too inflammatory. He had been the aggressor back in the Illawarra, and deserved to be kicked out. It would have gotten worse. Although David was pleased with tricking Tomo and getting him on the floor, the embarrassment Tomo felt would have added steel to his arms and granite to his jaw. The battle would have been brutal. He might have lost and finished up bloodied and breathless. Better not to have gone that far.

"You all right now?" asked Chalkie as they walked. The Harp Deluxe was only a ten minute walk away and David was already looking forward to another drink.

Taking David's silence as assent, Chalkie continued. "I was trying to apologize for not being a better friend."

"You've always been a good mate, Chalkie."

"Mates stick by their mates through good and bad and I sort of left you. Abandoned you when you told me that you were going to have an affair."

"Abandoned is a bit strong, isn't it?"

Chalkie stopped walking. So did David. "Do you think you could just shut up and listen?"

"I can do that," said David.

They started walking again, and Chalkie resumed his apology. "You know I destroyed my first marriage by cheating on Bianca multiple times. I was following my Dad's lead. I assumed she would put up with me like my mum tolerated my dad. But mum was from a different era. Women in those days didn't leave their husbands if they were having flings behind their back, or even if they were abusing them. They copped it and wore masks of bravery. Dad provided a stable home for her and us kids, and as long as he didn't mistreat her, he thought it was okay. He didn't want to leave her; he just wanted marriage with extracurricular activities. He didn't rub her face in it. He was discreet but she knew. He thought that was okay. I thought it was okay. Bianca did not think it was okay. It wasn't until she left that I realized I had done wrong. You remember how low I was at that time?"

"You were hitting the bottle hard enough to be labeled an alcoholic."

"Weeks went by in a liquor-fuelled haze. I didn't know who or where I was, or what I was doing. I loved Bianca. I still do. She's a good woman whom I treated badly. She didn't deserve that. I felt so guilty I wanted to kill myself. Bianca made me whole. She made me a better man. Then I ruined it with lust and a lack of self control."

"Ease up," said David. "Like you said, you are your father's son."

"That's an excuse, Dave. I did know it was wrong. The first time I had sex with another woman after I married Bianca, I was amazed at how guiltless I felt. I was nervous beforehand and kept telling myself to back out but I pressed on. I was like a man who walks into a building with flames lunging through the windows and the alarm warding him off. He knows the danger and goes in anyway. Not to save a life. He's no hero. He does it for purely selfish reasons. You with me?"

"That's all behind you now, mate."

They arrived at the Harp Deluxe and Chalkie pushed the door open, allowing David to enter. They found a vacant table. Chalkie said, "You know why I'm telling you this even though you've heard it before, so buy us a beer and we'll keep talking."

The Harp was a small run-down bar with a reputation for violence unmatched in the district. One wag on the Internet recommended it to those who were interested in being glassed and taken to hospital. The day time crowd seemed sedate enough and could have been doppelgangers of the men from the Illawarra Hotel, except for the absence of Tomo.

Once David returned with a couple of schooners, Chalkie said, 'You knew your affair with Julia was wrong when you started it. You were just like the guy walking into the burning building. The thing is when you get inside, and I know this from experience, you find out the flames don't burn you. There's no immediate danger. You can't even smell smoke so you think it's safe. The longer you stay, the more convinced you become that there's no impending disaster."

David took a mouthful a beer. "No offense, Chalkie, but are we going somewhere here?"

"Don't be a smart arse."

Chalkie was right to pull David into line. The analogy of a man entering a burning building for the purpose of satisfying his passions was a painfully accurate depiction of not only Chalkie but of David. Chalkie could not have been more precise in his portrayal of David's situation.

"I handled the situation badly and that's what I'm apologizing for," said Chalkie. "My response should have been compassion and grace, not condemnation and rejection."

"I felt rejected but condemned is a bit over the top, isn't it?"

"I listened to you talk about Julia and not even attempt to justify yourself, and I thought, damn, here we go again: another man who will follow his penis into hell. Another one bites the dust."

"Queen."

"Look," said Chalkie, "I can't be telling you how to live your life."

"But you are going to anyway," interrupted David.

"You're a grown man, even though you're not acting like one. It will end badly, despite whatever fantasy you've built in your mind. I can't stop you. I thought if I walked away it would jolt you into shame and repentance. I thought it would force you to change. I was the only one punished. I felt bad every day for avoiding you. I felt gutless. I handled it all wrong, mate, and I'm sorry."

David held Chalkie's gaze until it became awkward, then he looked away and drank more Victoria Bitter. David had understood the relevance of his affair to Chalkie's history, but had thought his friend's absence was an attempt to avoid bad memories. He'd never thought Chalkie might be punishing him or trying to force him to change. He didn't know how he felt about that. What did it say about Chalkie? What did it say about David? The long silence which engulfed them was perfectly calm and peaceful. Neither man seemed impelled to break it. There was nothing Chalkie had said that David could deny. The hammer of truth started tapping his fingers then bashing the side of his head. He felt dizzy, concussed.

Finally he spoke. "Shit."

Chalkie smiled. "Do you forgive me?"

"Nothing to forgive, mate. I get it. Thanks for telling me."

"Dave, I'm a Christian but sometimes I forget what that means. I forget that mercy triumphs over judgment, and I forget to extend grace to people, like I've had it given to me. It's pretty hard getting the balance."

"Don't be so hard on yourself."

"Sometimes we have to be hard on ourselves, Dave."

David raised his glass and tilted it towards Chalkie who mirrored his action. "To self control?"

"To self control."

"Where can I get some of that again?" asked David.

Chalkie pointed to the ceiling.

"Upstairs?"

"A little bit higher than that."

David glanced up at the ceiling and saw Julia's face. It faded and was replaced by Lilijana's. He wondered if she knew what he was doing. He wondered what her confession meant in terms of their relationship. Was it the start of something new? Was it fresh water about to wash through the stagnant pool of their marriage? Was it time to end the affair and take advantage of the wind of change? Even as he considered this, David reveled in the sweet memories of sex with Julia. Why should he give that up? Chalkie had given him solid reasons, yet he ached for his secret lover. He was addicted to her. Her skin. Her hair. Her taste. Her smell. Her voice. Her. Addiction blinded people and bruised them. Battered them. Addiction enslaved people.

"I'm trapped," said David, though he had not meant to speak aloud.

"I know a rescue specialist," replied Chalkie with an encouraging smile. "It starts with you, however. You've got a talent for making bad choices. You've always been that way. This is my final word of warning. Make a good choice and end this affair."

CHAPTER TWENTY-FIVE

David opened his eyes, and winced at the stabbing pain behind his lids. He lay still and mentally scoured his body for signs of decay, unexpected aches or stiffness in his joints. The physical examination was followed by deeply introspective questions. These all related to his mood and attitude. David could tell from this process what sort of day he was going to have.

There was a flatscreen television on the wall in front of him to the left of a large wall mirror, and set too high for comfortable viewing from the lounge. It would normally be switched on from the time David walked in and left to run until lights out and sometimes beyond that. The early starts often had him falling asleep with the television still running. It had not been used much the previous night however.

In the half light of dawn, David rolled onto his right side.

"Good morning, Julia," he said in a low murmur. There was no reply.

He watched her sleep, studying her features as he had the first time he laid eyes on her. This time it was an unhurried and unashamed admiration of the woman he had fallen in love with. David felt completely calm. As though he were only dreaming about waking up beside her, he felt no guilt. No regret. Julia had wanted to be with him and he had wanted to be with her. Memories of the previous night's love making flooded his mind. He felt a wave of warmth tingling across his lower stomach and into his genitals. Hard now, he considered rousing her but thought better of it. There was still time.

He pulled the covers back, rolled out of bed, and made his way to the bathroom. With a flick of the switch the ceiling exhaust fan roared to life and the light came on. He quickly switched it off and peed in the semi darkness, hoping not to disturb Julia.

Modern motels lacked the charm of the cutely kitsch versions, predominately built in the nineteen fifties and sixties. The antiquated exhaust fan, for example, was something you would pay extra for. The whole concept of a motel was naturally an American import. The first one in Australia was The Oakleigh Motel in Victoria, which was erected for traveling salesman and motoring holiday makers. Other motels sprang up across New South

Wales and Victoria. While they were called luxury hotels at the time, most were now considered a low budget option for travelers.

David was well acquainted with the motels of the New England region. Prior to his current job he'd been a sales representative for Chaucer pharmaceutical. Regular trips across the area had him spending at least one night a week away from home. The idea at first had appealed to him. A night alone, removed from the hustle and hassle of family: a little peace and quiet to refresh himself. Being able to sit and watch an entire television program without being interrupted, or needing to get up and do something. No telephone conversations or any of the raucous sounds which emanated from the kitchen. A rest. It was also a little lonely, and the lack of background commotion didn't feel quite right. Coming home, though, to the tension and clamor always made him wish he could leave again. This sense of discontent was unwelcome and unshakeable. Finally he decided to quit and find a job which kept him at home. He told Lilijana that he was sick of all the driving.

This particular trip was for a Dean & Branxton training seminar. Someone in the office mistook David for management material and offered him the chance to take some paid training. David had sold it to Lilijana as a great opportunity: proof of better times ahead. A management position would come with a pay rise and other fringe benefits. David simply had to attend the seminar and another one later this month, and then he would be moved into an office. He imagined this office would be spacious and air conditioned. He would sit behind an expansive regal-looking desk with nothing to do but answer phone calls and follow the latest cricket and rugby league news on the Internet. The walls would be lined with bookcases full of official manuals and lever arch files with typed labels, none of which he would read or ever touch. There would be a few framed certificates punctuating empty space with declarations of his achievements. People would need to make appointments if they wanted to talk. David had not required any cajoling to get him involved. His fantastic delusions provided the impetus to say yes and attend the seminar.

There was another reason he agreed to go and why he presented the opportunity to Lilijana in such glowing terms. An out of town trip afforded him the first chance in years to get away, to be alone. To relive those halcyon days when he traveled the state and for a day or two each week was a different man. This time he hadn't planned to be alone.

With as much subtlety as he could muster, David climbed back into bed and snuggled up to Julia. She stirred and turned her head. As he lowered his lips onto hers, a strange but sweet aroma entered his nostrils. Ravenous hunger welled and he wanted to inhale Julia, to take her deep inside himself. Enticed by the softness of his kiss, she pressed her body to his. Their hands caressed pleasurable pathways in the dark, and when their mouths met again, David could barely contain himself. The passionate fire that scorched his body as he and Julia made love was like finding a long lost child. For so long this suppressed emotion had been a distant stranger. David could not believe how powerfully his desire for Julia raged. It had been a very long time since he had made love to Lilijana with such abandoned intensity. The previous night with Julia had been sensational, better than he imagined in his wildest fantasies. This, right now, was something else. It was frightening.

Julia gently pushed him off her and onto his back, then straddled him. The grinding rhythm made David dizzy and he began to fear an explosion other than the orgasm which was approaching with hostile alacrity. She pushed harder and he responded as if in a battle. If war was this good, no one would ever seek peace. Finally he could wait no longer and had to hope she had reached her climax. He lost control and came inside her. Ecstatic spasms followed before Julia fell to David's side and exhaled hot heavy breaths into chest.

"Wow!" said David and instantly regretted it.

"Wow, indeed," said Julia in a tired breathless mumble. "So last night was just a warm up, was it?"

David felt a response would ruin the moment, which was just as well because he didn't know what to say. He assumed Julia had paid him a compliment.

"It's so beautiful to be totally lost in time," said Julia after a pause. "Feeling nothing else, thinking nothing, caring about nothing except the feeling of now. It's so peaceful."

Julia spoke of being lost and David related. He didn't know what planet he was on. Surely, he had died during the ferocious sex with Julia and moved into the afterlife where he was still in bed with her. She was talking, describing some sort of paradise, almost unaware of his presence. He had the odd disturbing feeling that he had just been used. Another thought trampled that one: he had used her too, and it was okay. Permission to fuck had been granted.

Julia kissed his chest and ran her hand down his stomach to where his hardworking erection had just begun to subside. He liked it but hoped she would shut up about peace and beauty. Needing to regain the upper hand, David ventured a rejoinder to Julia's musings.

"You know how we said at the beginning of—" David paused, not liking the sound of his words or even his own voice. "—this affair..."

"You can call it what you like. I'm loving every second."

Why couldn't she stop gushing? Bravely, he pressed on. "We said it could only continue as long as both of us agreed it should. Right?"

The sudden stiffness in Julia's body as she snapped away from him caught David by surprise. Immediately, he realized his mistake and tried to reassure her. "No, no," he said in a voice more urgent than normal. "I'm not saying I want out."

"What are you saying?"

"I feel like I'm never going to want out. I'm addicted to you and I don't give a shit."

When Julia punched his arm, it surprised David nearly as much as her reaction to his clumsy expression of affection. He was good with words. Words were his thing. Back in the day, when he taught migrants to speak English, he was never lost for words. An English language superman, even if he was the only person to think so. But Julia was like kryptonite. She made his head spin. Without even trying to beguile him, she enchanted David. He was spellbound. At another time in another place, he might reflect on how much control he surrendered to her. For now he would have done anything to never leave this cheap motel room.

"Why didn't you say that in the first place," she said. "You had me worried. I don't want to stop either."

The silence that followed was swollen with unspoken knowledge. Their affair would end. David did not want to leave Lilijana or even hurt her. He wished he could feel just a little bit guilty. It would have made it easier to resist this pool of lust and wanting to swim in it forever. This tryst had a shelf life no matter how much they might try to deny it.

"We'll have to though, one day," said David tentatively. "Won't we?"

Julia didn't answer and David realized the key to muting her verbosity was to shatter the fantasy with a sledgehammer of reality. He felt bad for spoiling the euphoria but it was too late. He couldn't stop himself now.

"You don't want to leave your husband and I don't want to leave my wife. We've already got pretty sweet lives. This is just icing on the cake for a couple of greedy lovers."

Julia's silence troubled him. Was the alternative any better? Gushy, poetic and romantic, or stony, chilly and silent? David wished for something in between. Julia was a woman prone to extremes. Seemingly self-controlled and calculating, she was tempestuous and dangerous. Yes, she was dangerous.

"Where are you taking me for breakfast?" she said as she sprang out of bed and headed for the bathroom. The exhaust fan drowned out David's answer. She returned, still clothed in nothing but beautiful flesh, and said, "We'd better discuss a new rule over breakfast. No more gloomy talk of reality and our other lives, okay?"

The light of dawn snuck into the room and illuminated Julia's body. Despite the weirdness of her behavior and his unshakeable suspicion that he might be having an affair with two women, David yearned for her again. Having sufficiently rested, his erection returned and he laughed.

"I don't suppose you want to do it again before we go, do you?"

"I don't know," she teased, "I'm pretty hungry." She twisted her hips this way and that, making her breasts sway. He noticed the hardness of her nipples.

"So am I," said David before grabbing her around the waist and pulling her onto the bed. "And I agree with your new rule."

***

Breakfast could not have been any less enjoyable. There were several cafes in town which served reasonably priced breakfast, as well as the ubiquitous McCafe. Julia had left the choice to David, who opted for the nicest café because it was a special occasion and he was unlikely to ever eat there, which meant he would not be remembered. It was funny how often he imagined that people would remember him when he was a completely unremarkable and therefore forgettable man. The longer he lived the more he wrapped delusional nostalgia around himself. He would never need an old fart's rug of memories to keep warm when he had such a thick quilt of fantasy to do the job. He was not imprisoned by his past. Julia, on the other hand, did appear to be bound by something in her past. He decided to investigate what he strongly suspected. Breakfast at a nice café, after a night and morning of wild passionate love making, was not, however a good place. His first mistake was to begin a sentence with the words, "You know before, when we were talking about the inevitable end..."

"I thought we agreed on a new rule not to go there,' replied Julia with half an eye on the pancake and banana draped over her fork. She took the mouthful and chewed it slowly without taking her eyes off him. Her eyes darkened with an unspoken threat that David couldn't interpret. He gulped and averted her stare.

Realizing the futility of pursuing this conversation with Julia in a state of animosity, David withdrew to his private thoughts. Although sex was and always had been the aim of this affair, it had actually destroyed it. The sex was fantastic, better than he had imagined, but something had changed. He felt like an Olympian who makes it to the final, wins the God medal, then wakes up wondering what to do now that he achieved his goal. The euphoria of victory turns out to be like a good meal: enticing in its appeal and pleasurable for a time but ultimately nonpermanent. Two hours later, the hunger returns as though the meal was never consumed. He wants it to last weeks or even years but knows it won't. The hollowness is gut wrenching. Knowing that hunger will render him useless for any purpose that does not feed it, makes him feel trapped. David had made a prison for himself. Right now as he looked at the beautiful Julia peacefully and absently drinking her coffee, he could not see a way to escape.

He remembered his conversation with Chalkie at the Harp Deluxe Hotel. He had seriously contemplated what his friend had said, but with the seductive lure of a whole night with Julia on offer, his resolved disintegrated. This trip was not just a lunchtime quickie. There was no rush. It was a golden opportunity from which no amount of reasoned debate could dissuade him.

It was only now that the feeling of powerlessness pounced on him again. A simple choice had to be made yet he didn't have the balls to break it off with Julia.

Julia broke out of her silence and crashed into his. "I've got some good news that I've been saving."

Who saves good news? What was the point of that? Bad news had to be delivered at the right time. Good news had an open invitation to walk through the door at any time.

"Aren't you going to ask me what it is?"

David suppressed a sigh. "Tell me your good news."

"That friend of mine with the cat is heading to Queensland for a week, and naturally she's asked me to feed her cat again. Remember the fun we had feeding that cat?"

He should have been pleased. He should have dived in with a salacious comment about pussies. He should have matched her emotional high, if not genuinely then at least with his best pretense. Had he done that, she wouldn't have scowled and resumed her death stare.

When Julia stood, grabbed her bag, and stormed out of the café, David just sat and watched her go. He was supposed to think it was fantastic that they would be able to have sex for seven days in a comfortable bed close to their homes. He should have felt that and expressed it to Julia, but a specter haunted those memories. The bad news about his dad being hospitalized had been dropped on him after one of those lunchtime trysts. His thoughts were scrambled. So much conflict now. Having failed to speak, which would have kept her from heading off to God knew where, he should have chased after her. Should have grabbed her and babbled sweet apologies and kissed her, because a passionate kiss wipes away every evil, rights every wrong. Yet he was frozen. His engine was running but he had forgotten how to change gears.

Seconds marched by as he sat there alone. He counted them to calm himself, to bring order to his thoughts. Didn't he know all along, right from the moment he chose to pursue Julia, that it would end badly? Guilt finally arrived, bringing a feeling of sick regret in his stomach. It burned like he knew it would. He'd deceived himself for so long that he'd believed it would be all right. He'd have is cake and eat it too. Nothing had changed at home as a result of his affair. His love for Lilijana had not diminished, nor had her intermittent affection. Although she had cried in his arms and made a fresh emotional connection, there were still question marks over their future. He had the best of both worlds. The question was whether Julia was still a world he wanted. He had conquered her. Did he want to continue to rule her? Had he ever ruled her, or had he been a slave? The signs of potential disaster had been there from the beginning. He had consciously overlooked them in favor of guilty pleasure. Bread eaten in secret is sweet. Lilijana had quoted that proverb to him with respect to his cigarette smoking, which he had quit many years ago. He never understood it at the time. He had liked cigarettes, but never thought of them as sweet or a guilty secret. Maybe Lilijana had meant that such pleasure was momentarily satisfying, even exhilarating, because it was an activity you wouldn't want others to know of.

David looked around the café. It was mostly filled with single people reading newspapers or work documents. There was a guy in a suit having a hushed conversation over his mobile phone, and another wearing a frown, banging away at his laptop. A woman with oversized glasses and thick brown hair was reading a book. Everyone seemed removed, as though they were in the place but not of it. Nearer the window, a young couple gazed into each other's eyes with an intensity that said: we are the world. Nothing existed for them but the moment and the tender togetherness they shared. He murmured and she smiled. David envied what he imagined to be their uncomplicated happiness. He wanted to stroll over, sit down and join in, to drink of their pleasure and slake his thirst, but he had to go after Julia.

He glanced at his watch and tried to work out how long she had been gone and how far she might have traveled. Of course, he had no idea. David paid his bill and stepped out onto the street, looking left then right, wondering which way she had gone.

CHAPTER TWENTY-SIX

As he veered off onto the exit ramp, just five minutes from home, David remembered his mobile phone. He had switched it off as part of his attempt to hide in the land of secrets. He hadn't wanted any reminders of his real life while he was indulging in his other one where there were no tears or pain. Although he recognized danger in disconnecting from the world, he justified his decision with typical flippancy. What could happen in a couple of days? I'm not that important. In the event of an emergency, Lilijana would have been able to call the motel. The world still turned.

David pressed the phone into life and waited with a modicum of discomfort. He thought about the trip: its highs and lows, and about Julia.

When she stormed out of the café, she had only gone to the car so David caught up to her quickly. But during those moments of uncertainty about where she was and what she was thinking, something changed. The spell had been broken, smashed. She had apologized for overreacting and kissed him with enough force to convince him of her contrition and willingness to put the matter behind them. They had returned to the hotel and made love furiously again before gathering their belongings and loading the car for a day of touring the wine country in the Hunter Valley. They had visited The Vintage vineyard and Peacock Hill in Pokolbin, and also taken in the famous Hunter Valley Gardens. Conversation was confined to wine, country driving and living, and other safe topics. Neither of them wanted to get serious. An unspoken agreement kept them rowing on the surface rather than diving into deep water. There was a moment when David had wanted to talk about what happened. He lost his nerve.

At the end of their trip, he had dropped her off at the commuter carpark at Asquith train station where she had left her car for discretion, and continued the journey home wondering how to end it with Julia, and whether to tell Lilijana about the affair.

The phone almost immediately signaled that it had received and stored messages. David knew at least one of them would have to be from Lilijana. He was almost afraid to listen. He was on his way home to her because that was where he belonged but a significant chunk of him was also roaming elsewhere inside Julia's handbag. To hear his wife's voice now would be... What would it be? he wondered. What was he so scared of?

David nearly ran the car off the road when he heard the message.

"Alen had an accident on his bike. He's going to be okay but I need to take him to hospital. Call me when you get this."

He called Lilijana immediately as he continued down the highway, barely cognizant that he was driving. He drove through the first red light and the second without seeing them. Lilijana's voice sounded tight.

"Is he okay? What happened?"

"Why did you take so long to call me?"

"I only just got the message. When did you call?"

David bounced into the driveway of 1010, narrowly avoiding the gate post and skidded to a halt centimeters from the garage door.

"This morning at ten past eleven."

"I gave you the number of the motel, didn't I?' David was doing a terrible job of remaining calm. He still had the phone pressed to his ear, held by his hunched shoulder, as he unlocked the front screen door and walked in. Lilijana saw him and hung up the phone. Only then did David realize he was still talking on his phone.

Lilijana sounded calm, but it was measured and obviously required effort. She was angry. "They said you already checked out."

David hugged Lilijana. She responded the same way a tree would have. As he held her he wracked his brain, trying to remember when they had left the motel. Just before eleven. "Yeah," said David. "Sorry."

Lilijana broke their awkward embrace and gently pushed David away. "Why didn't you answer your mobile?"

"I switched it off."

"Why?"

David wanted to know about Alen, not be subjected to an interrogation. His exasperation was beginning to manifest in his voice. He could have lied and told Lilijana the battery had gone flat and he had forgotten to pack the charger. Instead, he'd opted for the truth, which sometimes proved more trouble than it was worth. It was raising Lilijana's hackles. It didn't seem anywhere as important as the condition of his son.

"Who the fuck cares?" he blurted. "I want to know about Alen. Where is he? How is he?"

Lilijana seemed shocked by his outburst. Her initial reaction was to stare. After a melodramatic inhale and exhale she said, "We're going to have to talk later. Okay?"

David had no idea what she meant and didn't give a toss. "I want to see my son."

During the drive to Shellharbour Hospital, Lilijana filled David in on their son's accident. "He was riding to the corner shop to buy some bread and milk, and when he cut across the carpark, a car reversed and hit him, knocking him off. The driver jumped straight out to make sure he was all right, which of course he wasn't. He was able to tell the woman that he only lived up the road and he gave her our number. She called me and I ran down as fast as I could. I cut my foot because I didn't have time to put on my shoes. When I arrived a small crowd had gathered around Alen. I pushed through and saw his face covered with blood. I screamed but someone told me to calm down because it looked much worse than it was. Alen was crying because the shock had worn off and the pain was attacking. I told the faceless person what to do with their uninformed opinions about my son's health. Someone else said that an ambulance had been called and would be there soon. No one was to move him according to a nurse who happened to be there. She was paying close attention to Alen, while someone comforted the driver, who was still shaky from mortification. The ambulance arrived, the ambos did their thing and in no time they had him cleaned up and at least looking better. They suspected his wrist was broken and the cut to his head would need stitching but he would be fine. They loaded him in the ambulance and I ran back home to call you and get Danijela. Then we drove to the hospital. I was only at home when you arrived because, in the mad rush, I hadn't thought to grab overnight stuff for Alen. I didn't even know at that stage how seriously he had been hurt. I wasn't thinking straight."

"It's all right," said David softly.

That breathless recount used up the time it took to drive to the hospital. David had no time to think about what Lilijana could want to talk about. Something she had done or wanted to confess further? Something he had done or failed to do? David considered the matter but he was consumed by concern for Alen. Soon they were riding the elevator to the third floor. When the doors slid open, they stepped out. David followed Lilijana down a shiny white hall. Hospital smell invaded his nostrils and he was instantly transported back to his recent stay as a patient. That was months ago, but in some ways it seemed like years. That was before Julia had wrapped her tentacles around him. Before he had given Phil a touch up. Before he had been arrested. Before he'd acted like a complete tool at his father's wake. Before Chalkie dumped him as a mate. Before Lilijana went away and spun herself into a cocoon of refection then returned as a butterfly. Suddenly, he felt guilty and wished he had waited for Lilijana as a faithful and lovingly patient husband, instead of a selfish two-timing prick.

She stopped at the door to Alen's room, and allowed him to enter first. He looked at her and smiled before kissing her mouth and telling her he loved her. She smiled back but it was a typically enigmatic smile which he found slightly unsettling.

Alen was awake and watching television. His face lit up when he saw David, which made him feel like crying. He swallowed hard and rushed to the bed where he kissed and embraced his son.

"Ow," said Alen. "Careful, Dad, I've got a bit of a cut there." He pointed to his forehead near the place David had kissed him.

"A bit of a cut?" said David with mock incredulity. "I heard there was blood everywhere and the doctor had to sew up the hole with fifty stitches."

Alen laughed. "Only six stitches, Dad. Like a cricket ball."

David laughed and as Lilijana joined in, he knew his son was all right. He would recover. His wrist would heal. He would have a scar and a cool story to tell for years to come and embellish over time. David imagined Alen telling his mates how he was doing thirty k's through the carpark when a truck sent him flying How his head had been sliced open and needed fifty stitches to close it. His mates would call him a bullshit artist and laugh. Just thinking about his son growing into a man and still being alive, melted David's heart. This time tears rolled freely.

"It's not that funny, Dad," said Alen when he noticed the redness of David's face and the wetness of his eyes.

Lilijana stepped close and wiped his tears away with her thumbs. "It's not funny at all actually."

This was his life. This was where he should be grounded, and where his heart and mind should have been. Why did he search for extras to add to this perfect picture? He had a wife, two beautiful children, a comfortable home, a secure job and good friends. Why wasn't that enough? David stared through bleary eyes at Alen, and realized he was just plain greedy. He didn't fully appreciate what he already had. There was truth to Chalkie's words about the grass being greener on the other side. Unavailability was a turn on. Part of what made a woman attractive was that she belonged to someone else. There was also the mystery of a stranger who offered a smile that promised heaven. David considered all he had and realized his life was heaven. The only thing ruining it, the only sliver of hell poking through the cracks, had been caused by him: invited in by his foolishness.

Phil might have remained an eccentric and disagreeable neighbor but had David had turned him into an enemy, and Julia might have been a breath a fresh air which blew into his life for a couple of hours once a week to teach him about how to be a better communicator. Instead, he had transformed her into an object of desire and stupidly pursued her. David was not in the habit of trying to crack on other women. Despite what went on inside his head, he'd only engaged in mild and harmless flirtations. There was Mel of course, but she was a special case. That had been a one-off: an explosion of insanity. He looked at Lilijana, and was aware she had been watching him.

"What's wrong with you, David? He's going to be all right. Why are you still blubbering?"

Although he needed to talk, to release the polluted waters of his mind, he didn't know how to. How could he open that door now? He had slammed it shut and boarded it up. Beyond it lay a forbidden room in the house of his life. A confession seemed right and proper, even relatively simple, but David was powerless to speak. Each word burned to a crisp on his tongue by his fear of the consequences. No, this was not the time. Maybe there would never be a right time. Perhaps he would just live with the crushing weight of an awful secret. Lilijana was waiting for him to answer.

"I don't know," said David. "I'm just relived he's okay. Happy we are together. Stoked that everything is okay."

Lilijana screwed up her face. "Everything is not okay though, is it?"

Before David could respond, Alen said, "I have to stay here tonight, Dad."

"Why's that mate? You look all right to me."

Alen shrugged.

"You just want to tell your story to all the nurses, don't ya?"

He shrugged again.

Lilijana said, "Danijela, stay with your brother for a couple of minutes okay? I need to talk to Dad alone. Just out in the hall. We'll be right back and then Dad will take you home."

This was looking and sounding ominous. Lilijana had shifted into proprietary mode and this signaled serious intentions. Danijela nodded, not mystified as David was, perfectly accepting the take-charge tone of her mother's voice. Lilijana took David gently by the arm and led him out into the corridor. For a moment they just stood there and David's anxiety grew. She was justifiably angry about him turning his mobile phone off and no doubt still upset about Alen's accident. Not being able to contact David immediately had made things worse.

Lilijana spoke in a low measured voice. "When I called the hotel, the desk clerk said that you already checked out. I said, 'how long ago?' And she said, 'they left about fifteen minutes ago.' 'They?' I said questioning, because I was flustered and worried sick about Alen. I forgot you had said you were staying with Matt. Then she said, 'Yes, Mr. and Mrs. Lavender checked out fifteen minutes ago.' Stupidly, I said, 'I'm Mrs. Lavender,' and the silence on the other end was like a bomb going off in my mind."

She stared and he made a pathetic attempt to meet her gaze. He felt as though she had thrown boiling water in his face. He couldn't speak. His throat had been scorched and his lips and tongue melted by her unspoken accusation. Fighting the agony of hot guilt, David felt his knees jellify. He stumbled back to lean on the wall. Lilijana fixed him with an unrelenting look of betrayal, disbelief and fury. He had waited too long to pretend he could now attempt denial. David felt so hot his head swam. What could he say? Lilijana had also been rendered speechless by his admission. They stood there frozen and mute, their marriage pulverized by a meteor of infidelity.

"Mum," said Danijela, appearing in the doorway. "Are we going soon?"

No answer. David noticed Lilijana was shaking, trembling with emotional trauma.

"Mum?"

Somehow David found his voice but it sounded like somebody else's: pitchy and cracked. "Soon, baby. A couple of minutes. Go back inside please."

After a thoughtful pause, which included searching examinations, Danijela obediently left them.

"Lilijana," began David in that same strange voice, "I—"

"Don't!" she ordered cutting him off. "Don't."

More staring through stinging red eyes, blurry with tears. More silence. David felt like throwing up. He had never felt like such a complete shit. A monster.

"Mum?"

Lilijana turned at the sound of Tomo's voice booming down the hall from the elevator foyer. He approached rapidly and was soon by Lilijana's side, placing a consoling arm around her shoulders.

"What's going on?" he asked, looking briefly at David. "Is Alen okay?"

"He's fine," said Lilijana in reasonably calm voice.

"You look terrible. What's wrong?" Another accusatory stare at David.

Ignoring the question, Lilijana told David to say goodbye to Alen and take Danijela home. She said she would spend the night at the hospital and talk to him in the morning. Without waiting for him to answer, she walked into the room leaving David alone with Tomo.

"What have you done?" Tomo grabbed a handful of David's shirt front and jerked him against the wall. He glared at David, who remained silent.

"If this is your fault, I'm going to make you pay. I've warned you before that if you ever hurt my mum, I would make you fucking pay for it."

David's guilt-driven paralysis gave way to a rising tide of anger. He hated Tomo but he was angry at himself. He chopped down Tomo's arms to break his hold on his shirt then shoved Tomo across the hall. His stepson stumbled but didn't fall. David was just about to swing his fist into Tomo's head when Danijela reappeared in the hallway.

"Hi Tomo," she said sweetly. She was either oblivious or willfully ignorant. David thought the former was more likely. He stepped away from Tomo, who forced a cheerful expression.

"Hi, sweetie. What'd you do to your brother?"

She laughed. "Nothing, silly. He's too big for me to do anything. He fell off his bike. That's all."

"That's all?" said Tomo glancing sideways at David, perhaps to convey the message their business was not yet settled. "Must have been a big fall to end up in here."

"Yeah," she replied. "Somebody drove a car into him."

"I'd better go see if he's okay then, eh?"

"Okay, I'm going home with Dad. See you later."

David watched Tomo walk into the room and over to the bed where he exchanged a contemporary youngster's greeting with Alen, before wrapping Lilijana again in his arms. David felt excluded. He was observing another family through the window of their home as he stood outside in the cold wind of isolation. Was this the end? Had he just witnessed the destruction of his marriage? A brutal death for which he had been responsible. He stood and stared until Danijela tugged his sleeve and said, "Come on, Daddy. I'm hungry. Can we get McDonald's on the way home?"

"Sure," he said, automatically, but he didn't want to go home. It didn't feel right. Nothing would ever be right again.

CHAPTER TWENTY-SEVEN

Interrupted sleep was par for the course these days. David often went to bed anticipating noise from the neighbors. This made it more difficult to get to sleep in the first place. Anxiety was like a monster lurking in his bedroom. At the moment he collapsed into slumber, the door would creak ajar and a hideous beast would ooze from the darkness. The boogey man had never troubled him as a child. David's father had scoffed at anything pandering to unsubstantiated fear, despite his mother's protests. He could hear their recurrent conversation in his head even now.

"Stop pampering the boy. Do you want him to be weak? A trembling, bumbling boy all his life?"

"There's plenty of time for him to grow up. He's just a child."

"He'll always be a child unless we toughen him up. There's a shit load of things to be afraid of in the big bad world. He'll have trouble enough without battling imaginary demons."

"He's just a child. Why do you want him to grow up so fast?"

"Only the strong survive."

As he lay remembering his fathers' passionate pursuit of a lifestyle grounded in Darwinism, David wondered why it persisted throughout his life. His own experienced reality never swayed him from the belief that weakness was bad and should be shunned, while strength of mind and body was to be pursued with vigor. This world view had made Bill Lavender a hard man; unforgiving and uncompromising. David recalled how many times they'd argued and, even when he was old enough and had acquired some knowledge and a mind of his own, how seldom Bill had given ground. David had often wished for another father, even prayed on those rare occasions when he thought someone might be listening. The only answer he ever received was the mellowing of Bill Lavender with the advancement of years and onset of several ailments which he could neither refute nor escape.

The years had beaten a lot of the fight out of Bill Lavender. Not all, but enough to facilitate a more peaceful and enjoyable relationship in the years leading up to his death. He had died a stubborn old fool, leaving behind his obstinate mule of a son: equally foolish as well.

David looked at the clock on the tall boy at the far end of the bedroom. Ten minutes had passed since he'd slipped between the covers and snuggled up to the pillow. Lilijana probably slept fitfully, in the lounge chair by Alen's bed. She was where he wanted to be. David did not think he would ever be with her again. Anywhere. Why would she let him back into her life? His mind was full of turbid water: filthy dirty and swirling in wicked whirlpools. He was exhausted yet couldn't sleep. Momentarily, he thought of Phil and Naydine. The overblown neighborhood feud seemed so farcical now, it was almost embarrassing. He wondered if they would disturb his sleep tonight, as they had so often done in the past. Now sleep didn't seem desirable or important. The arrival of the bedroom carnivore was imminent, so he was keen to maintain a vigil. Why sleep when it won't last? Better to be alert when the monster comes and ready to do battle than groggy and uncoordinated from slumber. He looked around and smiled. Then the sandman knocked him out.

***

The sound which woke him was unusual. When David recovered his senses and could investigate the disturbance, he realized he heard cracking and popping. He thought he smelled smoke and heard more sinister sounds underneath the snapping. Hissing, and what sounded like gusts of wind. Fire.

He was out of bed in an instant, out the front door and across the yard to 1008. His thoughts were coming in a thick sludge. He couldn't remember what to do. Call triple zero? Check the house to see if there was anyone he could help? He was halfway to his destination when he suddenly spun around and ran back inside his house. Snatching the phone off the wall hook, he pressed zero three times then waited. The response was quick. After telling the operator he needed the fireys, he gave his address and listened as he was instructed not to do anything: especially not to enter the house. The fire emergency service would be there soon, he was told in no uncertain terms. He was thanked for the call and hung up.

A loud explosion had him ducking for cover. When he realized where the noise had come from, David rushed back over to 1008. The house looked okay. Although he could see the orange glow of hungry flames in the living room, the other rooms at the front were dark. That was a good sign. He tried to imagine what could have caused the explosion. Gas tank? An exploding gas tank would have sounded louder and done far more damage. David was staring at the fire and was therefore unaware that other neighbors crowded behind him. He felt useless, powerless, but he also felt the primal urge to help: to do something.

Without further thought, he bolted for the front door. He grabbed the door handle and screamed as metal seared his palm. He stepped back and struck at the door with his foot. It went through but the door didn't open. He tired to extract his foot and cried out as splinters stabbed his calf. He rammed his shoulder against the door, and it gave way. Falling through onto the floor, David took a second to gain his bearings. He had been inside before but not since Phil and Naydine had moved in. The living room was dark and filled with smoke. David decided to try the bedrooms and kept low as he went, half-crawling along the floor until he came to the first. The door was open and the smoke was acrid and dense. He pulled his shirt over his head and held it over his mouth and nose. Somehow he remembered the correct things to do. He moved efficiently through the house underneath the deathly blanket of smoke, on a search and rescue mission. He didn't know if there was anyone in the house. It seemed likely that if Phil and Naydine or any of their degenerate friends were here, they'd be passed out from alcohol and drugs. They wouldn't be aware of their impending incineration. David didn't like these people at all, but he wasn't going to stand around while they were burned to ashes.

The master bedroom was the last at the front of the house. The door was closed so David removed the shirt from his face and used it like an oven mitt to turn the handle. Once inside, he crawled toward the bed and felt over it from head to foot. Nobody was there. He spun around in ever decreasing circles making sure no one was there. Having satisfied himself, he left.

Sirens wailed outside. The wooden frame of the house whistled as it expanded in the heat. David's eyes were smarting so badly from smoke that he was virtually blind with tears. From memory, the bathroom was next. No sooner had he crawled through door than he bumped into a body. Fumbling over it to determine top from bottom, he recognized the ample curves of Naydine. He shook her and yelled at her, but she was unresponsive. He grabbed one of her arms and tried to drag her. She was too heavy. He shook her again and screamed some more, all of it useless. Naydine was either unconscious or dead.

Strong hands latched onto him, and he was lifted with little effort. He was jostled by the motion of running yet wasn't moving his legs. All he could manage was floundering, weak waving. Every now and then, one of his arms collided with something. He winced or groaned, and forever seemed to be bouncing, but then it stopped and he was lying on cool grass. David opened his mouth to tell his rescuer that Naydine was in the bathroom. A hacking cough erupted from his chest and burst through his parched lips. Soon there were other hands on him. He felt weightless as an oxygen mask engulfed his mouth and nose. He heard soothing words, telling him to breathe normally. They told him to relax, he was going to be okay. Then he remembered Danijela, whom he'd left sleeping in her room, and wrenched the mask away from his face.

"My daughter. Is she all right?"

"Where was she?"

"In the house."

"The burning house? Which room? Do you remember?" The questions were delivered in an urgent but calm tone of voice.

"No, my house," said David. "She was asleep when I came out to see the fire."

There was so much noise, a thundering cacophony, and the smell of fire permeated the air. David tried to sit up. Invisible hands pushed him back down. "Where am I? Where's my daughter? Danijela? Where are you, princess?"

"Daddy?"

Relief washed over him like cool water and he temporarily forgot the pain in his body and the frightening discomfort of taking short, shallow breaths. His angel was all right.

"She's okay with me, David," said Amy. "I'll call Lilijana, too."

"She's at the hospital."

"I know."

"Thank you," said David. The mask was replaced over his mouth and nose, and he was moving again. Floating. The noise and smell seemed to fade away. He wondered if he might be fading away but the peaceful timbre of the detached voice kept reminding him he was alive and okay. He believed it to be true. He repeated the words inside his head until everything fell dark and silent.

***

When he opened his eyes, David felt as if he hovered. He was aware of himself and his body but it was lighter and disconnected from anything solid. He wasn't on the bed below him. The sensation of floating and bobbing made him feel nauseated. He closed his eyes. He swallowed hard: a great awkward gulp.

"David?"

Lilijana's voice was soft and warm like a tender embrace. His mind flashed back to his anxiety attack and previous hospital visit. Confused and disoriented, he kept his eyes closed and wondered whether he was experiencing a memory or reality. It was hard to tell. He felt exhausted. No strength to speak or think properly, or even open his eyes. He desperately wanted to open his eyes to a new world. To Lilijana's smile. To forgiveness. To a new beginning. This was foolishness. Nothing had changed. Better to stay in the safety of darkness. She would be sympathetic and express concern for his wellbeing. Inside, she would be burning. The fire of betrayal which David had ignited would be scorching her soul, devouring her. The fireman were able to extinguish the inferno at 1008. Nothing or no one would be able to douse Lilijana's smoldering heart. So he kept his eyes closed and concentrated on looking asleep.

"David?" Lilijana persisted, as though she had seen some flicker of consciousness. "Can you hear me?"

How long could he hide behind his eyes? What was the point?

Her smile kissed him when he allowed his eyelids to flutter open. It was unnecessarily theatrical.

"Is everyone all right?"

"If by everyone you mean Danijela and yourself then she's okay and you will be fine. Just smoke inhalation and a broken wrist."

"How did I break my wrist?"

Lilijana ignored the question, which she obviously could not answer, and said, “Naydine died in the fire.”

The fire. The word drifted like smoke. He breathed it in. Felt it scratch his throat, gagging him. He tasted the bitterness on his tongue, eyes watering. He had crawled through the thick acrid haze to find his enemies. To save them. He had found Naydine prone on the bathroom floor.

“I found her.”

“She was already dead.”

Lilijana’s voice was now infused with an eerie coldness.

“What about Phil?”

“His name’s John.”

“Was John? Did he die as well?”

“He wasn’t at home.”

David thought about what she said and the way she was saying it. How did she know any of this? Then he recalled Amy saying she would look after Danijela and call Lilijana. She had already known that Lilijana was at the hospital. Everyone seemed to know things before him. He felt like he was always playing catch up with reality. Maybe that was because he had spent so much time and energy with his fantasy world and its queen, Julia. And why did she sound so heartless? She had only waited for David to wake before resuming her wrathful deportment. She had good cause to be angry. David would not have been surprised if she didn’t bother to visit him. She could have excused her absence by saying their children needed her and David was not seriously hurt. How had he broken his wrist?

Lilijana said, “Amy said the police were asking the neighbors if they knew where John was.”

“Is he a suspect?” asked David hopefully.

“I don’t know,” replied Lilijana dismissively. She moved to sit on the edge of his bed. Immediately she stood, as if a pin had punctured her buttock, and turned away from David. He waited.

Facing out the window, Lilijana spoke quietly. “Who is the other Mrs. Lavender? Your mother is dead and, as far as I know, your sister is still in the United States. I’m the only Mrs. Lavender who would be staying anywhere with you.”

David stared at his wife's back. He could see the tense hunch of her shoulders and the unnatural erectness of her stance. Was this a question he should answer? Did she even want an answer? The silence was heavy and excruciating.

He had established an alibi without expecting Lilijana to chase it up. Matt would have lied for him if she called but she had trusted him implicitly. Why did he check in at the motel as Mr. and Mrs. Lavender? To avoid the scrutiny of the staff? What business was it of theirs if a woman stayed with him? It wasn't illegal. Immoral? Sure, but what did he care about other people's morality? Wasn't he free to do what he wanted? Had he checked in under his name and said he had a guest, they would not have asked any questions. When Lilijana had called to speak to him after he and Julia checked out, the staff would have said Mr. Lavender and his friend when Lilijana asked who they were. Why did she ask that question? Why didn't she assume the word 'they' referred to David and Matt? It indicated suspicion on her part, didn't it? That was a question he wanted to ask, and he almost blurted it out as though she was on trial. By some miracle, he remained quiet.

"If the question is too hard, I'll rephrase it for you."

Now she sounded vindictive. David had never heard that tone and it was evidence he'd lost her. The air was so frosty that David held his breath, afraid that Lilijana had transformed the hospital room into an icy hell.

"Are you having an affair?"

"Yes," said David. He was too tired to play games.

"Anyone I know?" She stood rigidly with her back to him.

"No."

She turned and fixed him with a frightening glare. She was shaking as she said, "Why?"

David hesitated. No answer would mollify her. Anything he said would sound like a pathetic excuse for unfaithfulness. There was no justification for what he'd done. "I don't know," he answered finally.

It appeared she wanted to speak but didn't know what to say. David waited, mostly staring at the bed. He was ashamed and deeply sorry for hurting her. He had always known she would find out. He would say this and she would say that and she'd be livid, but she would forgive him after he repented in sackcloth and ashes. Nothing he predicted had prepared him for this. This was the end of the world.

"The police want to talk to you about the fire."

The subject change threw him. "What?"

"In their words, you are a person of interest and they want to talk to you about the fire."

"I'm a suspect?" David was incredulous until he realized that the history of unpleasantries between he and Phil and Naydine made the police suspect his involvement, even if arson and murder were a bit extreme.

Lilijana left without another word. David called after her but she kept walking. "Lilijana?"

CHAPTER TWENTY-EIGHT

"So the police woke up finally?"

Chalkie had known all along that David played no part in the dramatic flaming demise of 1008 Princes Hwy. Loyalty was a sweet thing to experience. One week had passed since his release from hospital and David had hooked up with his mates back at the pub. Matt had called it a debriefing, which was a touch melodramatic, but a hell of a lot had happened. He was grateful to talk. The silence at home filled the house with frosty air as Lilijana continued to punish him. She didn't say anything apart from what was needed for functional communication, and she was cold but at least polite. 'Please take the garbage out, David. Dinner is ready, David. I'm going to bed now. Goodnight.' Every single utterance was delivered with a simmering anger on which Lilijana was barely keeping a lid.

"I get that they wanted to talk to me. I didn't do myself any favors by starting a war with Phil."

"Have they found him yet?" asked Matt.

"He's gone. They say they're searching for him through all known contacts, at previous addresses and all that shit. If you ask me they don't seem especially hopeful. Not the detective I talked to anyway."

"Nice write up in the paper," said Chalkie. "Did you see it?"

"Yeah. How do the fire investigators work out what caused a fire? If everything's burned up, how can they possibly tell why it started?"

"Apparently because fire moves sideways and upwards. Depending on the structure, open windows and staircases can alter that. They can sometimes retrace the footsteps of the fire."

"That's cute,' said David. "Fire has footsteps. Very poetic."

"I was wondering," added Chalkie, "In what other directions could fire travel apart from sideways and up?"

"Down, I suppose," said Matt unaware he was being mocked. "Sometimes they look for a V pattern. Because of the way fire spreads, it can leave a V-shaped scorch mark on the wall or vertical surfaces. This can indicate origin as well. They also look for any trace of accelerants, which are almost always present when the fire was deliberately lit."

"I thought the paper said they had ruled out arson," said David.

"They ruled you out as an arsonist," said Chalkie. 'I think they still like the idea of someone causing the fire on purpose."

"Why?" asked Matt. "Because arson is sexier than accidental house fires which are usually caused by cooking, heaters or other electrical appliances, cigarettes, or Christmas lights in December and January?"

"Didn't you read that there had also been a fire in the last house your neighbors lived in before they moved to Chinaman's Hollow?"

"Is that right?"

"They didn't find that out immediately, which is why you were the prime suspect."

Their glasses were nearly empty and it was Matt's shout. He seemed more interested in enlightening them about the work of arson investigators. "By looking at the damage done to materials they can work out the intensity of the heat and this can also help them figure out where it started."

"After you buy another round," said David, "You can tell us what they do in the case of accidental fires where there aren't any accelerants."

Chalkie stalled his answer by placing his finger to his lips. "Beer first, Matt."

David thought that cigarettes were the cause of common house fires. How many smokers had fallen asleep in bed before stubbing out their butts? How many had dozed off from exhaustion or drunkenness on their lounges and allowed their unfinished cancer sticks to fall to the carpet and begin devastation? Given how much damage smoking inflicted on the body, he wondered, somewhat morbidly, whether being incinerated was worse than death by lung cancer. David was glad he'd given it up.

When Matt returned, Chalkie was ready with a question. "Suppose a particular fire started in a rubbish bin and was caused by a lit cigarette. How does an investigator know whether it was someone being careless when they dumped their ashtray in the bin, or if they deliberately placed a lit ciggie or a match in the bin to start the fire for the insurance money?"

"That'd be when the human element kicks in," replied Matt confidently. "Any detective worth a grain of salt could work out whether the fire was deliberate by talking to the people involved. Like they talked to you, Dave.

Despite your history of aggression toward Phil, they would have quickly gained some sense that you had nothing to do with the fire."

"It's a pretty big leap form a punch in the face to burning a man's house down," agreed David.

"Exactly."

"And what about risking your life to try to rescue whoever was there?" added Chalkie. "Why would you have done that if you started the fire?"

"Exactly," said Matt once more with feeling. He was doing an impressive job of convincing them. For a diesel mechanic, he sure sounded like an expert on arson. Maybe he had missed his calling.

"Who else could they have talked to?" asked David. 'Naydine was killed in the fire, and Phil's gone."

"She smoked, didn't she?" asked Matt.

"Yeah, but that doesn't tell us why the fire started."

"There are over ten thousand house fires in Australia every year, and seventy deaths. Most of the fires are accidental, so here's what I reckon happened."

"All right, Horatio, let's hear it," said David.

"Naydine was on the turps or smoking or injecting something." The hottie falls off her cigarette without her knowing and she passes out. Fire starts, smoke fills the house. She wakes from her drug-induced slumber and doesn't know what's going on. She doesn't know where the fire is but figures she has time to escape. The only problem is, she can't see anything and she's choking to death on thick smoke. Asphyxiation is the number one killer in house fires. In blind panic she looks for an exit then suffocates by the time you stagger in and find her on the bathroom floor."

"You're a barrel of laughs, Matt," said Chalkie.

"You should quit the workshop and become a detective, mate," added David.

Matt shook his head wistfully. "I'm too old to be changing careers."

"No you're not," said David. 'I'm quitting my job. I want to get back out on the road. I miss all the driving and being on my own."

He was a little afraid of returning to a driving job. It would take him away from home more, and provide opportunities to misbehave. He might even be tempted to take up smoking again, and he would certainly have to be careful with his eating habits. He had put on ten kilograms, the last time he drove as a sales rep. This caused him to doubt the wisdom of leaving his secure, close to home job, but he didn't say any of this because he was trying to be supportive.

"I don't want to change jobs," said Matt. "I like what I do. I'm all settled and in a nice groove. I'm contented."

There was a pause in the conversation. David thought of the air's heavy stillness before monstrous black clouds unleashed their brand of hell on the earth.

It was Chalkie who spoke next. "That's what got you in trouble, Dave. Discontent."

David's friend was dead right. He quit his job because he wasn't happy and that had led to meeting Julia. He had seen her as his savior when the new job hadn't delivered happiness and satisfaction. He had focused on Julia and pursued her as a distraction from the problems in his marriage. Not as a solution. His relationship with Lilijana was never going to be enhanced by his affair with Julia, but this was exactly what he'd told himself at the time. What a bloody idiot. He was the general of the legion of the asinine.

Without any words to offer, in rebuttal or defense, David raised his glass and titled it toward his mates. "To my loyal friends," he said, and the others shared in the toast. Nothing else needed to be said.

***

During the walk home, David thought about Julia. He hadn't heard from her in over a week. He didn't know if she knew he had been in hospital. The report of the fire had been in the local and national papers, and had made the evening news. It was a huge story. Local woman dies in house fire. Since the federal government's ill-fated home insulation scheme, every accidental house fire was linked in people's minds with faulty insulation. News reports referred to these incidents even when they weren't related. Still, it was possible she missed the whole thing. Not likely, but possible. Even if she had heard, there was no reason for her to contact him. The affair was over and they both knew it. The melancholy he felt was strangely comforting, like losing a tennis game he'd played well. This was how he felt, although his defeat in this case was ignoble, and he deserved to feel worse.

Music burst from the phone in his pocket. The chiming of bells and the crash of symbols from Iron Maiden's *Hallowed Be Thy Name* was the tone for his message service. Taking it out of his pocket he pressed a button and looked at the screen. It was a text message from Julia asking him to phone her as soon as he could.

He dialed her number and waited for her to answer. His heart was racing and he had stopped walking without realizing. What did she want? Just when he had been hammering the final nails into the coffin of their affair, preparing to bury it once and for all.

"Are you all right?" she asked.

The question was unexpected and David had no answer.

"David?"

"You heard about the fire?"

"Everyone heard about the fire. Are you all right now?"

"I didn't think I was ever going to see or hear from you again."

Her hesitation was telling. "I wasn't going to call but I just couldn't leave it like that."

David had not thought about the mechanics of how their affair would end. Even though they had talked about rules and agreed it would be over when one of them said it was, he never imagined how that would happen. What words would be used? Who would say them? Where would that conversation take place? Would there be one last torrid love making session? One for the road, so to speak. He hadn't considered any of that because he hadn't wanted it to end. Julia was waiting for him to speak. He didn't know what to say.

"I want to explain why I behaved that way the last time we were together. In Newcastle."

This had been an object of curiosity on his drive home from the trip. However, the rapidly unfolding dramas with Alen, Lilijana, and the fire, had conspired to steal his attention. He remained silent, allowing Julia to say what she wanted when she was ready to say it.

"My husband had just been offered a promotion that would necessitate a move. To Western Australia. He wanted to know if I was okay with that, and I balked. We had a long discussion about the pros and cons, and he was rational and sensitive while I was irrational and emotional. No surprises there. Eventually, he said I should sleep on it. There was no rush to make a decision as it wouldn't be happening for two or three months. I said that was fine and then I told him I was pregnant."

"Shit!" exclaimed David. "It's not mine, is it? Fuck me dead, tell me it's not mine."

"It's not yours."

"How do you know?" David started moving. He was walking on the spot, pacing backwards and forwards, cutting in tight circles. "How can you be sure?"

"Condoms."

"Condoms?" said David, trying to remember if they'd used one every time they made love. They must have used a lot of them. There must have been times when they were hurrying or recklessly spontaneous, and they weren't the most effective form of birth control. Was she on the pill? He had never thought to ask.

"Yes," said Julia calmly. "Thin rubber sheaths that are placed over the erect penis before insertion in the vagina."

"I know what a fucking condom is, Julia."

He was going out of his mind with panic and she was being flippant.

"I'm as sure as I can be that this child is my husband's," she said more seriously.

A thought entered David's mind. "I didn't realize you were having sex with your husband while you were with me."

"Not at the same time, but yes."

"Stop with the jokes," said David angrily. "Why aren't you worried like I am?"

"Listen David. I loved being with you and I don't regret the time we had."

Julia was delivering her break-up speech, even though their affair was over. He felt his heart being ripped apart. Hearing the words, her alluring voice, imagining the smell of her hair in his face as she ground herself against him. He felt like crying as she continued.

"I decided when I woke up that I was going to go with my husband to W.A., and we were going to start again. I convinced myself that things would be better between us, especially with a baby because they bring couples closer together. I didn't need you anymore, and I was going to tell you at some point during our getaway. Finding the right time proved harder than I imagined. My growing frustration for not having the courage to tell you made me angry, and that was what you experienced. It wasn't directed at you. I'm not disappointed. I don't feel guilty about what we did. Like I said, I have no regrets. I spent the past week trying to find the courage to make this call."

He was able to receive Julia's farewell with grace. She was right to end it this way. He thought about trying to arrange one last meeting but did not have the heart. Even the passion had died. He felt sadness and some grief. He, too, was without regret or guilt. They had found each other when they were both been lost and lonely. They had met each other's need. It was a simple transaction born of hunger and fatal attraction.

"Thank you for loving me," said Julia quietly. "Goodbye."

Julia choked at the end, so he wasn't surprised when she rang off without letting him respond. She was gone. Given the chance he would have thanked her too, and said he would never forget her. Tears welled in his eyes. He swallowed hard to dislodge a great gulp of emotion. When he recovered, he resumed the walk home and concentrated on Lilijana, though Julia was permanently lurking in the shadows of his mind. Would she haunt him for the rest of his days?

As he mounted the rise to 1010, a blast of Arctic wind swept over him. It was the frigid hostility of Lilijana projected from her ice castle, reaching out for him, calling him home. He shivered. The gust abated. He kept walking.

Apart from the businesslike questioning and commanding, Lilijana had spoken only once of the affair when she brought Alen home from the hospital. David had been released a day earlier with no lasting effects from smoke inhalation. The police had interviewed him, and said that Naydine was dead when he found her. Asphyxiation. She also received severe burns to her legs but these would not have proved fatal had she been able to escape the inferno. They had seemed satisfied with David's answers. Perhaps they felt sorry for him. Perhaps they had merely decided they were barking up the wrong tree. He didn't know and didn't care. David was sick of the police. He had caught a taxi home from the hospital while Lilijana stayed with Alen.

When she finally returned and found an appropriate moment, Lilijana sat beside David on the lounge and said, "So you have a mistress?"

"Had," corrected David.

She sniffed, as though the difference was inconsequential. The question of whether the affair was over did not alter its existence.

"Anyone I know?" she asked again.

David told her no, and then she stood and walked away. For two days she punished him with silent rage. Now, as he approached his home, he wondered when it would end. Something had to change. He needed her to talk to him, to verbalize her feelings, even it was vitriol and venom. Even if every word was like a sharp blade drawn across his flesh. Regardless of the pain, it would be better than this.

He stepped onto the verandah and retrieved his keys from a pocket. He didn't want to go inside but he couldn't stand outside. Where did he belong? Did Lilijana want him here? Maybe she hoped he would leave and save her the trouble of kicking him out. Their marriage was like a beautiful vase which had been knocked off its pedestal. It lay broken in pieces, each one with dangerous jagged edges. No one seemed willing to pick them up. They lay on the cold tiles as a testimony to the desolate failure of those entrusted with the care of that vase.

The door opened inwards as he pressed the key towards the lock, startling him. Lilijana was on the other side.

"Welcome home," she said, smiling broadly.

Taken off guard, David stood in the doorway. Did those words mean what he supposed them to mean, or was this some new tactic in Lilijana's war against him?

Lilijana rightly interpreted his paralysis as confusion, so she stepped forward, took his hand and gently pulled him inside.

"Are you still seeing her?"

David shook his head. "I told you it's over."

She looked at him with doubt. "I'm sorry that I let you down, and I accept part of the blame for the mess we find ourselves in, but it's hard to forgive you for taking it as far as you did. I don't feel like I can trust you now that you tell me it's over. I want to believe you, yet I'm not sure I can. I'm not at all sure you won't do it again."

David jumped in urgently, "I won't. I—"

"Don't say I promise," warned Lilijana, holding up her index finger with menace. "Your promises don't carry much weight with me right now."

This was excruciating, Lilijana twisting the knife, dominating the exchange, playing with him like a cat with a wounded mouse. He was defenseless. Crushed, but feverishly hoping she would forgive him and allow him to stay.

"I don't want to throw our life away, David. I wish I had not become such a workaholic and such a negligent wife. I wish you had not thought so poorly of me and so little of yourself that you ran to another woman. A part of me wishes I never found out. If Alen had not been in that accident, I would not have called the motel and I would have remained in the dark. Another part of me is angry for not being more aware. They say women know when their partners are cheating. I had no idea. I feel like an absolute idiot. But none of that changes that fact that I love you. You're essentially a good man, and I wouldn't find a better one no matter how hard I looked or how far and wide I searched."

She paused, and David held his tongue.

"This is going to be very difficult but I want us to fix what we nearly destroyed."

David glanced at the floor and pictured them kneeling together to pick up the shards of the vase. They carried them to the kitchen and David found a tube of Supaglue to reconstruct the vase. When they finished their silent collaboration, they stood and stared at their work. The vase was not, and might never be, what it once was. It was still beautiful and would function. The cracks would become less obvious as they grew accustomed to the memory of what caused them. This imaginary vase became David's symbol of hope. One day he would tell her about it so she could share in its poignant legacy. For now, he remained silent and received her forgiveness. It felt warm and he started to weep.

Lilijana led him to the dining room and gestured for him to sit down. She was going to make him a cup of tea and bring him some chocolate cookies she had just baked. Although it felt awkward, David received her efforts with grace. God only knew how long it would take before their marriage healed and the natural ease of a loving, trusting relationship was restored. However, they would try. They would learn to forgive, to release the bitterness, to allow resentment to be eroded by gratitude.

***

Many months passed. A new house had been erected on the ashes of 1008. Life had returned to normal, and their pain was slowly healing. David gained renewed enthusiasm for his job and his family: for life in general, and Lilijana thought less of herself. One afternoon, as David sat and sipped hot tea while perusing the newspaper, he looked through the window into the neighbor's yard. He watched one of the new residents of 1008 pulling her washing off the clothes line, folding it, just the way he did and laying it carefully in the laundry basket. He had not met the new neighbors yet. Lilijana had told him there were three: two young ladies and a man. David was looking at one of those young ladies, and he liked what he saw. He called to Lilijana in the kitchen, "Do we have any lemons on the tree at the moment?"

"I don't know. Why?"

"I thought I'd take a bag over to welcome our new neighbors."

Don't miss out!

Visit the website below and you can sign up to receive emails whenever D.A.Cairns publishes a new book. There's no charge and no obligation.

https://books2read.com/r/B-A-BPLPF-OJBSB

BOOKS 2 READ

Connecting independent readers to independent writers.

About the Author

Heavy metal lover and cricket tragic, D.A. Cairns lives on the south coast of New South Wales. He works as a ghostwriter, has had over 100 short stories published, and has authored eight novels, and a superficial and unscientific memoir, *I Used to be an Animal Lover.* His latest book is *The Secret to Happiness is Death.*

Read more at dacairns.com.au.

www.ingramcontent.com/pod-product-compliance
Lightning Source LLC
LaVergne TN
LVHW090938080826
845145LV00003B/798